Blue Heron Cove

BOOK ONE

LAKE BENTON

ALEXANDRIA VARIAN

To my husband, Bob. You have changed my life into an amazing adventure. This book wouldn't exist without your love and support.

To Vicky. Your constant encouragement and belief in me are something I will always treasure. Thank you for reading the rough draft for me. I hope you like the finished product.

"We have two lives, and the second begins when we realize we only have one."
~Confucius

One

Laurel muttered under her breath as her laptop chimed to remind her of the next meeting on her calendar. She glanced away from the email she was responding to just long enough to see what the upcoming meeting was about. Another meeting that could be dealt with via email. Finishing her reply, she clicked send and looked back at her inbox—only 203 new emails to deal with.

Sighing, she opened the next one, which made her blood pressure start to rise. Julie, in the sales department, never read her emails thoroughly nor filed them. Instead of researching something, she thought the best way to get an answer was to ask the same question repeatedly.

"Julie, I refer you to my email dated October 23rd at 4:34 p.m., where the information you're requesting was provided." Laurel clicked send with a bit more force than was necessary.

Sally, her coworker and one of her few friends at work, poked her head in the door.

"You know, hitting send like that isn't really like hitting the recipient, right?" Sally asked.

"Unfortunately. Why can't people just do their jobs? Read their emails?"

"Julie strikes again, huh?"

Laurel gathered her laptop and notebook and followed Sally down the hall.

"How did you guess? I don't know why her boss keeps her."

"I know. Not sure why people cover for her. She clearly doesn't do her job properly." Sally held the conference room door open for Laurel, and they both found their seats.

"Everyone, let's get started. We have a lot to cover today." The vice president of marketing said. "I would like you all to welcome our new marketing manager. Now, let's do a round-robin and introduce ourselves and our roles. Laurel, let's start with you, please."

Inwardly cringing, she smiled. "I'm Laurel. I am the system administrator, so anything with product and functionality of the website is me."

"I think we should also add that she has been here since the creation of this new division and therefore has a vast knowledge of sales and marketing, as well as our customer service department." The vice president clapped as encouragement.

"Yes, I wear many hats. If you need anything, please let me know." She clenched her fists under the table, hoping her smile appeared genuine.

The meeting lasted fifteen minutes past the hour it was allotted. Laurel walked quickly back to her office, thinking about all she had to get done today—in between meetings.

It was almost seven pm when she lifted the laptop from the docking station and slid it into her bag. Down the hall, she saw the light on in her boss' office. She pulled out her phone, hoping it would stop her boss from delaying her departure.

From inside the office door, she heard, "Oh, Laurel, going home already?"

Clenching her empty hand into a fist, she paused in the doorway. "Yes, going home already."

"Oh well, lucky you." Her boss barely looked up from her laptop.

"Not sure about lucky. I've been here since seven a.m. Good night." Laurel quickly turned from the doorway and walked out of the building.

Climbing into her car, she took a deep breath and slowly let it out. She stretched her neck from side to side and front to back. The tension reached into her shoulders. Looking at her smart watch, she saw that her heart rate was elevated.

What did she expect? She was working crazy hours with no end in sight. She couldn't possibly continue like this. She wasn't sleeping; she was at work twelve hours a day and working from home too.

She made her daily call to her mom as she left the parking lot.

"Hi Mom, how are you?

"Hi sweetheart, I'm good. You're leaving work late again, I see."

"Yes, another crazy day. Four meetings today and a total of 307 new emails."

"Oh my, do you really have to answer all the emails yourself? When do you get any work done?"

"Yup, just me. I attempt to get the work done in between everything else. They hired a new marketing manager. Not sure why they can't get me an assistant."

"Another new marketing manager. The other one certainly didn't last long. I agree, you need an assistant. They can't expect you to keep working like this."

"Unfortunately, they do expect it, and of course, the more I give them, the more they take advantage of me."

"Maybe it's time to push for the assistant again. I'm worried about you, sweetheart."

"Thanks, Mom. I have a one-on-one with my boss Wednesday, so I will make my plea again and see what happens. Anyway, how was your day? You sound good."

"I've had a good day. Amazing what a little energy does for mind and spirit. Not to mention the house to-do list. I did a bit of gardening and Linda stopped by this afternoon, so we sat outside and chattered away for a couple of hours."

"Aw, Mom. That's great. I know you love her visits. Now that she's retired, she will surely be stopping by more often."

"Yes, exactly. We had such a nice time. We're going to have lunch next week."

"Good."

"Oh, I picked up that new prescription today. We'll see if that makes a difference. I would love to have a little energy each day. Less coughing would be good too."

"Good, Mom. I hope it makes a difference too. You sound so good tonight. I love hearing you like this."

"Me too, baby. You must be almost home now. What's for dinner?"

"Almost there. I am making chicken Kiev tonight. One of the first dishes Dad taught me how to make."

"Yummy. I remember that first cooking class your dad gave you. Watching you two in the kitchen was always such entertainment. Him and his dad jokes, and you laughing at every one like you were hearing it for the first time."

"I still love those jokes. I tell them to myself now when I need a laugh, and somehow it feels like getting a hug from Dad."

"Aw, that's wonderful, sweetheart. He was a special man."

"The best!"

"Okay, so what are you having with the chicken Kiev?"

"I bought some beautiful heirloom tomatoes yesterday, so I'm going to make a burrata topped with some of my basil, which is growing like a weed."

"My mouth is watering. You'll have to make that for me next time."

"You bet. Okay, pulling into the driveway. Sleep well. I love you, Mom."

"Enjoy your dinner and get some sleep. I love you too, dear heart."

WALKING INTO THE KITCHEN FROM THE GARAGE, Laurel stopped dead in her tracks. Dishes were stacked in the sink and on the counter. When she had left for work, the kitchen was spotless.

Graham walked in from the living room. "Hi, babe."

"Hi. What the hell happened here?"

Looking around the kitchen, he shrugged. "Jeff stopped by, and we were hungry. So, we grilled a couple of chicken breasts..."

"You ate the chicken breasts that I took out for our dinner? I told you I was going to make chicken Kiev tonight." She looked at the basket where the tomatoes used to be. "Don't tell me you also ate the tomatoes I bought for the burrata."

Graham shrugged his shoulders again. "We were hungry. What's the big deal? You're the master chef. You can whip something else up for dinner."

"I can't believe you. You knew I was making us dinner tonight. You knew what we were having. There is other food here you could have eaten. I've been looking forward to that meal all day." Leaning against the counter, her shoulders slumped. "And look at this place. It's a mess!"

"Wow, you're in a great mood. It's just a couple of dishes."

"I've had a long day. We planned dinner together. I bought things especially for it. To come home and find the food eaten and the kitchen a mess is just too much."

"I think you're overreacting. It's just food and some dishes. Jeez."

"Does it ever occur to you to consider my feelings? Do you ever think about how your actions affect me?"

"Of course. I just think you're making this more of a big deal than it is."

Sighing, Laurel shook her head and walked past Graham into the bedroom. She changed her clothes and washed her face, trying to remove all traces of the day from her body.

Graham walked into the bedroom. Looking in the closet and the dresser, he turned to Laurel. "Have you seen my green sweatshirt? I wore it last week but can't find it."

"I've no idea. In the laundry basket, maybe?"

He crossed the room, opened the basket lid, and dug around in the dirty laundry. "Yup. Are you going to do laundry tonight?" He smiled sheepishly, which in the past had won her over.

"I can't believe you!" She glared at him until the smile dropped off his face.

"Fine. Never mind." Grabbing another sweatshirt, he walked to the doorway. "I'm going to help Jeff work on his car. See you later."

Hearing the front door close, she looked down at her hands. Clenched into fists again. Slowly, she opened them and took a deep breath.

How many times had she clenched her fists today? She was so stressed out. She needed to get a grip.

"I need to eat something and have a long soak in a bubble bath. That's what I need."

She ate an omelet and cleaned the kitchen because, while Graham didn't mind the mess, she did not want to wake up to it. After making a cup of chamomile tea, she slid down into the bubble bath and closed her eyes.

LAUREL WAS IN THE OFFICE AT SIX THIRTY A.M. THE next morning working on a product upload to the website. Graham had come home late, and she left before he was up.

Her phone chimed with a text from Graham.

Morning.

Deep breath.

Good morning.

She stared at the phone, hoping he would text back, not sure what she hoped for, exactly. An apology. Heck, she would settle for him just acknowledging her feelings. Or maybe even just... wishing her a good day.

Nope. He couldn't even do that. She was really starting to wonder if they were past the point of no return. Had their relationship run its course?

Her thoughts were interrupted by an email from her boss.

"I need to move our one-on-one to today. I'll send you a meeting request for 9 a.m."

More deep breaths.

Rehearsing her speech, she walked into her boss's office. After their normal agenda items were covered Laurel made her case for having an assistant. Her boss shut her down, claiming the division needed to make more money before she could authorize any more staff.

"I know we aren't profitable yet, but we all can't keep working at this pace. I don't mind working hard, but these hours and the expectations from the executive team are completely unreasonable."

"Laurel, I think you are doing a great job. We are all working long hours, but that's what's required right now. We will all benefit greatly when we reach our quarterly goals. There will be stock options available to you then. Just hang in there a little bit longer."

Defeated, Laurel walked back to her office. Sally poked her head through the door a few minutes later.

"Are you okay?"

"Come in and close the door."

Sitting down across the desk, she looked at Laurel. "What happened?"

"Well, I was just told that I can't get an assistant until we hit our quarterly goals. I just don't understand how they expect me to keep working like this. I'm giving everything I can, but I'm exhausted. I'm so stressed out. I have so many balls in the air, and most of them seem like bowling balls."

Sally's jaw fell open. "That's just crap. You have more on your plate than anyone, and it is all crucial! I don't know how you do it, truthfully. We would reach our goals if the execs didn't keep making knee-jerk reactions and constantly changing things."

"Exactly. Oh, sales aren't what we expected, so let's change the plan once again. Ugh, I just don't know how long I can keep doing this."

Sally stood. "I know I sound like a broken record, but hang in there. You are amazing, and it will pay off. I need to run to a meeting. Catch ya later."

"Thanks."

"Hi Mom. How was your day?"

"Hi sweetheart. Good. How about yours?"

"Not good. I had my one-on-one with my boss, and there's no chance for an assistant until we've met our quarterly goals. Like I have any control over that."

"Oh, honey, I'm sorry. You do so much for them, and they don't seem to appreciate you."

"I'm just so sick of it. I used to love this job. The excitement of the new division. The energy. The camaraderie. New ideas being shared and everyone thinking outside the box about how to make this a success. But now...now I just feel burned out and used."

"Perhaps it's time for a change then, honey."

"Believe me, Mom, I have been giving that a lot of thought lately."

"Okay, change of subject. How was your dinner last night?"

"Ha. Dinner didn't happen. Graham and his friend were hungry, so they grilled the chicken breasts and ate the tomatoes.

The kitchen was a mess. We argued. He went out. So, not a great night."

"Honey, you're having a rough week."

"And it's only Tuesday."

"Sounds to me like you need a fun weekend with your mom."

"Yes! I'm looking forward to our weekend together. Love our mommy-daughter time."

"I do too, sweetheart. You must be nearly home."

"Just pulled into the driveway. I love you, Mom. Have a good evening."

"Love you too. Get some rest."

"WHAT DO YOU MEAN YOU HAVE PLANS TONIGHT?" Laurel asked, hating the weakness in her voice.

"Yeah, I just have some plans with some friends. Nothing you would be interested in. What's the big deal?" Graham changed into a white button-down shirt and pulled out a pair of newish jeans.

"No big deal. Just that it's Friday night and we haven't really even seen each other this week, and I thought we could go to Valentino's for some dinner. We haven't been there in months."

"We were just there a couple of weeks ago, remember..." Graham suddenly looked uncomfortable. "I mean, it seems like only a couple of weeks ago. How about if we plan something for next week?"

"I have that stupid conference for work next week. You know how those things are. They start at the crack of dawn and go until midnight—if I'm lucky."

"What conference? Are you seriously not going to be around the house at all next week?" Graham's voice was heavy with what sounded like relief.

"What do you mean, what conference? It has been on the calendar for six months and I've been talking about it constantly.

Do you ever listen to what I'm saying?" Laurel's blood pressure rose at the not-so-unfamiliar conversation once again. "No, I won't be here except to sleep and change clothes. I can't believe you didn't remember that it's next week. That's why I have been even busier this week, trying to get ahead with my workload so that I don't get buried once the conference is over. That's why I wanted to have a nice evening out with you tonight!"

"I didn't forget...of course I listen. I just can't believe it is next week. Time flies, as they say," Graham said over his shoulder as he put on his best cowboy boots.

"Why are you getting so dressed up? Where are you going? Which friends are your getting together with, anyway?"

"Friends. Why so many questions? Don't you trust me? Remember, I always come back to you." He winked as he walked out of the bedroom, grabbed his phone, wallet, and keys, and headed for the door.

"But why can't I come with you?" Laurel knew she was pushing his buttons.

"Not your sort of evening, babe. Trust me." Graham opened the door and turned to look at her. "I'll be late, so don't wait up." And just like that, he closed the door and was gone. Again.

Laurel felt the tears coming but fought to keep them from falling. She was tired of feeling this way. When had things changed so much with them? Where was he even going tonight? Why so dressed up? She knew his friends. Dressing up was not their thing. She tried to push her suspicions away once again. If she let herself think about all the signs she had been seeing, the reality of the situation would be completely obvious—and that was something she couldn't cope with right now.

She grabbed her phone and ordered a pizza. Not quite the dinner she was hoping for, but she was not going to let this ruin her night. While waiting for the pizza to be delivered, she changed out of her work clothes and into her yoga pants and a T-shirt. She might as well have a productive evening so she could enjoy her weekend without all the normal chores. Putting on one of her favorite playlists, she grabbed the overflowing clothes hamper and carried it into the laundry room. Ah, what a glamorous life she lived. What a wild Friday night. Laundry, pizza, and well, who knew where this exciting evening would lead? She laughed as she sorted the dirty clothes.

Laurel carefully checked all the pockets, as she certainly didn't want to wash another pack of gum. Graham acted like it was her fault that she hadn't checked *his* pockets! It happened three years ago, and he still brought it up whenever he saw her starting a load of laundry. So, even though she knew it was his fault for leaving gum in the pocket of his favorite shorts, she always checked pockets thoroughly now.

Just as the doorbell rang, her fingers found a folded piece of paper. Distracted, she dropped it on the counter before answering the door.

"Oh my gosh, that pizza smells so good. Do you ever have grumpy customers?" She handed the man a tip and smiled.

"No, the job is kind of nice that way. I seem to bring smiles to people's faces. I know it's really the pizza bringing smiles, but I take a bit of credit." He laughed and waved as he turned around and left.

The scent of the warm pizza made Laurel realize how hungry she was as she set it on the counter. She looked at the piece of paper with a sideways glance as she reached for a wineglass. Pouring a glass of wine and taking a bite of pizza, her eyes returned to the folded paper again. If it wasn't anything important—and it must not be if he left it in his pocket—there was probably no harm in reading what it said. Then why did she feel guilty about looking at it? They had been together for years. They lived together. They didn't have secrets—did they?

This was crazy. She was doing laundry and just pulled it out of a pocket. The first thing anyone would do is unfold it and see if it is important. Why did she feel like she was doing something wrong, like she was intruding? Oh, screw this!

She wiped her hands on her napkin and reached for the piece

of paper. Her hands shook a little as she unfolded it and read what was written on it.

Laurel shook her head and tossed the paper back on the counter. All that was written on the paper was a list of items to get at the hardware store.

She felt a bit of relief, but still... Things weren't right with them. Lately—well, if she were honest with herself, for quite a while —she and Graham seemed to just exist together. They were both busy with their jobs, of course, but it was more than that. Early on in their relationship, she was sure they would be married by now. They had talked about getting married and what their life as husband and wife would be like. They both wanted it. Yet here they were, not married, and the subject hadn't been discussed in ages.

"Would I even want to marry him if he asked me now?" she asked aloud. She pondered that question as she took a bite of pizza. Then another sip of wine.

No. The answer came so clearly that it shocked her. She hadn't hesitated at all. She knew that even if Graham came home tonight and popped the question, she would say no. And she wouldn't regret it either.

If she had no desire to marry Graham, then why the hell was she still here with him? She stood, then sat again. Picking up another piece of pizza, she felt a sudden shift in her life. Her mind was all over the place as the truth made her face so many aspects of her life.

As she finished her pizza, she started jotting down notes and random thoughts that came to the forefront of her mind. Laurel knew she had to think this through. Well, not the part about Graham; she already had clarity on that. If she was going to leave, then she had to do it on her terms. She knew that if she told Graham, he would be a jerk and kick her out. His grandmother owned the house they rented. No, she needed to plan and somehow start the process without him knowing.

She started making lists. She didn't want to pack much. A

fresh start would do her good. And where would she move to? It would have to be a small apartment, probably. As much as she wanted a house, she knew she couldn't afford the rental prices right now. Maybe if she got the promotion at work that she had been hoping for, then she could look for something larger. Someday.

She switched the laundry out and went to the spare room to look for storage boxes. A couple of years ago, she had made it into her craft room—not that she seemed to have much time to be creative these days. Maybe that would change as well. That thought brought old dreams to the surface. Pottery had been her love, and she had once dreamed of creating her own collection and having a little shop someday. Throughout her teens and twenties, that was all she wanted. So, what happened? She had still been creating pottery when she and Graham met.

Oh God. *Graham* was the reason that she gave up on her dream. Over time, he had convinced her it took her away from him and their time together. Oh, he had been so charming and loving then that she wanted to spend every minute with him. So, she slowly let her dream fall away. What the hell had she done with her life?

Laurel felt like she was waking up from a bad dream. A long sleep. She suddenly felt that it was time to change her life.

Her ringing phone broke her out of her thoughts. Knowing it was her mom by the ringtone, Laurel leaned against the edge of a table and answered cheerfully. "Hi Mom! Your phone was busy when I called earlier. How are you feeling tonight?"

"Hi baby. I must have been on the phone with Linda. Well, not feeling great. It hasn't been a good day, but maybe tomorrow will be better. I just wanted to check if you're still coming by tomorrow."

"I'm sorry you're having a bad day. Have you spoken to your doctor again, or are you still waiting for him to call back, as usual?"

"Yes, yes, still waiting for him to call, but since it's after hours now, I'm guessing it will be Monday."

"What the hell is wrong with doctors these days?" Laurel knew there was no answer to that question. "Of course, I'm coming. I'll be there bright and early. How about I make you breakfast in bed?"

"Oh darling, that sounds lovely. I'll see you in the morning. I love you so much."

"Okay Mom, I love you too. Sleep well so we can have a full day of fun tomorrow." Despite the heaviness in her heart, her words were filled with as much cheerfulness as she could muster.

They disconnected the call, and Laurel whispered, "I have some big news to tell you, Mom." She felt a tear land on her cheek. She hated that her mom's health was so bad. Laurel knew the COPD was getting worse, and her mom did as well, but they both tried not to dwell on it. Her mom had taken a few bad turns over the past couple of years, but she had always pulled through with a positive attitude. Laurel knew that today not being a "good day" could easily be caused by a side effect of one of her mom's many prescriptions. They all seemed to inflict some irritation or discomfort for the sake of keeping her alive.

Laurel turned her focus back to the plan. She couldn't wait to tell her mom that she was finally leaving Graham. Her mom had tried many times to point out that she didn't think Graham was the right man for Laurel. But did Laurel listen? No. But she knew now that Mom was right, and she looked forward to seeing the huge smile on her mom's face when she told her about her decision.

Laurel began sorting and packing while the laundry tumbled in the machine and was surprised to find that she felt better than she had in a long time. A weight had been lifted off her shoulders.

She finished folding the laundry and tried to remember when everything around the house had become her responsibility. She did all the cleaning, laundry, most of the cooking, grocery shopping, and besides mowing the lawn, she took care of the yard. What the hell did Graham do around here?

Laurel realized just how one-sided this relationship had become. She shook her head as she put Graham's T-shirts into his drawer. While she was trying to get them in the drawer, another folded piece of paper fell on the floor. She bent to pick it up and opened it, thinking it was just another shopping list. She couldn't have been more wrong.

"I just wanted to tell you that I had an amazing time with you last night," the note read. "I don't think I've ever known anyone so romantic and attentive. I'm looking forward to seeing you Friday night. XX."

Laurel screamed and dropped the note. "Are you kidding me? I'm doing your friggin' laundry, and you're having an affair?"

She paced the bedroom, her blood boiling. She couldn't believe how blind she had been. How long had it been going on? Who was the other woman? How could she be so stupid?

Stop. Breathe. She'd already made the decision to leave. Finding out he was cheating on her only made her more determined to get out. She pulled out her phone and took a photo of the note, then tossed it back on the floor.

Taking another deep breath, she slowly let it out. She walked into the kitchen, topped off her wineglass, and grabbed her list. She sent her mom a text message that she'd decided to come tonight, but it would be late.

For the next few hours, she packed quickly and furiously. Knowing she couldn't take everything that night, she made sure to take the important stuff. Who knew how Graham would react?

She closed the door to her jam-packed SUV and walked back inside. Walking from room to room, she checked to make sure she hadn't missed anything. Holding back the tears, she wrote a note telling Graham she would be back to get the rest of her things. To be sure he understood why she'd left, she grabbed the piece of paper from the bedroom floor and left it on top of her note.

Two

Pulling into her mom's driveway, Laurel wasn't surprised to see lights on in the house. Her mom must have known something was wrong and waited up for her.

The front door opened as she reached for the door handle. Her mom took one look at her and pulled Laurel into her arms, hugging her tightly.

"I've just made a pot of tea. Sit down and tell me what happened."

Collapsing in a heap on the couch, the emotions Laurel had been holding in for the past few hours erupted. "Mom, he's cheating on me. I found this note in his drawer while I was doing his laundry." She showed her mom the photo on her phone.

"Oh honey, I'm sorry." Her mom caressed Laurel's back as she continued.

"How could I be so blind? How long has it been going on? Who is it? And why? What's wrong with me?"

"There is nothing wrong with you, sweetheart. Remember that! Graham made this decision for himself. It has everything to do with him and nothing to do with you."

"I'm just so angry. Why not just end things with me first?" Angry tears ran down her cheeks. "You know what's crazy, Mom?

Shortly before I found this note, I had decided to end the relationship. Things haven't been right for a while. We'd become more roommates than a couple. I was making notes of what to pack, where I could possibly find an apartment...then I found the note."

"Why don't you stay here? Seriously, this house is too big for just me. Your office is the same distance from here, so your commute wouldn't be any longer." Her mom hugged her. "It would be great to see more of you."

Laurel looked at her mom. "Oh Mom, that's a great idea. I never thought I would be moving home at this time of my life. But I would love to be here with you. Oh, the fun we'll have. Thanks, Mom. I love you." She hugged her mom tightly.

"I love you more. Now what do you need from your car for the night? You can unload the rest tomorrow."

"I'll go pull the car into the garage and grab what I need."

After moving her car and grabbing an overnight bag, Laurel got situated in the guest room as her mom settled into bed.

"Goodnight, Laurel. I love you," her mom called across the hall.

Laurel hung one last sweater in the guest room closet and went to stand in the doorway to her mom's room. "Goodnight, Mom. I love you too. See you in the morning. Thanks for being so supportive."

"Anytime. Sweet dreams. Things will look better in the morning."

Laurel returned to her room and climbed into bed, exhausted. Staring at the ceiling, she couldn't help but wonder what Graham's reaction would be when he saw her note.

ALTHOUGH SHE WAS EXHAUSTED, LAUREL SPENT THE night tossing and turning—playing and replaying scenes of her relationship with Graham in her head. The what-if scenarios went round and round. After dozing off, she would wake suddenly because of a vivid dream. Finally, she gave up on trying to sleep and walked out on the deck to watch the sunrise.

"Good morning." Her mom hugged her shoulders from behind.

"Good morning, Mom. Sleep well?"

"Not too bad. How about you?"

"Not great. I couldn't shut my brain off. Played the old what-if game most of the night. Can't believe I didn't know. I just feel so stupid."

"Have you heard from him?"

"I haven't even looked at my phone. Avoiding it seems better than facing the truth."

Her mother grabbed her by the hand and led her to the kitchen. "Today, we are going to forget about he-who-shall-remain-nameless. After we have a healthy breakfast, you can unload your car, and then we are going to shopping."

Laurel smiled at her mom. "Okay, what's this healthy breakfast?"

Her mom looked over her shoulder as she tugged open the freezer drawer and winked. "Strawberry ice cream! Well, it *is* dairy, *and* it has strawberries in it, so that's fruit."

That sounded just like her mom. Laurel laughed as she pulled two bowls out of the cupboard while her mom plopped the ice cream onto the counter. "I still don't understand why I could never have ice cream for breakfast when I was a kid."

"Ah well, now that you're an adult, you can have ice cream any time you want and for any meal." Her mom smiled.

"I do love the wisdom that you continue to instill in me."

Laurel emptied her car while her mom did her breathing treatments. Just before they went out, Laurel looked at her phone. Graham had called twice and sent several text messages, all claiming it wasn't what she thought it was—insisting they needed to talk.

She sent a text back.

> Nothing left to talk about. I'll come by next Saturday to pick up the rest of my stuff.

With that done, she grabbed her mom's portable oxygen tank from the garage, along with a couple of spares, and they set off to their favorite shops. They drove to Jackson, and with her mom's handicap placard, they were able to park right in front.

As they always did when they shopped together, Laurel and her mom encouraged each other to buy something they wanted but hesitated to buy for themselves. They also bought each other gifts. Just silly or simple things but special, nonetheless. They talked and laughed like the best friends they were. After exhausting their feet—and their wallets—they drove to the National Hotel for an early dinner.

Once they had placed their orders, Mom lifted her glass of wine in a toast. "Thank you for a lovely day. Now, when are you going to get back to your dream? Are you finally going to get back into pottery?"

"I was actually thinking about that last night, wondering why I gave it up." Laurel made a face and took a sip of her wine. "Well, we both know the reason. Gosh, I do miss it, but I think that ship has sailed."

"Why would you say that?"

"I'm in my mid-thirties, single once again, and well, I have a job now."

Mom made a "pause" motion with her hand. "One that you are not happy with, I might point out."

"That is true, but it pays the bills...which I will now be paying on my own."

"Just how many excuses are you going to use?" Mom leaned back in her seat as the waitress served their dishes.

"Mom, it's too late for me."

"Laurel, it is not too late for you. Look at me. Look at your dad's life. Both were cut short due to illness. It is not too late for you." Reaching across the table, Mom covered Laurel's hand with her own. "Just think about it, okay? That's all I ask."

"Okay, Mom. I'll think about it." Laurel gave her mom's hand a squeeze. "Love you."

"Love you too, sweetheart."

Their conversation traveled in many different directions while they enjoyed their dinner: family stories and gossip; talk of Laurel's dad; trips they had taken together; and lots of general reminiscing.

"I'm exhausted. You must be as well." Laurel said as her mom yawned.

"Yes, I think it is time to go home and unwind from our busy day."

"I was thinking the same thing. Staying with you is like having a slumber party!"

Her mom giggled, and just the sound of it made Laurel want to remember this day forever. It was always iffy that her mom would have enough energy to do these sorts of outings. Laurel treasured them so much.

When they arrived back at her mom's home in Addington, Laurel got her mom settled in her recliner and went into the kitchen to make tea.

When she walked into the living room with the tea, her mom was sound asleep in the recliner. Laurel set the tea on the table, then reached over and tucked a blanket around her mom. She grabbed another blanket and settled onto the couch to drink her tea. As she watched her mom sleep so peacefully, Laurel smiled. Then a tear slid down her face as she thought about their day. Their time together was so precious.

Pulling out her phone for the first time since the morning, she saw that Graham had replied to her text.

> I understand if you need some time to think
> things over. I really think we can work this out,
> babe. Just give me another chance.

Deciding not to reply to him felt like a small victory. *I feel like I've turned the corner. I made a decision, and I'm going to stick with it. There's no way I am going back to him.*

She texted her best friend, Maggie, explaining the saga of the past twenty-four hours and that she was staying at her mom's. The texts went back and forth, and Laurel felt even more empowered by the support she received from Maggie and her mom.

SUNDAY MORNING, LAUREL WAS ON THE DECK watching the sunrise again when her mom came out. One look told her that Mom wasn't doing well.

"Mom, c'mon. Let me help you. You've had a bad night, haven't you?"

"Yes, I just can't seem to catch my breath." Her mom allowed herself to be guided inside and sat at the kitchen table, trying to manage a smile.

"Let me check the oxygen setting, Mom. Maybe if we increase it a bit, that might help." Laurel found the oxygen concentrator in the garage. The oxygen tube was long and fed through a small hole in the wall. It allowed her mom to get around the house quite easily. She turned the dial up a bit, hoping it would help.

Back in the kitchen, she leaned over and hugged her mom. "Just take it easy, okay? We probably overdid it a bit yesterday. What can I help you with around here today?"

Reaching across the table, her mom squeezed her hand. "Hon, I'd like to go over some documents with you, okay? I just want to be sure you know where everything is when the time comes."

Laurel squeezed her hand back, holding back the tears that

wanted to fall. "Of course, Mom. Whatever you would like to do. I know you want to be sure everything is in order. I just hope that the time doesn't come for a long time."

"Oh honey, me too. But I want to be prepared. It will be hard enough on you anyway, so I want to make sure I make it a little easier, if I can."

Her mom smiled in a way that broke her heart. What would she do without her? Laurel lost her dad to a heart attack ten years ago. *Stop with the morbid thoughts, Laurel. Don't ruin the time that you have with Mom.*

After they finished breakfast, Laurel made a pot of tea to enjoy while they went through the documents. They discussed the living trust her mom had put in place, which would make probate easier. And her mom's attorney, Frank, had been a friend of the family for ages, so Laurel knew she had someone to turn to with any questions she might have.

It was emotionally draining to talk about what neither one of them wanted to face. Then her mom decided to rest in her recliner for a bit, leaving Laurel to putter about the house.

AFTER TWO HOURS, LAUREL LOOKED UP FROM HER book to see her mom's eyes were open. "You had a good nap. Do you feel any better?"

"Yes, my breathing is better. I'm tired, but better than I was this morning. How are you doing?"

"I'm good, Mom. I hate that things ended with Graham the way they did, but I'm glad that I got out."

"I'm proud of you, Laurel. I'm sorry you didn't get what you wanted from the relationship, but I know that the right man is out there for you. Someone who will love you and encourage you to follow your own path. Someone who will be there for you when you stumble and comfort you when the world seems too much."

"Thanks Mom. I would love to have what you and Dad had together."

"True, enduring love. We were soulmates, that's for sure." Mom smiled, as if remembering their life together. "And I still miss him every single day."

"Me too, Mom, me too."

"So, what are your plans now? Have you given any more thought to your job—or more importantly, your dream?" Mom leaned back in her chair and tried to take a deep breath, which caused her to cough.

Laurel reached for her mom's hand as the coughing eased. "Believe me, I am thinking a lot about it." She squeezed her hand. "Are you doing okay?"

"Yes, dear. I'm okay. But it is getting worse, and I just have no energy anymore." She shrugged her shoulders. "Nothing we can do about it but accept it."

"Oh Mom. I just wish I could wave a magic wand and make you all better. I hate to see you suffer so much."

"Sweetheart, I've accepted the cards life has dealt me. Of course, I wish it were different. I wish I could do the things I used to. I wish we had more time. I wish, I wish—but all that does is take the joy out of this moment, right now. I don't want to waste any more time on what-ifs. Life, for all of us, is too short for what-ifs."

Laurel hugged her mom and fought back the tears. The last thing she wanted to do was spend this precious time with her mom just crying. Who knew how long her mom would be around?

"I love you, Mom."

"I love you more, dear heart." Her mom tightened the hug.

That evening, while she watched her mom dozing peacefully in her recliner, Laurel sat on the couch and thought about what she had said. "Life, for all of us, is too short for what-ifs." Laurel reached back in her memories, trying to pinpoint when she had chosen different paths than what she had planned. She tried to examine what caused the shifts that changed her life. Maybe it was time to stop focusing on the what-ifs and figure out what she wanted for her life going forward. Thoughts swirled through her head as she drifted off to sleep.

LAUREL WAS STARTLED AWAKE BY THE SOUND OF HER mom's coughing. Rushing to her mom's side, she adjusted the recliner, so she was sitting up. "Mom, Mom..." She scrambled for the basket of medical stuff on the table. "Here, Mom, here's your inhaler. Can you try taking a puff?"

Her mom's shaking hands held the inhaler, and she took a puff. More coughing ensued.

"Try another puff, Mom, please." Laurel tried to keep the worry out of her voice.

"I...can't...seem...to...catch...my...breath." Mom grabbed Laurel's hand.

Laurel pushed the button on her mom's Life Alert and told the dispatcher she needed an ambulance.

"Mom, just take another puff. The ambulance will be here soon. We'll get you to the hospital and the doctors will help you."

The pleading look in her mom's eyes reflected how scared they both were. Squeezing her mom's hand tight, Laurel whispered, "I love you, Mom."

SHE WAITED FOR WHAT FELT LIKE AN ETERNITY WHILE the doctors and nurses in the ICU tried to stabilize her mom.

Finally, the doctor came out to talk to her. "Laurel, I'm sorry, but the COPD has taken its toll on your mom's lungs. She is on an NIV, which is a non-invasive ventilator, to assist her breathing. Hopefully, we can start to wean her off that tomorrow."

Laurel fought back her tears. "Doctor, what then? Is she going to pull through this time?"

"We're trying everything we can, but the COPD is quite advanced now. The damage to her lungs is extensive. I'm sorry. We are doing everything we can for her."

"Can I see her?"

"Yes. I'll check in on her later."

"Thank you, Doctor."

Taking a deep breath and slowly letting it out, Laurel tried to compose herself before going into her mom's room.

The nurse greeted her as she walked in. "She may seem a bit groggy, as we've given her a light sedation to make her more comfortable."

"Thanks. Is it okay if I sit with her?"

The nurse squeezed Laurel's shoulder as she walked by. "Of course, dear. She will know you're here with her. Let us know if you need anything."

She pulled a chair next to the bed and took her mom's frail hand in hers. Her mom lay connected to machines that dinged and beeped—machines that were keeping her alive.

"I'm here, Mom. I love you."

Her mom's eyes fluttered open as she weakly squeezed Laurel's hand. "I love you too, dear heart." She mouthed the words, but Laurel could feel them in her heart. Her eyes closed again.

Her mom slept while Laurel talked to her. "Mom, remember when you, Dad, and I put our hands in the fresh concrete at the cabin? We had so many good times there. Remember that fort that Maggie, Tim, and I built in the tree? They both send their love. I texted Maggie a little while ago. She offered to come to the hospital, but I told her I wanted to have you all to myself." She squeezed her mom's hand and watched her face for any recognition. Nothing. Just breathing. It might have been assisted by machines, but she was still here.

"I was thinking that when you get out of here, we should go

to the cabin for a few days. I should take some of that vacation time I have built up. We could sit by the lake and watch the ducks float by." She wiped tears from her eyes. "We could visit some of our favorite shops."

She looked down at her mother's hand clasped in hers. Her wedding ring was never removed, and it rested there as a reminder of enduring love.

A nurse came in and adjusted a setting on one of the machines. "You've been here a long time. I ordered a tray from the cafeteria for you. You need to keep up your strength."

Laurel managed a weak smile. "I'm not really hungry. Thanks though."

The nurse winked at her. "Listen, your mom would be telling you the same thing I am, so how about you try to eat something, okay?"

"Okay. Thank you."

As the hours passed, Laurel continued talking to her mom. The nurses came and went. When the doctor came back, they asked her to step out of the room for a few minutes.

"Mom, the doctor is here." She squeezed her mom's hand as she leaned over and kissed her forehead. "I won't be far away. I love you."

In the restroom, she splashed cold water on her face. The reflection staring back at her showed the fear and anxiety she was feeling. She couldn't lose her. It was too soon. She wiped the tears from her cheeks. She hated to see her suffer like this, though.

A few minutes later, the doctor found her pacing in the waiting room. "Laurel, have a seat." He sat next to her and looked her in the eye. "I'm sorry, but we've done all we can do. The disease has taken its toll on your mom. Her body is starting to shut down."

Laurel tried to hold in the sob, but it escaped. "What are you saying?"

"At this point, we are just going to make her as comfortable as possible. I'm sorry." When Laurel didn't respond, the doctor nodded, pushed himself to his feet, and disappeared down the hallway.

Taking a moment to compose herself, Laurel walked back to her mom's room.

"We've brought you in a more comfortable chair, dear," the nurse said. "Let us know if you need anything."

Laurel mumbled a thank you and sat in the chair, taking her mom's hand in hers. "I love you, Mom."

She fought back the tears so her mom could see how strong she was. "Oh, Mom. I wish I could make you better. I know it's been a rough road for you these past few years."

Leaning back in the chair, she looked at her mom. She tried not to focus on the data the machines were showing. She sat still and squeezed her mom's hand. "Mom, squeeze my hand." Nothing. "Mom, c'mon squeeze my hand, show me you're still here." No response. Laurel's heart was breaking.

She stood and kissed her mom's forehead, brushing a strand of hair away. "Mom, I know you're tired. It's okay to let go. I love you. I will be okay. Thanks for being the best mom and best friend I could ask for. I love you."

An alarm sounded on a machine. The nurse came in and turned it off and removed the oxygen mask. She touched Laurel's shoulder. "I'm sorry. Take all the time you need."

Mom was gone.

Laurel sat there, rocking back and forth, sobbing. "Aw, Mom. I love you. You and Dad are together again. I promise to make you both proud."

Three

Laurel walked into the house from the garage and stopped. The silence was so loud that it accosted her. She had only been in the house alone a few times in her entire lifetime—the times that her mom was in the hospital. That thought started the waterworks. She reached for the tissue box and plopped on the couch, letting the sobs consume her once again.

A short time later, the sound of the doorbell made her jump. She grabbed the tissue box and stumbled to the door. She had barely turned the knob when Maggie pushed the door open, closed it behind her, and wrapped Laurel in her arms. Maggie led her to the couch and held her as she cried.

"I know, kiddo. Just let it go. I know." Maggie rocked Laurel in her arms.

They cried together, holding on to each other and sharing the quickly depleted box of tissues.

"She was the best," Laurel said, a small smile breaking through.

"Yes, she was. She was my second mom. I'm going to miss her so much." Maggie blew her nose loudly.

"She loved having you and Tim as her extra kids." Laurel realized she'd forgotten about Tim. "Oh gosh, Tim. Have you told him?"

Maggie hugged her. "Yes, I talked to him on the way here. Not the smartest thing, 'cause we were both crying over the phone to each other. He'll call you tomorrow. He sends his love."

"Aw, where is he right now? I've lost track over the past couple of weeks."

"He just arrived in Dubai. Honey, I don't know if he'll be able to make it back for Mom's service. He has a huge business commitment there, and I don't think he can wiggle out to come back to the States right now."

Laurel hugged one of her mom's needlepoint throw pillows. "I understand. He's halfway around the world. I'll just have to wait a bit longer for one of his bear hugs." She hugged the pillow tighter.

Maggie pulled Laurel close. "His bear hugs are the absolute best. I miss him a lot, but I'm happy he's enjoying life and loves his work so much."

"Me too." She lifted the pillow to her nose. "This smells like Mom. Lavender, with a hint of citrus."

"It's weird how scents connect us to people or memories. For me, it's fresh baked bread. Anywhere."

"Your mom's bread. Oh my gosh, I always loved going to your house on the weekends when she baked bread."

They sighed in unison.

"Okay, so have you called your mom's brother or your cousins yet?" Maggie asked.

"Yes, somehow, in between the heavy sobs, I called Linda and Bill first so that they could be there for their dad. I'm so glad they still live in the same town as my uncle. Once I knew they were on their way to his house, I called him. Oh, Maggie, that call was so difficult. His baby sister. He tried to be strong for me, but I could hear his voice crack."

"Ugh, that is so hard." Maggie gave her a side hug.

"I also called my dad's sister. She and I cried together. Just talking to her felt like being wrapped in one of her hugs."

"Aw, that's nice. Betsy hasn't been out here in years, has she?"

"No, she said she regretted not making the effort when Mom was still alive. She hates that she'll travel out for her service instead." She took a deep breath. "Perhaps it's a reminder to us all, that we need to make more of an effort to spend time with those we love. Tomorrow isn't promised."

"Very true."

Laurel stood and gazed around the living room. Framed family photos adorned one wall, her mom's needlepoint, another. She ran her hand over the back of her mom's recliner. "I can't believe she's really gone." She took a deep breath and slowly let it out.

"Me either." Maggie walked into the kitchen. "I think we need to open a bottle of wine and raise a toast or two to your mom. When was the last time you ate anything?"

"I agree." Laurel paused, considering her stomach for the first time in a while. "Um, I'm not sure. It's all a blur right now."

Maggie opened the wine, and they made their toasts to Mom —one serious and one silly, because Mom would expect that from them. Maggie put a tray of food together and, even though Laurel said she wasn't hungry, they managed to devour everything.

Laurel called Frank, her mom's lawyer, and they agreed to meet in a couple days to review everything. She contacted the funeral home and arranged that she and Maggie would meet with them in the morning to plan the service. When she contacted work, she told them that in addition to four days of bereavement leave, she was also taking a couple of vacation days. There was so much to do, and work was the least of her concerns right now.

While Maggie called her husband Martin, Laurel went to her mom's bedroom. Standing in the doorway, she sighed. She slowly walked around the room, touching a photo here, lifting a book on the bedside table and putting it down again. She absentmindedly ran her fingers along the dresser as she looked around. The smell of her mom's perfume hung in the air. "Aw Mom, what am I going to do without you?" she asked aloud.

LAUREL MET WITH FRANK, AND HE EXPLAINED AGAIN everything about the will and the living trust. He assured her that her mom had set the trust up in a way that ensured it was easiest on Laurel. Once she cleaned out the house in Addington, it would be placed on the market. Laurel didn't want to live there, but she also felt she shouldn't sell it because it was where her parents had lived out the end of their lives. But that feeling stemmed from some misplaced connection that didn't need to be there.

As she got up to leave, Frank stopped her. "There is one more thing. Your mother gave this to me just last week. She told me that you'd want to read it back at the house." He handed her an envelope.

"Thanks, Frank. I appreciate all your help. See you at the service."

LAUREL WAS MENTALLY EXHAUSTED BY THE TIME SHE got home from her meeting with Frank. Her head was spinning with all the information they had discussed. There was just so much to think about.

She took the envelope and sat in her mom's recliner. Strangely, just sitting in her chair made Laurel feel like her mom's arms were wrapped around her. She slowly opened the envelope and read:

Dear Heart,

I know this is an awful time for you. Just remember that I lived a good life and I am now reunited with your dad. These past few years of illness have not been fun, to say the least, and now I am no longer suffering. Please take some comfort in that.

By now you have read my wishes for my estate. I have worked with our attorney, Frank, over the past year to put things in order for you. Hopefully, it will be a smooth process for you. As I said in my will, I want you to sell the house in Addington. I know you will not feel that you should do this, but you don't want to live there, and that's okay. It isn't where you belong.

You have your whole life in front of you to live your dreams. I know you have put those aside for too long now. It is time for you to start living your life on your terms. You know who and what I am talking about. I have tried to understand what you see in him, but I will be honest and tell you I don't understand. He is not the right man for you, and I think you know that. You are comfortable in your everyday life. Comfortable, but not happy. If you are honest with yourself, you know it is time for you to leave him. Yes, it will make your life messy for a bit, it's but nothing you can't handle, my dear.

We both know that your self-esteem and confidence have taken a blow, but you can, and you will, get past that once you are away from him. You are probably wondering why I am telling you this now in my final letter, but to me, it is that important. I've tried to talk to you about him, but you really didn't want to hear it, so I decided to change my tactic and just be there for you when you finally left him. Now, however, I am gone, and I really must encourage you to get out now. I fear that my death and thus my everyday presence in your life will only push him to crush your spirit even more. I don't want that to happen.

Breathe, my dear. I have more to share. I'm not sure what time it is that you're reading this, but I hope it is at a time that you can have a glass of wine. Oh heck, have one anyway!

I know people say not to make any major life-changing decisions when one is grieving, but I think now is the time! Time for change. You need to start living, so here are my thoughts.

1. Leave him. Just leave him. There is nothing left to discuss with him, and he will only twist things and make you feel guilty. So just leave him.

2. It is time to follow those dreams of yours, my sweet daughter. That means you need to leave that job as well. You are only there because it is a paycheck. Nothing more. Lord knows we've discussed this enough. I know, I know, this means major changes in all aspects of your life, but it is TIME

3. Pottery. Yes, that's right, pottery! It is your love. You wanted so badly to follow that dream of having your own collection and working in your own studio. Do it! Seriously, do it. Here's how it can happen.

4. Once you leave him, he who shall remain nameless, (c'mon, that made you smile a bit, didn't it?) and leave the job, why don't you move to the cabin? Seriously! You love it there, as we all have. That is our special place. We have so many memories of family times spent there. The cabin is the perfect place to make that dream come true. The studio/garden shed (your dad went a bit overboard with building it) is perfect for your pottery studio. Did I just see the lightbulb above your head flicker a bit?

5. The inheritance (sorry it isn't more, but hey, we enjoyed life) and the proceeds from the sale of the house in Addington should help you out while you get that dream going.

I hope I had the chance to tell you this before the end of my time. That was my plan. If I did, you may have thought it was the ramblings of Mom on pain-relieving meds, but after reading this, you now know I was of sound mind. Ha, ha…that made you laugh, didn't it?

Sweetheart, I've watched you go from a confident, strong-willed young lady to someone who questions everything she does. That isn't you. That is how someone else wants you to be. Don't let him do this to you any longer.

You have a lot to cope with now, and I know how tough it will be on you. I know Maggie and the rest of the family will be there for you. Lean on them, especially Maggie. She understands better than the rest what you are going through. I've always loved the bond you two share.

I implore you to start living your life on your terms. Your dad and I loved life. We took risks (some worked, some didn't), but our lives were richer for having those experiences. We may not have been rich in terms of money in the bank, but oh my, what a wonderful life we had. You can have it as well. And I truly believe that you will have a wonderful life. I believe in you, dear daughter.

Never forget that your dad and I are always with you in your heart and in your memories. We love you more!

Love and huge mommy hugs,
Mom

Laurel reread the letter for the third time and leaned back against the chair. Tears streamed down her face, and she wiped them with her sleeve.

Oh Mom, what have I done with my life?

HER MOM'S SERVICE WAS THE SEND-OFF LAUREL HAD hoped for. Lots of family and friends came to grieve, but more importantly, they came to celebrate her mom by sharing heartfelt stories. There were plenty of tears, but lots of love and laughter as well.

Laurel did a lot of soul searching that week, and when she returned to work, she gave her two-week notice. Her boss was shocked and told her she was just being emotional, that she shouldn't be making such a rash decision at this time. A couple of her coworkers voiced the same sentiments, although her closest friend at work, Sally, wished she were as brave as Laurel to escape.

Thankfully, the two weeks passed quickly. Laurel was working on the how-to manual that her boss had requested. Laurel had always documented the details needed for her system admin position. It was too important not to. So, it made the task easier, but she always loved it when bosses asked for a how-do-you-do-your-job manual. Shouldn't the boss know how to do the job?

On her last day, Laurel packed up her personal items from her office. She didn't tell anyone what her plans were, which probably made them think she was being irrational. Sally took her to lunch on her last day, and Laurel finally shared with her what she was going to do. Sally expressed her unconditional support, but Laurel could detect hints of envy in Sally's tone. At the end of the day, her boss never even came to say goodbye. She walked out of the office after four years without so much as a thank you.

LAUREL'S LAST OLD-LIFE TASK WAS TO PICK UP THE REST of her things from Graham's. When she pulled into the driveway, she had the strongest feeling that she didn't belong there anymore. After everything she had been through recently, living here seemed like a distant memory.

Graham stood in the open garage door. He tried to hug her when she approached him.

"Graham, please. Don't."

"C'mon, babe. We can work this out."

"No, we can't. I don't want to."

"Babe, you're just being emotional because of your mom."

"I'm being emotional because of my mom? Really?"

He reached out to touch her arm, but she walked past him. She quickly went around the house and garage, gathering the last of her stuff.

All the while, he followed her, trying to talk her out of leaving. "Listen, I know you're missing your mom, but she was sick for a long time. She is in a better place now. She would want you to be happy. Please come back."

She stopped abruptly, causing him to almost run into her. "She's in a better place? She's dead. How can you be so cruel?"

Graham grabbed her by the shoulders, trying to get Laurel to look at him. "I'm not trying to be cruel. Just—what am I supposed to say to make you feel better?"

Laurel drew in a deep breath and released it slowly as she looked Graham in the eye. She knew how angry it made him that she could remain calm when they argued. It always had and led to fights lasting longer.

"Nothing, Graham. Nothing at all. Please, just let me get my stuff loaded, and I'll get out of here."

"Babe, please, I don't want to lose you."

"You already have. A word of advice: The next time you cheat on your girlfriend, it would be best if you did your own laundry, so she doesn't find the notes from your lover while putting the laundry away."

Graham slammed his fist on the counter. "Fine! Go then! But don't even think of crawling back to me once you've come to your senses!"

"Don't worry, that thought will never cross my mind."

Graham grabbed his phone and keys and stormed out the door. His car started and backed out of the driveway, then his tires squealed down the street.

"Oh, that is so mature!" Laurel said aloud, rolling her eyes.

It was a huge relief the conversation was over, and she was thankful he had left. That would give her time to load the remainder of her stuff into her SUV and leave before he returned.

Two hours later, her SUV was loaded. She walked through each room one last time to make sure she hadn't forgotten anything. It was amazing how detached she felt as she wandered through the house. His house. Well, his grandmother's house. She paused in the living room and lifted a framed photo of them that was taken at his sister's wedding. It was a great picture of them at a time when she had thought he was the one. She placed the frame back on the mantel; it wasn't something she wanted anymore.

She couldn't believe how little she was taking, but how much of one's past was necessary for the future? With that final thought, she picked up her key ring, twisted the house key off, and placed it on the kitchen table. Picking up her phone and purse, she walked to the front door and closed the door behind her without another glance.

Four

Sitting in the driveway, Laurel looked at the cabin. So many memories flooded her mind. She and her friends used to draw chalk pictures and a hopscotch game on the driveway, playing in the sun until one of them yelled, "Last one in the lake is a rotten egg!" That would lead to a race up the porch to the deck that wrapped around the side of the house, then on to the lake. Giggles filled the air as they all tried not to be last. She was looking forward to reconnecting with her childhood friends who still lived in the area.

Laurel slid her fingers into her purse and touched the letter from her mom. Just the slight touch brought a smile to her face. She was doing the right thing. *Thanks, Mom.*

Taking the flagstone path to the porch, she strolled around the deck to the backyard. There it was. Her mom's beautiful garden. Purple irises, gladiolas, jasmine, and the trellis of red bougainvillea. The burst of color took her breath away.

Beyond the garden, the yard sloped to their dock on the lake. A small boat shed sat near the shore. It held fishing gear, paddleboards, life jackets, and a variety of flotation devices.

Her mom's studio/garden shed stood there, too, inviting her to make it her own. This was the place where her mom had found sanctuary, whether she was throwing pots or filling them with beautiful flowers.

Turning, she looked at the back of the cabin and the deck that wrapped around it. The heaviness of the past month lifted from her shoulders. Smiling, she unlocked the door to her new home.

Stepping inside felt just like that—home. This cabin played a role in so many special memories, and it was a place that she had always felt able to be herself. Setting her purse and keys down on the table, she walked into the living room and looked around. Opening the wooden window blinds, she loved how the after-noon sun filled the room. Laurel wandered through the cabin, opening the blinds and looking around the rooms. When she reached the door to the master bedroom, she didn't open it. Couldn't open it. Not yet. *Okay, I knew this was going to be hard, but gosh, I miss you both so much.*

Slowly, she walked back downstairs and stood at the open French doors which led to the deck. The sunlight was glinting on the lake, and the trees were full of birdsong. A deep breath in and out helped to shift her mood from the tears. Well, she had the rest of her life to stand and look at the lake. She'd better get the car unpacked. She walked from the kitchen into the garage and pushed the button to open the garage door. She moved her car into the double garage and started unloading her boxes. She'd made sure to label them as she was packing, so it would make the task of unloading easier. Some boxes would go into the house and into the room where they belonged, and others would remain in the garage for now.

An hour later, the car was empty, and she was exhausted. She closed the garage door and walked back into the kitchen. After making a cup of tea, she took her notebook and her phone out to the deck. Sitting at the table, she looked out at the lake. The sun had dipped lower in the sky, casting long shadows across the yard.

Sipping her tea, she watched a family of ducks float by the end of the dock. She picked up her phone and dialed Maggie's number.

"Hello! How are you?" Maggie asked before Laurel even heard the phone ring.

Laughing at her best friend's animated voice, she responded, "I'm good. The drive was easy, and I stopped in Baker and grabbed a few groceries so I wouldn't have to go back out once I got here. I've unloaded the car, and now I'm sitting here on the deck with a cup of tea. And you?"

"Ha, ha. Well, that's all great. Are you going to tell me what Graham said?"

"Ah, that. He reacted like I expected. He thinks I've lost my mind and told me not to even think about crawling back to him when I come to my senses. I assured him that I wouldn't even think about going back to him. He stormed out, which was exactly what I wanted. I loaded the car with the rest of the boxes, and I left."

"Wow, he really is clueless."

"Yes, he is. Anyway, I'm finished with him. I am now embarking on my new life. I wish Mom were here to see me do it." Laurel fought back tears.

"I know. I do too. Love you."

"At least she can see that I finally listened to her." A smile tugged at her lips once more.

"Ha, and we can hear her saying it's about time!"

Laurel heard a car coming up the driveway. She stood and walked toward the front of the house. "It seems I have company. I wonder who that could be. No one knows I'm here."

Maggie couldn't contain her surprise any longer. "Well, I wonder who it could be. Perhaps..."

Laurel screamed when she walked around the deck to see Maggie's car.

"You! How could you not tell me you were coming?" She gave Maggie a big hug.

"Martin and I thought it would be a great surprise if I came to help you get settled. You don't mind, do you?"

"Mind? This is the best surprise ever. I'm so thrilled you're here!" She squealed as she hugged Maggie again.

"Good! Listen, I brought some groceries and a fair bit of wine and cava to celebrate. Shall we unload the car?"

"You're the best friend ever!" Laurel grabbed a few bags from the back seat.

WHILE MAGGIE PUT HER THINGS IN THE GUEST ROOM, Laurel put the groceries away and put some cheese and flatbread on a tray, balancing it out with a bottle of cava and glasses.

They took the tray, sat at the table, and looked out across the lake. They sighed in unison at the view.

"I have always loved this view. It is so peaceful," Laurel said.

"Me too. How many summers did our families spend here together? So many memories."

"I know! We've had so many great times here."

"And now you get to call this place home. I'm really happy you're doing this."

Laurel exhaled slowly. "Let's just hope I'm talented enough to make a living with my pottery."

"You'll be amazing. It's time to restore your confidence, missy!" Maggie tapped Laurel's side with an elbow.

"I know. And with your help, I'm finding it again. How can one idiot cause so much damage in a short period?" Suddenly all Laurel's mistakes loomed over her, and all she could think of was the time she lost. "Why was I so stupid? Why did I let him do that to me?"

"Stop beating yourself up! He did enough of that. We all do stupid things in the name of so-called love. The important thing is to learn from those mistakes and not be afraid to love again. You'll put this behind you soon enough. Just focus on the future now." Maggie lifted a sleek green bottle off the table. "More cava?"

Laurel eagerly pushed her glass forward. "Yes, please. Do you remember when you first introduced me to Spanish cava?"

"I do. It was after Martin and I returned from our first trip to Spain. We did a tour of a winery and had a tasting. An ancestor of theirs had brought the method of champagne back to Catalunya. It feels like a bit of Spain when we drink it."

"Between you and Lena, my knowledge and love of wine and cava has really grown." Lena was a childhood friend who now owned a vineyard nearby.

"Oh, we need to get everyone together while I'm here. A 'Welcome Home, Laurel' celebration. I'll send a group text."

As soon as Maggie hit send, the replies started. Lena, Bailey, Cassie, Holly, and Joy all agreed: a celebration was needed. They would compare schedules and make it happen.

As the sun set and the temperature cooled, they went inside to put dinner together. As they ate, they talked about Laurel's plan for the studio and her pottery.

"Did I tell you," Laurel began, finishing a forkful of pasta, "my mom never got rid of her pottery wheel? She never gave up on me and my dream. I think using her wheel will help me keep her presence with me."

"Aw, that's a great sentiment. She will always be here with you. Just like your dad has been all these years. And just like my parents have been."

"Yes, gosh, we had the best parents."

Maggie lifted her glass, as if to toast to their parents. "We certainly did."

The next morning, Laurel was full of energy. She just couldn't wait any longer to start unpacking. Grabbing the corner of the box, she yanked on it, expecting the tape to tear open. While she gave it another yank, Maggie brought over a box cutter.

"This might help."

"Ha. Thanks." She cut the tape and opened the box.

Pulling out her beautiful ceramic bowl from the box, she smiled and set it on the coffee table. Then, opening the next box, she pulled out Marshmallow, her beloved stuffed animal. Laurel and her mom had found the cuddly lamb on one of their many mother-daughter weekends away. That made it even more special to her. She hugged Marshmallow and apologized for keeping her in a box for so long. She muttered about it being a stupid time of her life and nothing Marshmallow had done. Yes, she knew it was a stuffed animal, but didn't everyone talk to their stuffed animals?

"Okay, let's go check out your pottery barn. That has such a good ring to it." Maggie turned to Laurel with a gleam in her eye. "You should use that as the name of your company."

Laurel laughed. "Um, except I think that name is already taken and very successful."

"Oh bother. We'll come up with something else then."

They went out the French doors to the deck and walked the short distance to the garden shed. Laurel suddenly stopped when they reached the concrete step to the doorway.

"Maggie, look." She bent and placed her hand over her child-size handprint in the concrete. A few tears fell, hitting the three handprints below. "This was one of the memories I talked to Mom about in her final hours."

Maggie hugged her. "So many of your favorite memories live here with you."

"That's beautiful. Thank you."

Laurel put the key in the lock and turned the handle. She slowly opened the door and flicked on the light. The scent of garden dirt and damp clay greeted them as they both stopped in the doorway.

"Oh wow!" Laurel breathed. "I forgot how perfect this shed is. The skylight and windows... Look at the light in here. And the tile floor will be easy to clean up. This is going to be great!"

"I know! You are going to create magic in this space," Maggie said.

"Joe from the youth center will be dropping off the kiln tomorrow morning. He'll also move Mom's old pottery wheel from the garage to the studio. I'm so glad she never got rid of it. She hadn't used it in years, but like I said, it's obvious she never gave up on me and this dream of mine. I couldn't believe my luck when I saw they were selling the kiln on the town's marketplace website. And Joe, being the wonderful guy he is, said he would deliver for free. I love the people in this town. It still feels like small-town America, where people help their neighbors."

"So, how can we make this room work for your studio? Let's take some measurements and figure out what you need and then go do some shopping!"

They measured and chatted and looked at some photos Laurel had saved in her "Dreams Come True" folder. The room was bigger than she imagined starting out with, and she couldn't wait to get everything set up.

Off to town they went, first to the second-hand furniture store, as Laurel really wanted to keep with the rustic feel of the cabin and its location. They found some great shelves Laurel could use and a neat little desk that would match perfectly. Next stop was the hardware store for some other bits and pieces.

"Let's stop at Lyman's Bookshop & Café and grab some lunch," Maggie suggested as they loaded the car.

"Sounds great! I'm starving, and it will be great to see Holly and Joy. I was so touched that they came to Mom's service."

Maggie smiled and took Laurel's hand. "When we all spent our summers together here, our parents were so close as well. It was as if we all gained each other's parents. What a blessing that time was, and how amazing that as adults, all of us are still close."

"That's so true. I remember feeling lucky being accepted by the people who lived here year round. Lena, Cassie, Bailey, Holly, and Joy's families all embraced us. They never treated us as summer folk."

"I know. Gosh, the fun us girls had together. It will be great to see them all."

"I've always envied Holly and Joy and their bond as sisters." Laurel slung herself into the driver's seat of her SUV as Maggie closed the passenger side door. "When we were kids, they always made me want a sister."

"They *are* amazing. Those two have so much fun working together, and they keep adding new products and experiences in the bookshop. Holly is now giving kids cookie-baking lessons, and then the kids are selling them in the shop."

"Aw, that's great. I bet the kids love that! What do they do with the money they make?"

"Oh, that's the best part. The kids took a vote and decided that all the money should go toward buying books for kids in town who cannot afford them."

Laurel practically melted in her seat as she pulled the SUV onto the road. "Have I told you how much I love this town, Maggie? I still can't believe that I now get to call it home."

"I'm just so happy this has all worked out. We'll get you all settled, and then you need to get to work creating!"

"That's the scary part now. What if I'm not any good? What if no one wants to buy my less-than-perfect pottery?"

"Laurel, you are going to do great. Why do you doubt yourself so much these days? Oh, yes, I know why. Well, it's time to put jerk face behind you and move on."

"I know. I know. I just—"

Maggie put up a hand. "Seriously, Laurel. Stop listening to his lingering voice in your head. He no longer has any control over you. He is out of your life. No more looking back. You're not going that way!"

"Okay, got it." Laurel pursed her lips for a moment, then smiled at Maggie. "Thanks for the pep talk. You're right."

They pulled into the café parking lot and made their way inside. As soon as the bell jingled on the door, Joy came around the counter to greet them.

"Holly, look who's here!" Joy called out over her shoulder. Then she reached out to hug them both. "Oh, Maggie and Laurel! We are so happy to see you. Laurel, how are you doing? We miss your mom."

"I'm doing okay. I have my good days and bad days. I miss her terribly."

"She was a wonderful lady. We always loved when she came to the cabin and stopped in here to visit," Holly chimed in, getting her chance at the hugs.

"Thank you both so much." Laurel hugged each of them again. "I'm really excited to be here, and I love that I'm home now."

Joy led them to a table and handed them their menus. They all chatted for a few more minutes and talked about the little celebration at the cabin they were planning to throw before Maggie went back home the following week. Then Holly went back to work, and Joy got Laurel and Maggie some sparkling mineral water as they looked over the menus.

"I'm suddenly really hungry. I'm not sure what to order; it all sounds so good," Laurel said.

"I'm getting their cobb salad. It reminds me of the one at Rosine's in Monterey. Remember that place? Their desserts were amazing. I always had a salad, so I could tell myself it balanced out the calories." Maggie winked over her menu.

"I do remember that place. Last year, when I was down there for Maureen's wedding, we had lunch there. The place is still incredible. Okay, that's easy...cobb salad for me as well."

Joy took their order and brought back a glass of Sauvignon Blanc for each of them. "It's from the Marlborough region of New Zealand. I think you'll love it."

"You do know us well, Joy," Maggie said. "Thank you."

"Enjoy," Joy said, and walked away to greet another customer.

Raising their wineglasses and clinking them, Laurel and Maggie said in unison, "Cheers! To following dreams!"

After lunch, Laurel and Maggie headed back home to start work on the studio. The second-hand store was due to deliver the furniture at four that afternoon, and they wanted to get the rest of the room prepped. As they worked together, they talked about childhood memories of their families together. They laughed and shed a few tears.

The shelves and desk were delivered right on time, and once they were in the studio, the reality of what was happening suddenly hit Laurel. "Wow, am I really doing this? Look at this place. It looks like it was meant to be my studio. I can't believe this is really happening. I'm equal parts excited and petrified!"

"Laurel, stay right here. I have something to finish off the room." Maggie rushed out of the studio. Coming back in, she told Laurel to close her eyes. "I have a surprise for you." Laurel heard a muted thump and then Maggie told her to open her eyes. On the desk sat two little clay bowls.

"Oh Maggie! That's perfect. Gosh, how old were we when we made these in summer camp together? Thankfully, my pottery has improved a lot since then." Laurel laughed at the misshapen bowls.

"We were both just silly little girls then. I just thought they would be perfect on your desk as a reminder to never give up. Things will improve and get better with a bit of practice."

"Thank you so much! For everything. I couldn't have done this without you!"

Maggie flapped her hand as if to wave away the compliment. "Yeah, yeah, yeah. Whatever. I just did for you what we've always done for each other: support and encourage. It's what we do. Now, let's go finish cleaning out the corner in the garage where the kiln is going to go."

A couple of hours later, they were sitting on the deck, glasses of wine in hand and toasting to their day. They had accomplished a lot and, although exhausted, the excitement of what they were doing renewed Laurel's energy. Over dinner, they made a list of what they wanted to get done the next day after the kiln was delivered.

LAUREL WAS UP AT SUNRISE THE NEXT MORNING. SHE made herself a cup of tea and took it out to the deck with her journal. Wrapping a shawl around her shoulders, she sat watching the sun creep through the trees and climb over their crowns. As she sipped her tea, she wrote in her journal—a morning ritual that, unfortunately, had been pushed aside due to her busy life-style. This dream of hers for years now had a plan, and she was starting to really believe it was going to happen.

After she wrote her goals and gratitude list, she made bullet-point entries of what they accomplished yesterday. Then she set down her pen and took a long sip of tea and listened to the bird-song for a few minutes. Picking up her pen, she continued writing —but this time she wrote about her feelings.

I've made it another day. I miss Mom so much, and there are times that the littlest thing will start the tears falling. The past few weeks have been so busy, which I think is helping me cope, or maybe not quite face everything that has changed in my life.

I'm feeling stronger every day, and with Maggie's help, my confidence is getting better. It still amazes me how I let him manipulate me and bash my self-esteem to nothing. I never thought I was the kind of person who would find herself in that position. What was wrong with me? How could I become that person, the one who—even though I knew what he was telling me was wrong—still let it seep in and become my inner voice as well? What scares me the most is that I don't know how to prevent this from happening to me again. How do I trust men again? He was so charming and attentive at first. Were there signs at the beginning that I missed? I always thought I was a good judge of character, but now I'm not so sure.

Graham's sister, Sara, texted yesterday and asked what happened with Graham and me. I told her it just didn't work out. Period. End of story. Who knows what Graham told his sister, or anyone else for that matter. Hopefully, people who know me will not believe his side of things. It felt weird not explaining what had happened or where I was going, but I just need some distance between that mess and my new beginning right now.

On more positive thoughts, I am absolutely in love with this place. I'm writing while sipping tea on the deck, watching the sunrise. How perfect is that? I really live here now. That's still hard to believe. Mom was right: This is where I belong.

Maggie has been so wonderful through all of this. I love our time together. What am I going to do when she heads back home in a few days?

The voice inside my head just told me: "You are going to work your ass off on your dream. That's what you're going to do."

With that, she closed her journal and went inside to take a shower. Maggie would be up soon, and they had a busy day ahead of them.

Joe arrived at nine a.m. with the wheel and kiln. They placed the kiln in the corner of the garage that was (thankfully) sealed off from the rest of the garage. It had been used as a workshop at some point and turned out to be the perfect place for the kiln. Joe and his son moved the pottery wheel into the studio and, after a few nudges left and right, Laurel declared the spot to be perfect.

After Joe left, Laurel went back to the studio and sat at the pottery wheel, pretending she was throwing pots. She was so excited to get started.

Maggie came back into the studio and laughed at her. "You know, you will never be able to use that if we don't get a move-on and run our errands. One of which, may I remind you, is to buy some clay. C'mon, let's go."

Laurel laughed as she got up from the wheel and followed Maggie out of the studio. She was almost giddy at this point. "Oh my gosh, this is all happening so fast. This dream of mine is almost within reach now."

"It'll be happening sooner if you get your stuff and we get going." Maggie gave her a high-five.

They drove to Willow, the town about thirty minutes away, to pick up the long list of tools and the clay Laurel would need to get started. Oh, that store was dangerous. Laurel wanted just about everything, but Maggie kept Laurel focused on the necessities to start with.

"I know, I know...stick to the list." Laurel laughed as Maggie took yet another item out of her hand and placed it back on the shelf. "I have so many ideas of pieces that I want to make, and there are so many different techniques I want to try."

"I understand, but you don't need it all right at this moment. You're the one who told me to keep you on task, and that's what I am doing. You would buy the entire store if I let you."

"Okay, okay. I think we're done. That's everything on the list. Let's get out of here before I go crazy."

By late afternoon, they had finished setting up the studio. Laurel snapped a couple of photos and leaned against the door frame.

"Wow! Look at it. It's beyond what I imagined. Do you think I can really do this? Make a living with my dream? What if I can't create what I've been dreaming all these years? What if I've forgotten how to do this? What if no one buys them? What if I spend all my savings while waiting for—?"

Maggie wrapped her arm around Laurel's shoulder and pulled her into a hug. "Yes, I know you can do this. I have no doubt that you will be successful and yes, make a living. Handmade items are all the rage now. People want something that is unique and made with love. We just need to get your website up and running."

"I've just never been without a regular paycheck, so if I think about it too much, I get a little freaked out."

"I know, but you'll be okay. Trust yourself for once." Maggie smiled at her. "We've earned a glass of wine. Come on."

They took their wine outside and sat down in the Adirondack chairs at the edge of the lake. In the distance, they heard the splash of a fish jumping. A chorus of birdsong caused them both to watch the trees. The gentle lapping of the water against the sand offered a sense of calm.

Laurel sighed. "This view never gets old. Remember when we were kids and our dads helped us build that tree fort? I think some of the wood is still up there in that tree, but the tree has grown so tall."

"Wasn't that the same summer they built the shed for your mom?"

"Oh, I think you're right. She wanted a simple shed she could use for gardening or pottery or whatever. Our dads went all out! Bailey's dad found the tiles for it and helped put the floor in. That was such a fun summer."

"Summers were always fun because our families were together again. Our parents sure knew how to have a good time."

"Just like we do." Laurel clinked her glass to Maggie's. "They were good influences, not to mention wonderful parents. I wish they could see us now."

"I think they can see us. They are watching over us." Maggie shifted in her chair and sighed. "I remember after my parents' car accident, Tim and I came and stayed here with your parents. They were such a huge comfort to us and helped us with all the arrangements. More importantly, they were just here for us. Their love and guidance really helped both of us cope with our loss."

Laurel reached over and squeezed Maggie's hand. "Gosh, that was such a difficult time. We were all so shocked about the accident. I'm glad you both found love and comfort here." She looked from Maggie back to the lake. "I sure wish they were sitting here with us so we could talk to them about all the exciting things happening in our lives. Imagine what they would say."

"Ah, if only that could happen."

Laurel took a sip of wine and watched a lone fisherman paddle his boat across the lake before she replied. "I think my parents would say that it's about time. My life certainly took a few wrong turns, didn't it? I mean, first Dave and then Graham. I can really pick 'em, can't I?"

Maggie squeezed Laurel's hand. "You haven't mentioned Dave in a long time. And to be honest, you were very young then."

"Well, he was one of those wrong turns in my life, wasn't he?" Laurel stood, walking a few steps before turning around. "Seriously, you would think after that relationship I would have sworn off men all together."

"Ha, that doesn't sound like any fun at all. Most of us have had a bad relationship or two, ones that make us wonder what the hell we were thinking."

"Yes, and we are supposed to learn from them and not make the same stupid mistake again. But that's exactly what I did. I fell for two smooth-talking guys who then turned out to treat me like crap. They both did a number on my self-esteem. Ugh, when I think about what I put up with, I get so angry with myself."

"Listen, you got away from them. They're in your past. Time to move on."

Laurel sat back down decisively. "This time I *am* swearing off men! Seriously, I'm done! I make such bad choices, and I really don't want to do that again. So, no more."

Maggie reached over and touched Laurel's arm. "If you say so. But I think the perfect guy is out there for you. You just haven't met him yet. Don't close yourself off to the chance of true love. You've learned what you don't want or need, but just don't put that wall up too high."

Shaking her head, Laurel replied, "Nope. I'm done, and I'm okay with that. Let's change the subject."

Maggie squeezed Laurel's hand, and they both fell quiet, looking out at the lake.

A blue heron glided over the lake before landing at the edge, beneath a tree. Laurel and Maggie both sat very still as they watched the heron walk along the water's edge toward the dock, his eyes focused on the water. He stopped and stood statue-like, never taking his eyes off the lapping waves. In the blink of an eye, he dipped his beak into the water and pulled it back up, clutching a small fish trying to wriggle free. He swallowed the fish and turned to walk back along the waterline.

They watched until he was out of sight, then Maggie leaned over toward Laurel and whispered, "You know that was a good luck sign just for you, right?"

"What are you talking about?"

"You don't know the story of the blue heron? Hold on." Maggie dug her phone out of her pocket and googled "great blue heron good luck" and when she had the results, she handed her phone over to Laurel. "Read this...this is the new you!"

"According to North American Native tradition," the website explained, "the Blue Heron brings messages of self-determination and self-reliance. They represent an ability to progress and evolve. The long thin legs of the heron reflect that an individual doesn't need great, massive pillars to remain stable, but must be able to stand on one's own."

Laurel read it, then read it again, and handed Maggie's phone back.

"Maybe I need to hang that in my studio to remind me. Well, to help me believe that this is the new me."

"If that's what it takes, you got it! I'll print it out tomorrow."

Laurel laughed. "Let's go make some dinner. I'm starving."

They picked up their wineglasses and, with one last look across the lake, turned and walked toward the cabin. At the edge of the garden, the birdbath was occupied by a few goldfinches having a last dip before settling in for the night. A few frogs seemed to be having a singalong in the distance. The fragrance of the jasmine drifted through the air. Laurel smiled as they reached the cabin door. She was really beginning to believe that she would be okay with her new life on the lake.

Five

They worked alongside each other in the kitchen in synchronized harmony. Maggie sliced the vegetables as Laurel prepared the chicken and wok for the stir-fry. Once the chicken was browned, Maggie added the vegetables and drizzled in the Szechuan sauce while Laurel used two wooden spatulas to constantly stir everything.

"Tomorrow morning while you work in the studio, I'll go pick up groceries and wine for our girls' night." Maggie grinned. "It'll be great to have everyone here for dinner. It's been a long time since we've all enjoyed an evening together."

"I can't wait to see everyone! We've been so busy since I arrived. I haven't seen Lena or Bailey yet. Or Cassie! So much to catch up on." Laurel continued cooking the stir-fry.

Maggie warmed the bowls and poured them another glass of wine. As she set the table, she said, "I'm so glad you'll have them all close by. They're such a fun bunch of crazy ladies!"

"Me too." Laurel set the bowls of stir-fry on the table.

Over dinner, they chatted about the menu for the following night and what Laurel was going to work on in the morning.

"I think I should start with something easy, just to get warmed up. It's been so long since I've thrown any pots. I thought

I'd start with a bowl that I had sketched out about a year ago in one of my daydream sessions." Laurel drummed her hands on the table lightly. "I have a sketch pad full of ideas."

After they washed up, they made a pot of tea and took it into the living room. As they stretched out on the two couches, they both picked up their phones to check their social media.

THE NEXT MORNING, LAUREL WALKED INTO THE STUDIO and looked around. The shelves that she and Maggie had found looked like they were made for this space. She visualized them stacked with her finished pieces. She put her sketch pad on the desk and flipped it open to the bowl she wanted to create. Yes, a bowl was simple, but it would have a unique pattern that wouldn't be easy to achieve. She laid out the tools she would need on the platform next to the pottery wheel, then she sliced a slab of clay and kneaded it.

As Laurel slowly worked the clay on the wheel, she focused on the texture, forming it with her fingers. Memories started to gently ease their way into her mind, like the time her mom taught her how to create pottery.

Laurel's mom was sitting at the wheel, forming a piece of clay in her fingers. Laurel hovered close to her, mesmerized by the movement of the wheel and the rhythmic dance her mother's hands played against the clay. It seemed like magic, the way her mom worked a lump of clay into a bowl or vase. Her hands were always moving, yet never rushed. They pulled the clay up with one hand and shaped the outside with a plastic wedge, the two working perfectly together.

Her dad had appeared at the door holding a small stool that he made for Laurel. Stopping the wheel, Mom moved her stool back a bit while Dad placed Laurel's new stool between Mom and the wheel. Laurel climbed onto the stool, sitting very still. Mom placed her hands over Laurel's as she gently brought the wheel to life again.

She could sit for hours watching her mom as she explained what she was doing at each step. They would play their favorite music and sing along. The hours passed easily when they were together in the studio. She loved that time with her mom. What she wouldn't give to have one more day.

A tear gently escaped from the corner of her eye. Instead of taking one of her hands off the clay to wipe it away, she let it fall. She remembered the day her mom helped her make her first bowl. Dad had been working on building a small boat in the driveway, and Laurel and her mom spent the day in the studio. Mom had sat Laurel in front of her on the stool at the wheel.

With her hands placed gently over Laurel's, they had made her bowl. Laurel had to start over twice, but in the end, she got the feel of the clay in her hands and was able to form the shape of the bowl.

That day was one of her favorite memories and she returned to it often, whether for comfort when needed or just on ordinary days when she would place something in her special bowl on the coffee table. That's why it was the first thing she unpacked when she arrived here at the cabin: She wanted to keep it with her always.

As she worked and molded the clay in her hands, she smiled at the memory. *Mom and Dad, I miss you so much. I wish you were here, but I know that you're cheering me on as I finally follow my dreams.*

Working the clay was therapeutic for Laurel. She loved the way it felt in her hands. She loved the way *she* felt. It wasn't long before the high-sided bowl was the shape she wanted. She stopped the wheel, took the thread, and cut the bowl from the stone. After placing it carefully on the drying board, she then sliced a small piece of clay. Slowly, she molded it in her hands and then laid it flat as she cut out the image she wanted. She cut the rounded edges of wineglasses and in between them cut out the edges of a wine bottle. On each glass she cut in an M, and on the wine bottle she cut in "Dream Vintage."

She carefully attached it to the bowl and stood back to look at her first creation in years. She liked it. She really liked it.

Now, all she needed to do was keep Maggie from seeing it before it was ready.

BEFORE MAGGIE LEFT TO DO THE GROCERY SHOPPING, she talked to Martin on Skype. They had talked on the phone the night before they each went to bed, but when they started their days in different places, they liked to do a quick video call. It wasn't even close to being as good as waking up next to each other, but it helped to begin the day seeing each other's faces.

"Good morning, sweetheart," Martin greeted Maggie as his face appeared on her screen. "I miss kissing those lips of yours, ya know?!"

"Not half as much as I miss you kissing them," Maggie replied. "Did you sleep well, my dear?"

"Yes, only because I dreamt of you all night. What wonderful dreams they were! It was raining, and we spent the entire day in bed...and I was..." Martin told her some of the details of what those dreams entailed, and Maggie started to blush.

"Oh, Martin, how am I going to think of anything else all day?" She sighed, unable to keep the smile from her lips.

"Don't think of anything else but what I'm going to do with you when you get home." He smirked and blew Maggie a kiss.

"You are insatiable, Martin!"

"Yes, and you *love* it!" He laughed.

They talked about what each of their days looked like and about an important meeting with a new client that Martin had that afternoon.

After a few minutes, Martin smiled at her. "Okay, we both

have busy days ahead of us. Have fun with the girls tonight and call me before you go to sleep."

"I hope your meeting onsite goes well," she replied. "It'll probably be a late night. Are you sure you want me to call? You'll be asleep."

"Yes, do call. Even if I just get to hear your voice before nodding back to sleep. I love you so much."

"I love you too, darling. Have a great day!" Maggie said, and they signed off. Then she walked into the kitchen to grab the grocery list and wrote a note to Laurel before heading out the door. "Didn't want to disturb the artist at work. I'm off to do the shopping. Text or call if you think of anything else we need. Xoxo."

Maggie drove into the parking lot of Sal's Sunny Sprouts grocery store and parked. Grabbing the reusable shopping bags from the backseat, she walked toward the entrance just in time to see Dorothy, an old neighbor, coming out the door. Maggie's instinct was to duck and hide, but she squared her shoulders and kept going. Maybe she'd be pleasant for a change.

"Maggie, I heard you were in town. Have you put on weight?" Dorothy asked.

"Hi. No, I haven't put on weight. How is your family?" Maggie gritted her teeth, trying to be nice.

"Hmmm, you look like you gained some weight to me. I guess you would know, though." Dorothy looked Maggie up and down. "The family are fine."

Maggie had had enough. She had known the woman all her life, and she couldn't remember one pleasant conversation with her. "Now, I really must be going. I've a very busy day and must keep on task. Take care. Bye now." Then she turned and walked inside before the miserable woman could reply.

Lily, Sal's daughter, greeted her from the customer service desk. "Good morning, Maggie! Lovely to see you."

Maggie walked over to give her a quick hug. She said, "I saw you talking to Mrs. Grumpy. What kind, sweet conversation was she offering today? I swear I will never understand why she is so mean to everyone. Lord knows, we all try to be pleasant to her, but it's never returned."

"I know! It's sad, but she's always been that way. Her husband and son are so sweet! How do they live with such a sourpuss?" Maggie sniffed. "Today's focus was on how much weight I've apparently put on since she saw me last. Even when I told her that I hadn't put on any weight, she didn't believe me."

"How sweet of her to be concerned." Lily rolled her eyes. "Just ignore her."

"Believe me, I try to let everything she says to me go in one ear and out the other."

Their conversation was cut short as a customer approached the desk to inquire about a special order.

Lily waved. "See you later. Have a great day."

"You too. Bye!"

Maggie had shopped at Sal's for ages. She was thankful that, unlike chain grocery stores, Sal didn't feel the need to rearrange the store every few months just to get customers to buy more items. She knew the store well and was able to navigate the aisles quickly and efficiently to get everything on her shopping list. Before long, she was through the checkout and back at her car.

Her next stop was the wine store. She waved to Henry, the owner, as she walked in. Maggie had known him for years. Lake Benton was a small community and, even though she hadn't lived here for years, her connections to the residents were still strong. She headed towards the Spanish wine section, where he joined her a few minutes later.

"With all your travels to Spain, I'm not surprised to find you in this section. Hello Maggie, how are you? How is Martin doing?"

"I'm doing well. Martin is great. Very busy with work, but you know how much he loves it," Maggie said. "Laurel and I are having some friends over this evening, and I thought it would be great to have them taste some wines from Catalunya. How are you?"

"I'm doing well, thanks for asking," he said. "You certainly know what wines you would want to share from that region, so I'll leave you to browse. Let me know if you need help."

Maggie thanked him and then turned her attention to the shelves stocked with wine in front of her. Being familiar with the different wines of Catalunya, she quickly picked a few to share with the girls later that evening. She paid for the wine, said goodbye, and loaded her bulging shopping bag into her car before heading back to the cabin.

LAUREL HAD JUST FINISHED PLACING THE LAST OF THE bowls she had created on the drying board when she heard Maggie drive up. Maggie laughed as Laurel approached the car to help unload the groceries.

"What's so funny?" Laurel asked.

"You are! You should see yourself! You are almost floating with happiness," Maggie said.

"Oh Maggie, I've had the most incredible morning. It all came back to me much easier than I thought it would. It just felt so, I don't know, familiar."

Maggie gave Laurel a hug and stood back to look at her. "I knew it would. You have a gift. One that's been buried for years. I'm thrilled you're finally back to being *you*!"

As they put the shopping away, Laurel told Maggie about the pieces she had created.

"I can't wait to see them!" Maggie said, her eyes twinkling with excitement. "Let's have some tea, and then you can show me."

"Not yet. I want to wait until the pieces are done." Laurel bit her lip. "You understand, right? I just want these first pieces to be finished before I show anyone."

"Of course, I understand. I'll try to be patient."

"Thanks, Maggie. Okay, let's get things ready for our dinner party tonight."

THE DOORBELL RANG SHORTLY BEFORE SIX O'CLOCK. Maggie opened the door to find Lena and Bailey, their arms laden with goodies. Lena held a bottle of wine and a box of local chocolates. Bailey had fresh, homemade bread.

"Cassie will be here shortly. She had a last-minute call with a new client," Lena said.

"Well, that's a great excuse. How exciting." Maggie led them into the kitchen.

Laurel wiped her hands on a towel and walked around the island to hug them. "Oh, it is so good to see you both. Bailey, your hair is so cute! When did you cut it?"

"A couple of days ago. You know, since meeting Lena when we were kids, I have always wanted my curly red hair to be as long as hers." Bailey tugged on Lena's long braid that hung down her back. "After many years of straightening it and, well, fighting it on an almost daily basis, I finally gave up. I decided to embrace my curly red hair with this short cut. I love it. Why did I waste so many years trying to be like her?" She winked at Lena.

"I have an idea." Lena hugged Bailey around the waist. "I would trade hair with you any day. I've always loved yours."

Maggie was just about to offer them wine when the doorbell rang again. She was greeted by the laughter of Holly and Joy. "Hello! Welcome you two." Maggie hugged them both. "Please come in. We're just waiting on Cassie to arrive."

Their laughter filled the entryway as they walked toward the kitchen and greeted everyone.

Two minutes later, the doorbell rang again.

"Sorry I'm late, everyone," Cassie said as Maggie led her into the kitchen. "I have a new client and they asked for a call at the last minute."

"No worries, Cassie. We haven't started the party without you," Laurel said.

Maggie got everyone's attention by simply mentioning wine. "Now listen, I know we have our favorite winemaker here tonight." She bowed her head slightly to Lena. "But since I'm counting down the months until Martin and I head off to vacation in Spain, I thought I would introduce you to some of the wines we'll soon be drinking there. Y'know, just to make you feel like you're on vacation as well."

That elicited a mixture of laughter and groans. The ladies were always envious when Maggie and Martin went on their yearly two-week vacation to Spain.

Maggie explained the different vineyards and wines and poured everyone their chosen wine, then Lena held up her glass for a toast. "To us, and to our friendship. We're aging as well as a fine wine!"

"Cheers! Salut!"

Maggie chimed in, "Here's to Laurel! To your new life. To your regained confidence. To following your dream! Welcome home!"

"To Laurel! Cheers! Salut! Welcome home!"

Laurel beamed at them all. "Thank you. I'm so happy to finally be living near my childhood besties."

"We're happy to have you back here for more than a long weekend," Cassie said.

Laurel grabbed the platter of appetizers and led everyone out to the table on the patio. Looking around at her friends as they chatted away about everyday happenings, a sense of belonging washed over her that had been missing from her life. As they all took their places at the table overlooking the lake, the golden light of the sun sinking behind the hills cast a glow over everything. A silence fell over the table as they all noticed the sunlight. That's what living in such a beautiful place did—it made everyone stop and take notice. Sometimes it simply took Laurel's breath away.

"So, Cassie, tell us about your new client." Bailey passed the basket of bread.

"Well, I really can't believe it, but my new client is Brady Tech. They just moved into the old mercantile building. I'm doing their rebranding campaign for them. I can't believe they chose me to do it."

"Brady Tech! Wow! They're supposed to be an up-and-coming force in the AI arena," Joy said.

"Yes, and this rebranding campaign is crucial, so I can't screw it up." Cassie laughed, but it sounded a little brittle, like she was doubting herself.

"No way! You're not doubting yourself already! You won this account, and you know you can do this," Lena said.

"I know, I know. This really is a piece of cake. I just want to do it right. And I will!" Cassie smiled.

"I've met the owners briefly," Bailey chimed in. "One of them bought a piece of property on the other side of the lake. I'm designing their new home. We're meeting next week to walk through the contract before I get started. Oh, and let me tell you... both owners are drop-dead gorgeous! And single, ladies!" She looked at each of her friends around the table pointedly.

Maggie laughed and said, "I wonder which of you single ladies will scoop them up."

"I'm out of the running. Brad and I are getting serious," Bailey said.

They all laughed and joked about who would end up inviting them to the town festivals and who would soon have a boyfriend.

"I'm kind of sorry I won't be here to watch this all unfold," said Maggie.

"When are you heading back home?" Joy asked.

"The day after tomorrow. I need to get home. I have a deadline with my editor."

Laurel leaned over and put her head on Maggie's shoulder.

"You've been a godsend to me. I couldn't have done this without you. I guess it's time for you to go home to your hubby and time for me to get my act together."

Maggie put her arm around Laurel's shoulders and hugged her. "You're going to be fine. And look at this support group you have here. I know you'll be in good hands."

"Don't worry, we'll take care of her," Bailey said.

"Yes, we will." Everyone chimed in and raised their glasses. "To Laurel!"

"Thank you, everyone!" Laurel smiled.

There was something about being with a group of like-minded friends that made time slow down. Laurel couldn't deny the feeling of contentment that bloomed as she listened to her oldest friends share their latest news.

Joy told them she and Holly had devoted an area in the bookshop where local artisans could sell their products. Lena mentioned Hank, the winemaker, several times with her update on the winery. Bailey talked about Brad, the projects she was working on, and how it felt to be living in her grandparents' lake house, which they recently left to her. Holly shared that the children's cookie-making class had raised enough money to buy not only books for the children who couldn't afford them, but also a couple of laptops that the children could use in the bookshop. Cassie was excited about her new client and confessed that she dreamed of starting a new line of journals and notecards.

Laurel shared with them her vision for her pottery and how she had no idea how to sell it. Joy suggested selling it in their gift section of the bookshop when she was ready. Maggie showed them the illustrations she had just received for her new children's book.

As the night air grew a bit cooler, they moved the party to the living room. Maggie and Lena opened some dessert wines and Laurel served up plates of blueberry tart and peach-and-blueberry crumble.

Then Joy finally asked the question that they had all been

thinking: "Laurel, so what happened with Graham? Are you okay?"

"It's okay if you don't want to tell us, but we're here to support you if you need us," Holly chimed in.

"Consider us your safe haven," Joy added.

Laurel sat up straighter and sighed. "Thank you. I appreciate you all. Well, let's just say that I finally came to my senses. We had really been just existing together for a while, and he was spending more time with his *friends* than he was with me or at home. He went out one night, and I suddenly realized that I didn't want to be with him anymore. I started making notes and plans while doing laundry that night. Then I found a note in his drawer from the other woman."

"What?"

"Are you joking? What a jerk!"

"You are so better off without him!"

"Yup. I packed everything I could that night, and I went to my mom's and, well..." Tears were now falling and Laurel stopped to wipe them away.

She suddenly felt herself enveloped in a huge group hug. Tears, hugs, and supportive words were spoken before they all settled down again.

"Sorry, my emotions are still pretty raw," Laurel said.

"Aw, don't be sorry." Bailey rubbed Laurel's shoulder with a gentle hand. "We just want to be here for you and help in any way we can. Just know that if or when you need to talk, any one of us is here to listen. Not preach, not judge—just listen and support."

"Thank you. I really appreciate that."

"Coffee, anyone?" Maggie stood and looked around the room, taking orders, then motioned for Laurel to follow her.

In the kitchen, Maggie gave Laurel a big hug. "You have a great support system with these ladies. They would do anything for you."

"Thanks, I know. Believe me, I am so thankful for them, especially now."

"I'm glad they'll be here for you." Maggie reached out and squeezed Laurel's hand. "Let's get these coffees going."

As the clock in the living room struck midnight, everyone started gathering themselves to leave.

"Thank you for a wonderful evening, Laurel and Maggie. So much fun." Lena hugged them both.

Everyone hugged and talked about what a wonderful evening they had as they headed out the door. Joy called out as she and Holly got into their car. "Maggie, stop in for a coffee tomorrow before you leave."

"We will," Maggie said as she and Laurel waved goodbye.

They were both quiet as they worked together to clean the kitchen. As Laurel dried the last wineglass and put it away, she sighed.

"That was a great night. I hadn't realized how much I needed that—how much I need all of you. I've missed being involved with everyone more than I knew."

Maggie smiled. "It was a great night. Such a marvelous group of friends. We're lucky to be so close after all these years."

WHILE LAUREL WROTE IN HER JOURNAL THE NEXT morning, Maggie packed so they could just enjoy the rest of their time together. They enjoyed a cup of tea on the patio and watched as the blue heron made his way along the shoreline, fishing for his breakfast. They talked about how much patience he had as he stood still and stared into the water.

"If only we could learn such patience in our own lives. Imagine what that calmness must feel like." Maggie said.

Laurel sighed. "Oh, Maggie... I'm hoping that's what we'll both learn with our lives. No more rushing about and trying to be what others want us to be. Just focusing on what *we* want and need for us. That isn't selfish."

"No, it isn't selfish. It's more like self-preservation."

"That's exactly what it is," Laurel agreed.

At just that moment, the blue heron dipped his head quickly into the water and pulled it back up with a small fish wriggling in its beak.

"That's us making our dreams come true!" Maggie laughed.

"Exactly!"

Laurel told Maggie about her thoughts on how she could get some easy pieces done quickly so that she had something to sell.

Maggie hummed, tilting her head as she considered Laurel's plan. Slowly, she presented a counterargument: "I don't think you should rush to the market with basic pieces. What if you just focused on what your style is going to be? Create a vision and a style that will be recognizable. While you do that, you can work on social media and get a marketing plan down on paper. Remember, you're following *your* dream, not someone else's dream. You're not desperate for money right now, so don't go about this the wrong way."

"Wow." Laurel sat back in her chair and looked at Maggie. "I hadn't thought of it that way. I'm just so focused on my lack of paychecks coming in that I feel like I need to do something fast to support myself."

"Honey, listen. You have a roof over your head. You have money in the bank. You have always supported yourself. You have always had only yourself to depend on, and you have always been just fine!"

"And that little speech is why you're my best friend in the whole world. You tell me exactly what I need to hear." Laurel beamed at Maggie. "Thank you."

"You're welcome. Now, don't forget what I said." Maggie winked. "Okay, let's go get pampered with mani-pedis."

They spent the next hour and a half relaxing at the nail salon. This was a tradition that started many years ago when their moms were still alive. All four of them would go to the salon together, and these were some of the highlights of Laurel and Maggie's friendship.

Instead of looking at their phones, they talked. They never ran out of things to talk about, dreams to discuss, memories to reminisce about. Sometimes they even talked about a book one had read that the other just had to read because it was so good.

Once they finished at the nail salon, they walked down the main street and popped into a couple of their favorite shops—another tradition they held. In Yuba Blue they found some candles and browsed through all the quirky books on display. This was always one of their favorite places, and they could spend ages in there looking at all the gadgets, homemade soaps, silly cards, unique jewelry, and clothing.

"What a fun morning. How about lunch at Lyman's Café? Then we can figure out what we want to do the rest of the day," Maggie said.

"Sounds good. I think you should pick what we do this afternoon. After all, you're the one who's going to be leaving."

"Hmmm, okay. I'll give that some thought while we eat. Let's go."

Before they sat down, they wandered around the bookshop. They each bought a couple of books and spent some time looking at the handmade items local artists were selling in the gift area. There was a good range of different items, but one thing that they both noticed was the absence of any pottery or ceramic items.

"Perhaps this is an option for you, Laurel. Remember what Joy said last night?" Maggie nudged her encouragingly as they walked towards the archway that led them into the café.

"Hmmm. Perhaps it is. Hopefully, there will still be space when I have something to sell." But even Laurel could hear her lack of confidence in her voice.

"Oh no you don't. No getting wishy-washy on this now," Maggie replied.

"Listen to her, Laurel," Joy said, laughing as she came up behind them. "I meant what I said last night. Once you're ready, we could certainly include your pottery in our gift shop. You're a local artist now."

"You're serious, aren't you?" Laurel asked.

"Yes, I am. We've seen local artists really get noticed in our shop. When you have a couple of pieces ready, bring them in."

"Okay, thank you, Joy. I'll do that." Laurel smiled.

"Now, let's get you a table." Joy motioned them to a table near the window.

Once Joy left, Laurel leaned across the table and whispered, "Oh my gosh, I'm about to burst over here. This is so exciting! I have the first place to sell my pottery."

"Do you know how great you look right now?" Maggie clapped her hands together. "Happy. Excited. Confident."

"Yes, yes, and yes." Laurel leaned back and tapped her hand on the table to bring the point home. "I've got this."

Six

L aurel stood at the end of the driveway, waving as Maggie drove out of sight. She treasured their wonderful time together. They'd bonded even more, if that was possible.

As she turned to walk back up the driveway, she glanced next door and noticed the for-sale sign had been bannered with a large red SOLD. Who had bought the old Johnston place? It had been vacant since Mr. Johnston passed away the summer before. His daughter had moved to New York City as soon as she graduated from college and had never looked back. She was not someone who enjoyed the quiet lifestyle that the lake community offered. She loved all the noise, the hustle and bustle that was city life. Mom had told her the house had been on the market for months, but it needed serious renovation, so it had proved difficult to find a buyer.

She glanced next door one more time, then the old Johnston place slid out of sight as she continued up the driveway. Walking around to the back deck, she admired the garden. Her mom certainly had a green thumb. When she was a little girl, her parents had designated a corner of the garden just for her. Her dad even bought her little pink gardening tools.

Smiling at the memory, she was confident she could keep the garden looking beautiful. Before going inside, she put fresh water in the birdbath and made sure the birdfeeder didn't need filling. She turned to look at the lake and smiled. It was just her now. Her and her new life. She was finally following her dreams and living in her favorite place. *I can't believe this is all happening.*

The sound of almost frantic chirping broke her chain of thought. In a nearby tree, a couple of birds chirped rapidly, as if admonishing her for standing so close to the birdfeeder.

"Okay, okay. Sorry I was in your way," Laurel said to the birds. "Remember that I'm the one who fills the birdfeeder and bird-bath now." She walked to the back door, pausing to gaze at the lake once more before stepping into her new home.

In the kitchen, she flipped on the electric kettle to make a cup of tea. While waiting for the water to boil, she washed the dishes from their early morning breakfast. When she sat with her fresh cup of steaming tea, she saw an envelope with her name written on it. On the front, in big festive letters, it said, "WOOHOO YOU!" The exuberant exclamation brought a smile to her face as she opened the card and read Maggie's chicken-scratch hand-writing.

Laurel,

I'm so proud of you for making this new start in your life. I know you've had a rough time and no doubt you may stumble going forward, but you will survive and thrive. Change can be daunting but also amazingly rewarding. You've got this girl! Welcome home.

Lots of love and hugs,
Maggie.

Laurel wiped a stray tear from her cheek and took her tea and the card out to the studio to place on her desk.

After sliding into her desk chair and taking a sip of tea, she thumbed through some sketches of pieces she planned to work on this week. With a red colored pencil, she sketched and shaded the flower she had previously drawn. The red hibiscus would be raised on the vase, making it a centerpiece with or without flowers in it. Laurel spent the next thirty minutes working on her sketches, adding details and colors.

Ready to start throwing pots, she grabbed her phone and hit play on her Kenny Chesney playlist. She sliced the clay, laid the sketch she would be creating next to her, and sat at the pottery wheel. Taking a deep breath, she used her right foot on the pedal to bring the wheel to life.

Once again, she felt as if she were one with the clay. Her hands moved in a rhythm that came so naturally. As she manipulated the clay with her fingers, she sang along to the music. She worked for a couple of hours and managed to create the number of bowls she had wanted to. With the bowls set on the drying board, she stretched her back and arms.

Taking a quick break to get a glass of sparkling water, she returned to the studio to start on the next batch. A couple of hours later, she stopped for lunch. After placing the last item on the drying board, she stood back to admire the results of her productive morning and felt proud of her work. *Maggie is right. I've got this.*

While she ate her lunch, she made a list of things to do: items to pick up at the store, things to research for her business, and some bullet points for social media. As she looked at the to-do list, she felt overwhelmed at all that needed to be done. Finishing her lunch, she moved the plate aside to make a revised to-do list. This time, she listed her tasks in order of priority, and that made it look less daunting. It was still a long list, though.

She walked to the end of the dock. From there, she could see a good portion of the lake. There were a few kayakers, as well as a couple people on paddleboards. She really needed to get out on the water again. Cassie had taught her to paddleboard last summer, and she loved it.

A couple of ducks landed on the lake, looking so graceful. She stood there for a few more minutes and then reminded herself she had a lot of work to do. Daydreaming would have to wait.

BY THAT EVENING, LAUREL WAS PLEASED WITH WHAT she'd accomplished during her first full day of making her dream a reality. She didn't even care that her body was going to feel those long hours bending over the pottery wheel in the morning.

Taking her notebook and sketch pad with her, she turned off the lights and closed the studio door. It had been a productive day. Now she desperately needed to unwind and let some of the tension out of her shoulders. She made a cup of tea, grabbed her book, and sat on the couch. She texted Maggie a quick message, not wanting to take her attention away from Martin on her first night home.

> Just stopped for the day. Got lots done. Exhausted. Cup of tea and book time before I make some dinner.

Her phone pinged with Maggie's reply.

> That's great! So proud of you! Make sure you rest. You're in charge of your schedule now. Remember to take care of yourself. Martin is just making dinner. Then an early night. Love you so much!

> Thank you.

Laurel shot back.

I loved your card, by the way. Don't worry, I am taking care of myself. This being-in-charge-of-my-life thing is great! Enjoy Martin's yummy cooking. Thanks again for everything. Chat tomorrow. XX.

Laurel drank her tea as she read a couple chapters of the latest book in a romantic suspense series Joy had recommended. Afterwards, she poured herself a glass of wine as she made dinner. As she sat down to eat, her phone chimed with a text from Graham. She finished her dinner before picking up the phone and reading his message.

I hear you quit your job. What the hell is going on with you? And you left me because of some stupid note. You really need some professional help. You obviously have no idea what to do with your life.

She opened her contacts, scrolled to Graham's name, and chose the Block Contact option. Thankfully, Graham had never been fond of social media, so there weren't any accounts to block there.

Laurel put her phone down on the coffee table and sighed. "Done."

With that, she got up and walked to the window, taking a moment to watch the birds on the bird feeder. As she stood there, she noticed she was standing a bit straighter. She felt stronger and a bit more confident. *It's about time you took your life back and think for yourself. No more letting others dictate how you feel or what you do. It's time.*

When Laurel and Maggie talked the following evening, Maggie was shocked by what Graham had texted. "What a jerk! I can't believe that guy."

"Well, you'll be happy to know that I blocked his number."

"YES! Good for you!"

"Thanks Maggie—for everything. I couldn't have done this without you."

"I'm happy to help and just thrilled that you are out of that relationship."

"Now that he's shown, once again, who he truly is, I'm just glad that it's over. I'm ready to put this—and him—behind me."

"Okay, let's change the subject, then. How are you doing in the *pottery barn*?" Maggie giggled as she asked.

"Ha, ha. That sure is a catchy name, isn't it?" Laurel traced a seam on the arm of the couch, smiling to herself. "But I've chosen Blue Heron Pottery for the name. In fact, today I asked Frank if his office could assist me in setting up the business. I could do it myself, but I figured I'd like one less headache right now."

"Great name. I'm sure his help will make the process much easier. I can't wait to see your collection, so send me some photos when you are ready."

"I will. So, how are you?"

"I'm good. I've been busy plotting out a book idea I have." Maggie told her about the story. "It's about twins, a box of mementos they find behind a barn, and the unlikely friendship they form with a lonely old man.

"That sounds great. Can I have an autographed copy when you publish it?" Laurel asked.

Maggie laughed. "Of course."

They talked for a while longer, and Maggie asked, "Laurel, are you doing okay? Y'know, with this Graham stuff?"

Laurel sighed. "I'm okay right now. I'm sure I'll hit some rough patches, but you know, you and I are the same when it comes to closing a door in our lives. When we make the decision to stop, end, or leave something or someone, we don't waste time looking back. I'm glad today's little drama is over, and now that I blocked his number, I don't have to hear anything more from him."

"Good to hear. I'm proud of you. I know this has been hard, but you deserve so much better."

"Thank you. I appreciate all you love and support."

"Ditto."

At the sound of her stomach rumbling, Laurel said, "Okay, I need to make some dinner. It's been a long day."

"Sounds good. Have a good night. Love you."

"Love you too."

Seven

Laurel decided to make some changes around the cabin before she started cleaning out her mom's house in Addington. She knew the house would be a big project, and some of her mom's things would be coming to the cabin, so it was best to have the cabin in order first.

Laurel worked on the living room first: Clearing some knick-knacks and books from the built-in bookshelves was the first step to making this her home. She had created the studio the way she wanted, but it had been years since it had been used. Making changes to the cabin itself was harder emotionally, but she didn't need all the extra stuff that had been collecting here for years. She kept some sentimental items, and when she mentally struggled with getting rid of something, she swore she could hear her mom or dad telling her to do it. *Make this your home. The memories will always be there.*

Some things were there only because it was a second home and thus didn't get cleared out as often—like the toy box that still held some of Laurel's barbies and other toys. She finished the living room and tackled the kitchen next. There were items in the kitchen that should have been tossed ages ago. How many

Tupperware containers did a person need, and where the heck did the lids go for half of them?

With the cabin being located on the lake, family and friends gave her parents anything with a lake-related picture or phrase on it. And bless her mom's heart, she could never part with them. What if the gift-giver came for a visit? She had to keep it just in case. Laurel had teased her mom many times that if Ellen, her mom's second cousin, who had visited once, suddenly came for a visit from the East Coast, then they would deal with it then. But her mom held on to the gifts anyway. It wasn't as if she liked them all. Some of them were quite tacky, but Laurel found them all tucked away in cabinets and drawers.

By the time she finished the kitchen, she was pleased with how much she had purged. She had boxes and bags of stuff to be donated and piles for recycling and the dump. She moved them out to the garage and stacked the other items just inside the garage door to take to the dump when she finished the rest of the house.

The bedrooms were the next rooms to be attacked. She started with the two guest rooms first, as she knew those would be relatively easy. One of the rooms used to be hers growing up. There were still mementos from her childhood. It was the room she stayed in whenever she visited as an adult as well. It was where she had unpacked her suitcases when she arrived this time, when she hadn't been able to face her parents' larger bedroom quite yet.

But the time had come. Laurel needed to transform this place from a holiday cabin into her home—a home that, no matter how many years passed, would always hold special memories of her family. With that thought to brace herself, she walked across the hall to her parents' room and slowly opened the door.

The room seemed different to her and not how she remembered it. Her mom's bedside table was cleared of her ever-growing stack of books to read. The bed had new sheets and a duvet more to Laurel's liking than anything her mom would have had. When she opened the closet door, she couldn't help but let a small gasp escape. Her mother had cleared all her clothes out.

Tears started to roll down her cheeks as she walked to the dresser and opened the top drawer. Empty. She frantically opened the remaining drawers to find them all empty. She turned and looked back at the bed. It was then that she noticed an envelope on the pillow. *Oh Mom, why? Why did you do this without telling me?*

She wiped the tears on her sleeve and walked over to the bed. She sat and picked up the envelope. More tears escaped as she saw her name written in mother's beautiful cursive handwriting. She hugged the envelope to her heart before opening it. It read:

My Dear Heart,

I love you. Please always remember that. I know this is a horrible time for you, so I wanted to make some of it easier if I could. I hope you are reading this letter because you have left "he who shall remain nameless" and have moved here to start following your dream. Somehow, I know this to be true. You just needed a little push in the right direction.

I know you have a lot to deal with right now, and you are going through so many changes. The last time I came to the cabin, I knew it would probably be my last visit. Oh, I can't tell you how many tears I cried on that deck looking at the lake. But to be honest, I was also at peace with the inevitable. I want you to know that.

Knowing you, you are clearing out the knickknacks and books and other items that I could never part with. Not that I didn't want to get rid of some stuff, but I was, if nothing else, a great procrastinator when it came to purging. I would always think of other things to do, like work in my studio or read a book by the lake. Please know that I didn't mean to leave you such a mess to clean up. On a positive note, you can get rid of anything you want. Please do what you like with anything and everything, both here and at the house in Addington. I did make some notes with a couple of items at the house—a few things to pass along to a few family members and friends. Other than that, it is completely up to you.

You do not need to hang on to anything that you don't want. This is your home now, and this is the start of a new life for you. Start fresh! Oh, and don't cuss me out too much as you are purging. Lol. I love you.

Now, as to the master bedroom. I took everything out of it already so you could make this your bedroom. I know that may seem difficult, but it is just a room. Make it your own. Please.

I hope that you have reached out to Maggie and are allowing her to be there for you when you need her. Being an only child makes all of this that much harder, as you have no one to share the burden with. I wish I could give you a big hug right now, sweetheart.

I'm proud of you. I hope you know that. Remember that you can do anything you put your mind to. Follow your dream. Make a new life for yourself. Don't grieve so long that it stops you from living a wonderful, joy-filled life! You deserve it. Oh, and don't settle!

Be happy, my love. I'll always be in your heart and let's be honest...my momisms will live on as little whispers in your head.

All my love forever and always,
    Mom

Laurel reached for the tissue box on the nightstand and pulled a couple to wipe the tears flowing down her cheeks. As she blew her nose, she wondered why she couldn't cry and look as beautiful as Demi Moore in *Ghost*. Instead, she knew without looking that her face was red and blotchy, and she would most likely wake up with swollen eyes.

Oh Mom, I am trying. This is so hard. I miss you so much. I promise to make you proud.

Sniffling as she wiped more tears away, she carefully tucked the letter back into the envelope. She would add it to her keepsake collection in the cedar chest. Slowly pulling herself together, she stood. Enough of this blubbering; she had work to do.

With her mother's blessing, she moved her stuff from the guest room into the master bedroom and went about making it hers. It still felt weird, but she knew it was just another step she had to take in the grieving process.

She thought back to when her dad had died and how both she and her mom would have good days and bad days. Even on a good day, it shocked them how a smell or a song or some little thing could set them off once more. They'd had each other then, but now it was just her. Laurel grew up a lot when her dad died, and she found herself being strong for her mom and helping her walk through the grieving process. Laurel's heart was broken too, but she'd needed to take care of her mom—so that's what she did. They had always been close, but that time brought them even closer. Laurel saw a vulnerable side to her mom she never knew existed.

Moms are strong, confident, and capable in the eyes of their children. But Laurel learned that her mom was also broken sometimes, unable to see her self-worth as a widow, and she didn't know what to do with her life. It had been difficult to see her mom go through the heartbreak of losing the love of her life. But Laurel and her mom had somehow held each other up in those days, and they took things one day at a time. That was exactly what Laurel had to do: take it one day at a time.

Eight

U p at sunrise the next morning, Laurel picked up her phone before heading out the front door for a walk. As she wandered the trail around the lake, she occasionally stopped to snap a photo of a flower or an interesting-looking leaf that she might later use on a piece she was creating. She loved this time of the day. The world was so still, except perhaps for the birds chirping their morning songs. This morning, the water on the lake was like glass.

Thanks to Maggie's help getting the studio set up, Laurel was ahead on her plan of getting her business started. She had chosen Blue Heron Pottery as her company name after the encounter she and Maggie had sitting by the lake; she wanted the magic of that moment to permeate everything she created. Laurel filed the paperwork that afternoon with Frank's help and received her business license. Cassie was creating a logo for her, and once that was done, Laurel would order her logo stamp for the bottom of her pottery.

Cassie called her the next day to tell her she had a few logo mockups for Laurel to look at. When they met at Lyman's Bookshop and Café later that afternoon, Laurel was over the moon with what Cassie had created.

"Oh Cassie, these are amazing." Laurel spread three of the designs out on the table in front of her. She knew almost immediately which one she liked best, but she kept an open mind while they went over everything.

"I'm glad you like them. I loved the story that you shared with me about the blue heron. It was easy to create the images for you."

They discussed certain aspects of the designs and what would work best for different social media platforms. Cassie had also created a sample of a logo stamp for each of the designs so that Laurel could visualize how they would look on her pottery.

"Okay, I love them all, but this is the one that I love the most." Laurel held up the printed version. It was a blue heron standing in shallow water. It looked just like Laurel's memory of the one she and Maggie had seen.

"Perfect. I'll email you a Dropbox link with all the file types you'll need." Cassie smiled at Laurel.

"Great, and an invoice," Laurel replied.

Cassie rolled her eyes. "I told you I wouldn't charge you."

"Yes, and I told you that I would pay you!"

After a brief staring contest, Cassie rolled her eyes again. "Okay, you win."

Laurel smiled and winked. "Thank you for doing this. I can't stop saying this, but I am so excited!"

"I know that feeling. I still get it every time I sit down to create a new design."

"I'm also scared to death!"

Cassie laughed. "Yup, I know that feeling as well. Especially with a big new client like Brady Technology. I mean, I know what I'm doing, but I really don't want to screw up this contract."

Laurel leaned forward. "Is the owner as gorgeous as everyone says?"

Cassie blushed, and Laurel knew instantly what the real problem was.

"Ah, I understand. You like him, don't you? That's why you're nervous about it."

"No, no." Cassie drummed her fingers on the table. "Well, okay, maybe just a little. Yes, he is gorgeous, but it's so much more. He's so down to earth and lacking an ego, which is really refreshing. He's very hands-on..."

"Oh, is he now?" Laurel laughed.

"Not like that. Although I wouldn't mind finding out." Cassie wiggled her eyebrows. "Seriously though, he is so different from anyone I've ever met. He's extremely intelligent and worldly, and yet, he seems interested in what I have to say."

"Why would you say something like that? Why shouldn't he be interested in what you have to say?"

"I don't know. What have I ever done? I mean, I've lived in this town my entire life, except for college. What would he find interesting about me?" Cassie looked down at her hands and then back to Laurel.

"Cassie, being interesting to someone has little to do with the fact that you've lived in this town. It has everything to do with your intelligence—your creative, free spirit that led you to start your own graphic design business. The fact that your smile lights up a room, and you are one of the most compassionate people I have ever known."

"Wow, Laurel, thank you. That's so sweet." That wonderful smile of Cassie's reached her eyes.

"I'm just telling you the truth. You are an amazing woman. Don't ever doubt that." Laurel reached across the table and squeezed Cassie's hand. "Now, tell me more about him."

Cassie leaned forward and opened her mouth, then closed it and sat back in her seat. "Let's change the subject. I don't want to lose my focus on my work there. I need to finish that before I let myself get lost in any fantasies of a love life."

"Okay, good point. Speaking of focusing on work—" Laurel put a hand on her bag, "—I really should get going. I have to run up to Jackson to pick up some things. The traffic is bound to be awful at this time of day, but I really want to get started early tomorrow, so I need the supplies."

"Yes, I need to get back to my office and get some designs mocked up."

"Thank you *so* much for my logo and all the artwork. I'm really looking forward to seeing them on my website."

"I'm so glad you like them. I will email the files as soon as I get back to the office. Please let me know if you have any questions. Some file types work best on different social platforms, so if anything doesn't look right or you need help, just give me a call, okay?"

"Perfect. Thank you again. Don't forget to include the invoice," Laurel winked.

"Yes, ma'am! I will." Cassie collected her papers and stood. "Let's get together for dinner next week, okay?"

"Sounds like a great idea. Let's do it," Laurel said as she gave Cassie a hug and they walked out to their cars.

Laurel's trip to Jackson didn't take as long as she anticipated. The traffic wasn't too bad, and she was able to get a parking spot on the main street. She shopped at the three stores she needed to and thankfully got everything that was on her list.

As if being pulled along by memories, she found herself standing in front of the National Hotel on Water Street. Laurel and her mom often stopped there for a bite to eat or a glass of wine while they were wandering the little shops of this town.

As she stood on the sidewalk looking up at the grand old hotel, the tears slid down her cheeks. She thought about her mom and the fun times they shared on their weekend trips. A sob caught in her throat, and she wiped away the tears. A part of her wanted to go inside, but it was just too soon. She glanced up at the hotel once more before turning and walking back up Water Street. Occasionally, she stopped to look in a storefront window. A few tears still fell down her cheeks, but she made no attempt to wipe them. She could hear her mom's voice in her head, saying, "Sometimes tears need to fall to help us heal."

She parked in the garage and walked into the house through the adjoining kitchen door. Suddenly, feeling mentally exhausted, she made a cup of tea and took her journal out to the deck.

Laurel sat at the table and opened her journal. She looked across the yard to the lake and sighed. The loss of her parents suddenly weighed on her emotions. It was as if the floodgates opened—both in the speed at which she put the words to paper and how the tears fell. When she finally put the pen down, she was surprised to see that she had written six pages. Emotions that she thought she had been dealing with fairly well suddenly felt raw.

As much as she was making a new life for herself, she was missing the two most important people in her life. It struck her again how much of her life was spent just settling and existing. She wished she could turn back the clock and show her parents what she could accomplish before she lost them. Laurel spent the next few minutes quietly berating herself for wasting time. She knew she couldn't change the past, but she certainly could and would make sure her future was something she loved and that her parents would be proud of.

Having finished her pity party for one, she stood. *Enough is enough.* A few deep breaths later, she started to feel better. Deciding to spend a little time puttering about in the yard, she scrubbed the birdbath and pulled some weeds. The new plants and flowers she had planted were growing well and bringing some additional color to the yard. Now that it was no longer just a holiday home, she was thinking of other improvements she might want to make. Around her, birdsong filled the trees and helped to lift her spirit.

CASSIE EMAILED THE GRAPHICS SHE CREATED FOR Laurel's website and other social media accounts. Laurel had the website theme set up and placeholders for the graphics, and she hoped it would be easy to drop the images where she wanted them. Thankfully, technology had progressed, so setting up her website was pretty simple. Her social media accounts were set up, so she simply needed to add the images Cassie created.

Admiring her website landing page, Laurel held her breath and hit the publish button. She texted Maggie the link and asked her to have a look at it. Within a couple of minutes, she received a text.

> OMG! This looks incredible! I'm so proud of you!

> Thank you for all your encouragement. I love the images Cassie created. They make the site just pop. Do all the links work on your end?

> They're great! Cassie is amazing. Yup, all the links work. You're in business.

> Woohoo! I'm equally scared to death and unbelievably excited!!!

> You've got this, Laurel! Have you spoken to Joy yet about selling pieces in the bookshop?

> She's coming by in a couple of days to look at what I have and discuss details. ACK! LOL.

> Oh, that's great. I can't wait to hear all about it.

I'll let you know. Thanks again!

You're welcome. Now get back to the wheel.

Laurel set her phone on her desk and laughed out loud. She'd never felt so proud of herself. She was starting to believe she could really do all this and make a living from it.

She already found it hard to remember what her daily life used to be like. The dead-end job, the relationship where she was unable to be her true self, the way the days and weeks seemed to drag on—it was all burning away like mist in the sun.

One thing she missed, though, was her mom and their daily chats. She remembered how they would discuss the troubles of the world and agree on how any issue could be solved. They would often say to each other, "If only they would listen to us!" She was thankful every day for her mother's letter that encouraged her to change her life.

THE NEXT MORNING, LAUREL SPENT SOME TIME ON THE dock working on some sketches. She had noticed work being done on the house next door but had yet to meet the new owner. The only views she had of the house were from the road or from the dock. As Laurel looked over at the house, one toe making ripples in the calm lake water, she saw a man in the yard. Of course, that was the exact minute that he looked over and caught her looking at him. She tried to look away quickly, but she caught his wave out of the corner of her eye and she didn't want to be rude, so she waved back. Laurel started to look down at her sketch pad, but she noticed the man walking down the slope of his yard toward the lake.

"Hi," he said as he reached the lake's edge. "I'm your new neighbor, Aiden."

Laurel stood and walked over to the property line where he was standing. "Hi, welcome to the neighborhood. I'm Laurel."

"Thank you. It's a pleasure to meet you." He smiled, and his gorgeous green eyes sparkled.

Laurel made herself look away from his captivating gaze toward the building behind him. "I'm guessing you have some major upgrades being done on the house. I know the Johnstons hadn't done much to the place over the years."

Aiden laughed. "That would be an understatement! It's almost like stepping back in time. I'm hoping to do most of the work myself. I've made some headway on it already."

"Oh, wow, is that what you do for a living?"

"It hasn't been, but I'm making some changes in my life, so I'm looking to do this sort of thing going forward." Aiden looked down at his work gloves. "It's so satisfying to see the improvements and changes one can make with their own hands. Working on the house is reminding me of that."

"Ah, I can understand that feeling."

Aiden's gaze dropped to the sketch pad still in her hand and his eyes lit up. "Are you an artist?"

Laurel laughed. "Well, thankfully, I'm better at making pottery than I am at these rough sketches."

"Oh, you're a potter? How wonderful."

"Yes, I've just restarted it recently. So, I'm still in the beginning stages of getting my business going."

"Do you have a studio in town?"

"No, actually, my studio is right over there." Laurel pointed up the yard to the retrofitted garden shed.

"That's great!" Aiden said, and by the intensity of his gaze, Laurel could tell he meant it. "You get to be creative right here in this beautiful setting. I can see there must be so much inspiration here for you."

Laurel took in their surroundings. Her eyes traveled from her home, which held so many happy family memories, to her studio, then back down toward the lake with the morning sun glinting across it and the trees alive with birdsong. "Yes, it is inspiring. I've always loved it here, and I'm thankful that I can now live here and make my pottery."

"Oh, so you knew this area before you bought the house?" Aiden took off his work gloves and stuck them in the back pocket of his jeans. "I hadn't even heard of Lake Benton until a friend of a friend told me about it and mentioned the house being for sale."

"Yes, this is actually my family's cabin. We spent a great deal of time here when I was growing up." Family memories flashed through Laurel's mind. "Who told you about the house?"

"Brad. He owns the local boat works. He said he'd learned about the sale from his girlfriend..." Aiden scratched the back of his neck. "Gosh, I don't remember her name."

"Bailey! She's a friend of mine! And Brad is a great guy! What a small world." Had fate played a hand in Aiden buying the house?

"Yeah, Brad has been a big help in pointing me in the right direction for materials and resources. My friend Geoff introduced us. Geoff bought a boat from Brad a couple of years back, and they've become good mates."

Laurel nodded knowingly. "Small towns are great like that. Even though I spent a lot of time here growing up, I've also been away awhile. But that hasn't changed the friendships I have in this town. It was like coming home and being welcomed with open arms."

"It sounds as if you love it here." Aiden tilted his head a bit and smiled.

Laurel returned the smile. "Yes, I do. Even though it's changed a bit over the years, it still has that small-town America feel to it. The fact that it's surrounded with all this spectacular natural beauty makes it a very special place."

"Well, I look forward to exploring the area. First, I had better get some more work done on the house. It was wonderful to meet you, Laurel." He reached out his hand. "I'm happy to have such a lovely neighbor."

Laurel, sure she was blushing, reached her hand out and felt a bit tingly as his large hand enveloped hers. She continued smiling, hoping he hadn't noticed her blushing. "Well, thank you. Again, welcome to the neighborhood. If you need anything—" She felt herself blush more. "—you know, to borrow some sugar or something, just ask." Laurel laughed a little as she pulled her hand away.

Aiden joined in. "Yes, well, I might need some when the kitchen is finished. I'll keep that in mind. Thank you."

They both lingered there for a second longer, then nodded at each other and turned away toward their respective yards.

Laurel picked up her glass of water from the edge of the dock and took her sketch pad back to the studio. She knew she had to get inside for a while so she wouldn't stare back at Aiden's house.

Oh God, why did he have to be so gorgeous? Laurel tried to shut that thought down immediately; she didn't need any distractions. She wasn't looking for a new relationship, so what was the big deal? But she couldn't help but think about how Aiden was tall and ruggedly handsome, had gorgeous green eyes, and was good with his hands—for renovating, of course. *Laurel, get a grip.* He was just her new neighbor, not a new prospect.

Laurel chose a playlist on her phone in an attempt to quiet her thoughts of Aiden. She hoped that some classic rock and some work in the studio would help to get him out of her mind. Oh, but he was difficult to get out of her mind.

AIDEN WALKED UP THE STEPS OF THE DECK AND OPENED the sliding door to the living room. Its current state didn't conjure up thoughts of being cozy or welcoming, but he would change that. He went to work pulling up the last of the old carpeting and hauled it outside to the dumpster he had rented.

Laurel was beautiful—not in a striking way, but more like the beautiful girl next door. And those little freckles across her nose, the way her eyes lit up when she talked about Lake Benton.... He could be in serious trouble here. She seemed so down to earth and comfortable in her own skin, which was so refreshing after Lydia and her friends. *Don't even start thinking about Lydia. You promised yourself not to bring thoughts of her into this new life. She doesn't deserve space in your head anymore.* So that left him with Laurel.

Aiden sighed and walked back inside, trying to clear his head. He grabbed the utility light and plugged it into the wall socket near the kitchen. He shone it along the floorboards as he walked up and down each one. None of the boards seemed to squeak when he stepped on them, and the wood all seemed to be in good condition. That was good news. His plan was to sand and seal the existing wood floor. That would allow the natural colors and character of the timber to come through. He wanted the cabin on the lake to be rustic and natural. The Johnstons had covered almost every inch of the floor with carpet, and it really took away from the cabin feel.

A cabin on the lake should be easy to take care of. Friends shouldn't feel guilty tracking in a bit of sand or dirt from enjoying the natural surroundings. Sandy feet from frolicking in the lake, a bit of dirt from hiking the numerous trails around the area— none of it would hurt anything if tracked inside.

Not that Aiden was a slob or messy. Not at all. He appreciated everything having a place and being in its place, but he certainly didn't fret over a bit of dirt that could be cleaned up. Lydia had been so uptight about that sort of stuff.

No shoes were to be worn in her apartment. Towels were to be folded perfectly after use (which meant they never air-dried properly, as far as Aiden was concerned). Every counter was wiped down within an inch of its life. No one ever felt comfortable visiting, as they were afraid to touch anything and have to hear Lydia's cleanliness speech. She had a cleaning service that came twice a week. What they cleaned for several hours two times a week, Aiden could never figure out. It got to the point where his friends declined any invitations if the gathering was at Lydia's.

Of course, that wasn't the only thing people didn't like about Lydia. Lydia had an air of superiority and could be very condescending, even to her best friends. His job as a financial advisor for one of the largest global investment firms came with an image. The social circle Aiden became part of when he was with her was of a certain elite status. People had more money than most folks could dream of—and all the airs that came with it. Looking back, Aiden could now see that most of the women were like Lydia in a lot of ways: high maintenance, accustomed to the best of everything, thought they were better than anyone else. To be honest, the men were no better. They were always competing to see who had the latest high-priced toy and how much they had made with their day-trading jobs, flitting from one woman to another, as if they had to compete at that as well.

Lydia had been a friend of his then best friend's sister. She was considered a real catch by most of his friend's standards. In hindsight, he knew that they were all just judging by superficial standards. Once Aiden got to really know her, he found Lydia just as shallow as those standards.

When Aiden allowed himself to glance back at his former life, he felt embarrassed and disappointed in himself. He wasn't brought up in that world, but once he was making that crazy amount of money, he tended to look down on his simple upbringing. Oh, the arguments he and his dad had had about his new lifestyle. Both of his parents were proud of how he had excelled in university and had been on the fast track in the financial world, but what they couldn't understand was how quickly his personality and morals seemed to change.

While Aiden and his dad argued about it, his mom did her best to gently remind him of what was truly important in life. His parents' standards had nothing to do with how much money you made, how many toys you had, or whose yacht you spent the weekend on. They had never met Lydia and wouldn't have approved of her if they had.

Walking back into the kitchen with the utility light, Aiden turned it off and laid it on the counter. He turned to look around the kitchen. He had already pulled up the ancient linoleum and replaced the few floorboards that needed to be removed. The old oak cabinets had been removed, stripped of the many layers of paint under the years of grease and grime of the kitchen. He would stain them a light color and rehang them on another wall once he had replaced the lower cabinets and the appliances. Aiden was struck by a memory of his dad teaching him how to strip, sand, and stain old cabinets at his grandparents' house. The memory made him smile as he got back to work.

LAUREL'S PLAN TO GET AIDEN OUT OF HER HEAD WAS not working. How could a brief encounter mess with her mind so much? There was just something about him that she found intriguing. Why the change in lifestyle? What did he do for a living before? What would it be like to...

It was enough for her to send Brad a text.

> Hey Brad. How's it going?

Hi, good. How are you doing?

> I'm doing okay, thanks. Just wanted to tell you that I met my new neighbor, Aiden, today.

That's cool. I wasn't sure he had moved in yet. Aiden's a great guy. Really interesting too. He has a lot of work to do on that house, huh?

He seems nice. Yeah, he said it was like going back in time. The Johnstons never updated anything. Anyway, just wanted to tell you that we had met.

Great. I'm glad you will have him next door in case you need anything. Gotta run. A client just walked in. Take care of yourself.

Okay, bye.

Setting her phone down, she looked out towards the lake, remembering their earlier conversation. Well, if Brad says Aiden was a great guy, then it was enough for her. At least she knew he wasn't a creep. No one wanted some weirdo living next door.

Nine

After several long days of making more pieces, Laurel loaded the kiln and crossed her fingers as she fired it. She was excited to see how these turned out. Building up her stock had been her focus, and now that both the kiln and the drying rack were full, she felt ready to set up a meeting with Joy to discuss a display.

Having taken photos during the process, she shared those on her social media accounts. It was great to find that her followers—though there weren't many yet—liked seeing the creation part of the process.

After a long day of being cooped up in the studio, Laurel needed some fresh air. Time in the garden was her reward.

Laurel had only seen Aiden a couple of times since their meeting last week, and each time, they had only waved from a distance. Today, as she dug in the boat shed by the lake for some gardening tools, she heard Aiden call out. To whom she wasn't sure, but she poked her head out of the shed and looked toward his yard.

There was Aiden chasing a small dog around the yard. Upon a closer look, Laurel could see that it was a puppy with something in its mouth. Aiden was trying to coax it to drop the object and as soon as he took a step towards the puppy, the puppy ran in another direction. Perhaps frustrating to Aiden, but the puppy thought this was a great game. Laurel walked around the shed and closer to the property line to get a better look.

Aiden was a good sport; he wasn't yelling at the puppy but talking to it and trying to reason with it. It was like he expected the puppy to stop in its tracks and respond by dropping whatever the item was in its mouth. Of course, that didn't work, and the puppy zigged and Aiden zagged across the yard. He tried distracting the dog with a fake throw of an invisible object, but the puppy was too smart for that old trick. Then Aiden got down on his hands and knees, trying to entice the puppy into a closer game.

Laurel put a hand over her mouth as she tried to stifle her laughter. The puppy waddled a little closer to him. As he reached out to grab the object out of the puppy's mouth, the puppy took off again. Aiden had been reaching quite far, and the puppy's sudden movement caused him to lurch forward and tumble onto the grass.

Laurel couldn't hold her laughter in anymore. The sound of her laugh got the puppy's attention as well as Aiden's. While Aiden glanced over his shoulder, looking in Laurel's direction, and stood, the puppy—an adorable chocolate-colored Labrador—wandered right over to Laurel.

"I'm glad you find this funny," Aiden said, laughing himself.

Laurel crouched down as the puppy dropped the object from its mouth and met her with sweet puppy kisses.

"Oh my, aren't you just the cutest puppy? Was Aiden picking on you? Was he trying to take that away from you? No, that's not very nice, is it? No." Laurel plopped down on the ground and pet the puppy as it crawled all over her lap and licked her hands and face. She continued her conversation with the puppy as Aiden walked up and retrieved his wallet, which the puppy had dropped.

"What are you, the dog whisperer?" Aiden asked, as he took in the sight of Laurel getting puppy kisses.

Laurel laughed. "Well, obviously! Oh, Aiden, she's so cute! What's her name? When did you get her? Oh, and why are you picking on this sweet little girl?"

The tone of her voice brought more puppy kisses, as if in approval of her last question.

"I'm not picking on this little hairy monster." Aiden laughed while reaching over to pet the puppy. "She took my wallet and bolted."

"What's her name?"

"Sophie. She stole my heart three days ago. The SPCA had an adoption event outside of the hardware store. I really tried not to look, but this sweet girl did the little head tilt and yawned at the same time and, well..." Aiden shrugged bashfully. "I caved."

"Aw, Sophie...you're so adorable. Full lab?" Laurel asked, looking up at Aiden.

"Yes. Hopefully, she will be a water dog like most labs."

"You haven't taken her down to the water yet?"

"No, I've been letting her get settled and used to the house first. Oh, and before you ask, she is now in charge of me and the house."

Laurel laughed again. "Well, that is as it should be. Girls rule."

Aiden smiled and sat down on the ground next to Laurel. "Of course, you do."

Sophie climbed from lap to lap, getting lots of attention. Aiden leaned over to his left, grabbed a stick just within reach, and threw it. They watched Sophie waddle-run across the lawn after the stick. She brought it back, but just as Aiden reached for the stick, Sophie took off again.

Laurel couldn't help but grin. "I believe this is where I came in. You have a bit of work to do on the ol' 'Drop it' command."

"You think so?" Aiden tried again to get the stick from Sophie. "Yup, I think you are right."

After a few more minutes of running around, Sophie dropped the stick and laid down in front of Aiden with her head in his lap.

Aiden gently smooshed Sophie's face in his hands and raised his gaze to Laurel. "I'm a goner. Look at that face and those eyes." He dropped his gaze again and peered at Sophie. "On second thought, never look in her eyes. She'll melt your heart and you'll be under her spell."

Laurel smiled, reaching out to ruffle Sophie's ears. "I should have been told that important piece of information before. I'm afraid I'm already under her spell."

"Well, I guess we're in this together." Aiden offered Laurel a heart-stopping grin. "So, what's new with you?"

"I've been busy in the studio creating lots of soon-to-be gorgeous pieces. Friends of mine, Joy and Holly Lyman, own the bookshop and café in town. Joy offered to display my pottery in the bookshop." Laurel picked at a tuft of grass with her free hand. "I was nervous when she suggested it, but I'm feeling more confident now. I'm going to meet with her and discuss the details."

Aiden considered her for a moment, and Laurel felt her cheeks heat. "Do you have any idea how much you light up when you discuss your pottery?" he asked.

"Ha, I still get a bit giddy about finally doing this." Laurel sighed, trying to slow her heartbeat. "How's the reno coming along?"

"I'm making good progress, actually. The kitchen is the focus right now, so you can imagine what fun that is."

"If the kitchen is torn up, where are you cooking and eating?"

"Ah, well, grilling mostly—or takeaway when I can't be bothered to do anything more."

Before she could chicken out, Laurel blurted, "Hey, why don't you come over for dinner tonight?"

Aiden looked at her again, and she couldn't help but notice the Sophie-esque tilt to his head. "I don't want to put you out, Laurel."

"No, no problem at all. It would be nice to share dinner together."

"Well, thank you," he said, seeming genuinely touched. "That would be great. I just bought a couple of steaks. I could bring those over and grill them here."

"Sounds perfect. Is there anything you don't eat?"

Aiden grinned. "No, I pretty much like everything."

"Okay, I'll make a couple of side dishes, then."

"I really appreciate this, Laurel. Thank you."

Laurel reached over and booped Sophie's nose. "Bring her along."

"Are you sure?"

"Of course." Laurel stood and waited as Aiden did the same. Sophie was snuggled in his arms. "Say, six thirty?"

"Perfect. See you then."

Laurel turned back to the shed for her garden tools while Aiden and Sophie walked back to his house. Once inside the shed, she leaned against the door frame. *What did you just do?* Just being neighborly, she told herself. *New life. New me. No regrets.* She spent the next couple of hours working in the garden and jumped into the lake for a swim when she was finished.

AIDEN WORKED ON THE KITCHEN ALL AFTERNOON, BUT he found it difficult to stop thinking about dinner that night. Trying to tell himself that it was just dinner between two neighbors didn't really help. He was really looking forward to learning more about Laurel. When the time came, he fed Sophie and took a shower. Then he grabbed a couple of toys for Sophie and stuffed them into his jacket pockets.

"Sophie, are you ready? Shall we go see Laurel?"

Sophie spun in a circle and ran to the door, looking back over her shoulder at Aiden as if to say, "C'mon dad!"

"Okay, okay. Looks like you're as excited about seeing her as I am. Let's go." He carefully opened and closed the door, holding a dish with the marinating steaks in one hand.

Sophie stayed close as they walked across the backyard.

Laurel's garden glimmered as solar lights in the darker areas blinked to life. It was still too early for sunset, but there were some clouds moving across the sky that made it seem much later.

They were greeted by Laurel as soon as they reached the deck. Well, Sophie was the first one who got the attention, Aiden noticed.

"Hi there, Sophie." Laurel bent down and scratched Sophie's ears and kissed her head. What would kissing Laurel be like? He smiled and pushed that thought from his head.

"Hello."

"Hi Aiden, welcome. Let's go inside."

Laurel opened the door and followed Sophie and Aiden inside.

"Wow, it smells incredible in here. So, are we ready for me to get these on the grill?"

"Yes, the potatoes are almost done, and I've just thrown a salad together. I thought we would eat outside, okay?"

"Sounds good. I'll go fire up the grill."

Laurel handed him the grilling tongs and pointed to his jacket pocket. "Did you bring some toys to play with if you get bored talking to me?"

"I never leave home without them. You never know when—" Sophie heard the squeak of her toy as Aiden pulled it from his pocket and started circling his legs. "Okay, okay. Here you go." Aiden dropped the toys onto the floor next to Sophie.

"She really is the boss of you."

Aiden chuckled as he nodded and walked outside.

Laurel talked to Sophie as she pulled the dishes and silverware out and placed them on a tray to take outside. "You're such a good girl, yes you are."

Sophie paused, playing with her toy for a brief second before tossing it up and pouncing on it when it fell.

Everything was just about ready, so Laurel picked up the tray and walked toward the French doors that led to the deck. Just as she reached for the doorknob, the door flew up and Aiden rushed in, carrying the platter with their steaks. His hair was wet, and his jacket looked quite damp.

"What happened to you?" Laurel asked, not being able to stifle a giggle. "Did you have a fight with the hose or something?"

"I'm so glad you find this funny," Aiden said, laughing himself. "Those clouds that have been building over the lake, well, they just opened up."

"What! That's crazy. It wasn't supposed to rain tonight." Laurel put the tray on the dining room table. "Let me grab a towel for you."

"Thanks." Aiden put the platter on the counter and took his jacket off.

Laurel returned with a towel and took his jacket from him and hung it on the coat rack in the front hallway. "Well, I guess that means we aren't eating alfresco tonight. Just give me a minute to set the table."

She returned to the kitchen to find Aiden briskly towel drying his hair as he stood by the door. He turned and caught her staring at him. Putting the towel aside, he set the table.

Laurel could feel herself start to blush, so she quickly turned to the oven. "Um, let me just get the potatoes."

"Potatoes. My weakness," Aiden said.

"Well, I hope you like au gratin potatoes. Or maybe it's better if you don't, because that just leaves more for me. My weakness."

They both laughed as Laurel put the dish of bubbling au gratin potatoes on the table and they each reached out their forks, trying to get to them first. Aiden stopped, as if remembering his manners. "Ladies first."

"Well, thank you. You must be a true gentleman if you would risk not getting any potatoes!"

"I was hoping you would share some with me." Aiden said with a wink.

"Okay, maybe just a small portion. I mean, you did bring the steaks—and grilled them—so the least I can do is share some of *my* potatoes." Being cheeky, Laurel winked back.

Having served himself a modest allotment of potatoes, Aiden took a bite and a low groan escaped his lips. "Oh, wow, these are amazing!" Taking another bite, he closed eyes. When he opened them, he said, "I'm not kidding, these are the best au gratin potatoes I have ever had."

Laurel giggled. "Well, thank you. And if you think that compliment means I will let you have a second helping, then you are highly mistaken." They both reached for the serving spoon in mock desperation, then Laurel relented and sat back in her chair.

Laughing, they settled into an easy banter with a freedom that made it feel to Laurel like they had known each other for years. The conversation over dinner covered many topics. Aiden told Laurel about the renovations, and she could tell by the way he talked about it that he loved what he was doing. He spoke passionately and told her in detail about some of the precision work he had had to do to make things work in the old house.

"Some of the work is more than I had imagined, but nothing is too bad. I'm still on schedule—well, at least the schedule I came up with. Another couple of weeks for the kitchen, and the new appliances should be here at the end of the month, so that works perfectly."

"Please tell me that you tore out the dark-brown paneling in the living room," Laurel said.

"What? You don't like that dark-brown paneling? It's so, oh, what's the word...retro."

"I think the word you're looking for is more like repulsive," she mumbled, but not as quietly as she thought.

"Repulsive? Really? I like it. In fact, I was thinking of putting down a shag rug as well," Aiden said. "Perhaps a dark-brown plaid couch."

Laurel looked up from her plate, met Aiden's eyes, which were crinkled at the corners, and they both burst out laughing.

"Maybe you should stick to the remodeling and leave the interior design to someone, uh, perhaps a bit more qualified," Laurel said, catching on now. "Or possibly just someone with some taste."

Trying to keep a straight face, Aiden said, "So, that's a no to the shag rug, then?"

"Definitely!"

"Bummer, I was thinking an avocado green rug would look nice..."

Their laughter filled the room as the conversation continued while they ate. Sophie had found a spot nearby and had fallen asleep with both of her toys tucked close.

After they finished dinner, they cleared the table and, against Laurel's objections, Aiden helped her clean up the kitchen.

THE RAIN HAD FINALLY STOPPED, SO AIDEN POPPED outside to clean the grill. He used the steel bristle brush and gently scrubbed the grates. When he finished, he walked to the French doors and let himself in. He found Laurel on the phone and motioned that he would step back outside. She motioned for him to stay and held up her finger, indicating she would be just a moment. He picked up his wine and took a drink while he turned and looked out at the lake. The moonlight was obscured by the passing clouds. The light from houses across the lake cast dappled reflections on the water. Aiden took in the view with a sense of contentment. He smiled to himself, thinking about how much his life had changed since he moved here. It had been just a few short months since he left his previous life, and so far, he had no complaints.

"That's really not my problem anymore." Laurel paused to listen to the person on the other end of the line. "He's the one who caused this, not me." Another pause was accompanied by a roll of her eyes. "Ted, I can't believe you're sticking up for him."

Aiden turned around to look at Laurel. Not that it was any of his business, but he didn't like the sound of this conversation. He watched her face as the conversation continued.

"No, I am not going to talk to him. I have nothing more to say. No, no, listen..." Laurel turned and met Aiden's gaze for a moment before looking away. "Ted, I'm not sure what Graham has told you, and frankly, I don't care. I have no intention of getting back together with him. I should have left a long time ago." Another pause. "Well, if he's that depressed, maybe he should talk to a therapist. No, I am not heartless, and neither you nor Graham are going to make me feel bad, Ted. I'm done. Goodbye."

LAUREN ENDED THAT CALL AND TURNED TO FIND AIDEN walking toward her, concern evident on his face.

"Hey, are you okay? That sounded a bit rough."

"Sorry you had to hear that. Yeah, I think I'm alright." Laurel put her phone down on the counter. A quick glance at Aiden told her they both had noticed her hand shaking as she released the phone.

"Do you want to sit down?" Without waiting for her to reply, Aiden led her into the living room and held her arm as she sat down.

Aiden returned from the kitchen with the bottle of wine and her glass.

"I'm really okay," Laurel said.

Aiden topped up each of their glasses and handed one to Laurel. She took it in both hands, still shaking a little. Aiden then sat in the overstuffed chair to the left of where Laurel was sitting.

Laurel lifted the glass of red wine to her lips and took a small sip. "I just can't believe that conversation. The nerve..." She took another sip and put her glass down on the coffee table.

Aiden watched her as she gathered her thoughts, shook her head, and then looked up and gave him a weak smile.

"Do you want to tell me what that was all about?" Aiden asked gently.

"Ah, well, that was my ex-boyfriend's best friend. Not a bad guy, but at times gullible to my ex's lies." Laurel shook her head again. "It appears that Graham, my ex, is not coping with my leaving him. He's depressed, apparently, and telling people that I just walked out. That I didn't even try to talk to him and work together on our problems. He misses me terribly. Blah blah blah.

"Oh, and evidently, he is so distraught about our breakup that he has been missing work. Ted said that he was over at Graham's the other day and the house was in shambles. Dishes piled up. Clothes strewn about." Laurel lifted her wineglass again but didn't take a sip. "I'm sure that's because *I* used to do everything around the house. As for him being depressed, this may sound mean, but I think he's just feeling sorry for himself and wanting others to feel the same way."

Aiden listened and watched Laurel closely as she recounted the phone conversation. He didn't interject. He just listened.

Laurel continued. "So Ted was asking if I would talk to Graham. How he thinks that would help is beyond me. Graham told him that if he could just see me, he knows we can work this out. Oh, and what about the other woman he was seeing? What happened to her?"

Laurel stopped and looked over at Aiden. He was leaning forward in his seat, as if to not miss a word she was saying.

"Oh, I am so sorry." Laurel felt sheepish. "Just rambling on like that. I'm sure the last thing you want is to listen to my drama."

Aiden put his wineglass on the coffee table and looked Laurel in the eyes. "Laurel, you have no reason to say you are sorry. If anything, I think you probably need to talk about what just happened, and I'm here to listen, if you want."

"Thank you. I am..." Laurel looked down at her hands in her lap.

"You are...what? Sad?"

Laurel looked up at Aiden and offered a twisted smile. "No, I am actually feeling...angry."

"Angry?"

"Yes, angry at Graham for playing these games, for trying to manipulate me once again. I guess he figured it always worked in the past, so why wouldn't he try it again?" Laurel lifted her wineglass and then set it down again. "And that thought makes me angry at myself for being so stupid for so long."

"Aw, c'mon," Aiden said, reminding Laurel of Maggie. "We all do silly things in the name of love."

"Well, that may be true, but when I look back on what I put up with..." Laurel sighed. "I realize how much time I wasted, and I'm disappointed in myself."

"Those feelings mean that you've grown and have learned from your mistakes. That's a positive step."

Laurel giggled. "What are you, a relationship guru?"

Aiden laughed, sitting back in his armchair, and taking a healthy gulp of his wine. "Far from that. I've made plenty of mistakes in my life. And, at times, I still beat myself up over what I did. But I'm getting better at putting that behind me and chalking it up as lessons learned."

Laurel swirled the wine in her glass, watching the slow spiral as she considered his point. "That's a good way to look at it. Lessons learned."

"Exactly. Listen, you can't go back and change things. The best thing you can do is learn from those mistakes and try not to make them again."

"Good point." Laurel smiled at Aiden as she lifted her wineglass.

"Oh, and the best revenge is to live a happy life—without them." Aiden leaned forward and raised his glass in a toasting motion. "To the best revenge."

Laurel clinked her glass to Aiden's. "To the best revenge."

"That's the spirit, Laurel. It will get easier. I promise." Aiden leaned back in the chair and smiled at her.

She looked at him and caught the sparkle in his eye. "What?"

"I'm just happy to see you smile again after that phone call."

"This smile is thanks to you. Thank you for listening. I didn't mean for the evening to turn into this mess."

"Seriously, you must stop apologizing. The call was not your fault. The way it made you feel was completely valid."

"Sor..." Laurel's cheeks heated, "I mean, thank you. I really need to work on not using that word so much."

"I could get you a jar and every time you say 'sorry' you have to put a dollar in it. That might help."

"I don't know if I can afford that right now." Laurel laughed at herself. "Okay, reset to the evening. How about some dessert? I think we've earned it."

"You know, I have a very serious rule that I hold myself to." Aiden started.

Laurel leaned forward, poised to stand. "Oh, do tell."

"Never, under any circumstances, should I say no to dessert."

"Ah, a kindred spirit. Great! I made a peach-and-blueberry crumble earlier today."

"Yum, that sounds wonderful." Aiden followed Laurel into the kitchen. He refilled their wineglasses as Laurel reached into the cabinet for bowls.

She spooned a serving into each bowl. "A little vanilla ice cream to top it off?"

"I refer you back to my 'very serious rule:' never say no." Aiden grinned.

Laurel couldn't help but giggle as she added a dollop of ice cream to each bowl. She grabbed two spoons from the drawer and put everything on a tray. "Shall we sit outside? It looks like the rain has passed." She grabbed a towel from the living room closet to wipe off the chairs, balancing the tray on one arm as she did so.

"Perfect." Aiden picked up their wineglasses and followed her out the French doors to the deck. Sophie trotted out the door right behind him.

Aiden took the towel from her arm and wiped off the chairs while Laurel placed the bowls on the table. Sitting down, Aiden leaned his face over the bowl. "Wow, this smells amazing."

"It is one of my favorite dishes, and I love that it serves both as a dessert and as breakfast."

Aiden lifted a spoonful to his mouth and let out a groan. "Oh, this is incredible. The combination of peach and blueberries is perfect. And the cinnamon in the crumble..." He stopped talking to take another bite.

"You seem to be enjoying it." Laurel laughed.

"I can see what you mean, that this would be great for breakfast."

"Well, I'll be sure to send you home with some so that you can try it for yourself." Laurel leaned back in her chair and looked out at the lake. A sigh escaped her lips.

"You okay?" Aiden looked over at her.

"Yes, I am, thanks to you. I've really enjoyed this evening. Thank you for listening to me after that phone call and for the pep talk. I really appreciate it."

"Anytime. I've enjoyed this evening as well," Aiden said. "Little did I know when I bought the place next door that I would be lucky enough to have a neighbor who's an incredible cook. My kitchen remodel might need to be delayed so I can partake in more of your cooking." He winked at Laurel as she reached over and slapped his arm playfully.

"Maybe you should have kept that a secret. A month from now, if you're still claiming the kitchen remodel is taking longer than you expected, I'll know why."

"Can you blame me, though?"

"No, I suppose not. For me, it's sometimes easier to make a meal for two people instead of just me. So...we can certainly do this again."

"I would love that. Thank you." Aiden smiled warmly at

Laurel. Then he looked at Sophie, who was pawing at his pant leg and sniffing the air. "On that note, I think Sophie and I should call it a night."

Laurel attempted to hide a yawn as she stood and looked at her watch. "Oh, I hadn't realized how late it was. Let me grab Sophie's toys from inside."

She returned with the toys and a small container with a serving of peach-and-blueberry crumble for Aiden's breakfast.

"You really are spoiling me now." Aiden took the container. "Thank you again for a great night and incredible food."

"Enjoy your breakfast. Thank you for the steaks and, well, everything. I've had a great time." Laurel bent to pet Sophie. "You be a good girl now, okay? See you soon."

"C'mon Sophie. Let's go home, girl." Aiden looked back over his shoulder before he went around the side of the house and out of sight.

Laurel smiled to herself, remembering that line from a Clint Eastwood movie: "If she looks back, that means she's interested." *Must mean the same thing if he looked back.* Grinning like a Cheshire cat, she locked the door and turned off the lights before heading up to bed.

Ten

Joy arrived just after six p.m., and they walked out to the studio. Laurel had arranged a table with some of her completed pieces. The vase held a red hibiscus from the yard. In the large centerpiece bowl, she placed a mixture of seashells and sea glass surrounding a large conch shell. The blue mugs and smaller bowls were set on yellow placemats.

"Oh Laurel, these are beautiful. You have a gift, my friend."

"Thank you, Joy. I'm happy with how these all turned out."

"And the way you have placed everything with the little touches of the flower, the shells, the color of the placemats to show off the blue of the dishes...it's perfect."

"Great. Thanks. Let me show you some other items I'm working on." Laurel showed her the new place settings, along with several different candle holders. She also shared sketches of pieces she planned to make.

Joy gasped at a sketch of a large vase adorned with humming-birds and shaded with an array of bright colors. "When you make this one, I want to buy it. Will it really be this colorful?"

"Deal! Yes, and if you want different colors, just let me know."

They talked about how to display them in the store and discussed both retail and wholesale prices for each item.

After an hour, they had agreed on what Laurel felt was a great business partnership.

When Joy left, Laurel called Maggie. "Joy and I have a business agreement. She loved everything. My hands are shaking so much."

"That's fantastic! I'm so thrilled for you! Congratulations." Maggie paused. "What are you doing? You sound like you're jumping up and down."

"Thank you. Oh, yeah, I guess I am a little hyped. I'm pacing the deck." Laurel laughed at herself. "Oh, hold on a sec."

"Okay," Maggie said.

Laurel waved over at Aiden, who was in the yard with Sophie. "Aiden, hey I've got your dish from the steaks last night. I'll bring it over in a few."

Aiden waved and gave a thumbs up before he turned back to Sophie.

"Laurel, who is Aiden?" Maggie asked.

"Oh, my new next-door neighbor. He bought the old Johnston place."

"Okay...and what was that about steaks last night? Spill it! I want all the details."

Laurel laughed as she walked into the studio so their conversation wouldn't be overheard. "Well, we met last week—or the week before, sometime—and then yesterday morning he was in his yard with his new puppy, Sophie. Oh, Maggie, she is just the cutest little lab."

"Back to the man, then you can tell me about his puppy."

"Okay, Okay. Well, he's remodeling the kitchen, and of course that makes it difficult to cook, so I just invited him over for dinner. We had a great evening. He's a nice guy."

"Well, well. Haven't you been busy?" Maggie teased. "Tell me more."

"Brad is the one who told him about the house, so I texted him after I met Aiden and just casually said we had met. I just wanted to make sure he wasn't an axe murderer or something.

Brad said he was a great guy and interesting, so I figured it was safe
to invite him to dinner. And, before you start, I was just being a
good neighbor."

"Of course you were." Maggie snickered.

"He's cute too. In a tall, ruggedly handsome sort of way."

"Laurel, are you a bit smitten?"

"I don't know. He's sweet, but I don't know if I'm ready for
that again."

"Sounds to me like you're getting closer to being ready for
something new. There's nothing wrong with that. You deserve all
the happiness in the world."

"Thanks. We'll see what happens. For now, I'm enjoying
having a new friend and great neighbor."

"Ha! Gosh, I've missed hearing your excitement. Welcome
back to you!"

"Funny, I feel like I'm becoming myself again. And I love it!"
Laurel smiled to herself, then remembered the other thing that
happened last night. "Oh, and can you believe Ted called me last
night, while Aiden was over?" She told Maggie what happened in
detail, trying not to fume about it.

"Seriously, that man needs to get a clue," Maggie muttered.
"Sounds like you handled it perfectly, though."

"Yes, hopefully that's the end of it. Oh well. Not letting it get
to me. I'm just happy I'm out of that relationship."

"Me too. Listen, I must run. Have fun with Aiden," Maggie
teased.

"Ha ha. Bye." After she hung up, she walked over to Aiden's
to return his dish.

He was tied up on the phone, so she just left it on the deck
and returned home.

Once her tea was ready, she slipped on a sweater and walked
outside to the deck. The sun had dropped low behind the trees,
and the evening was cool. A few birds stopped by the bird feeder
for an evening snack before flying up into the trees and chirping
excitedly to each other about all their day's happenings.

The lake was still and quiet. With her hands wrapped around the mug of hot tea, she listened to the frogs sing their nightly chorus and smiled, remembering her mom's love of frogs. They used to sit out here and make up conversations that they imagined the frogs having. They would try to outdo each other by being ridiculous and then laugh hysterically. Ah, such special memories.

She put the mug on the table and opened her notebook. For the next twenty minutes, she did a brain dump, just getting everything down on paper. Once she looked over what she wrote, she made more intelligent notes, and added items to her designs and to-do lists. Laurel loved this exercise. It helped clear her mind, yet made sure she captured everything on paper.

Closing her notebook, she picked up her phone and mug and walked inside. Locking the door behind her, she felt an amazing calm come over her. She was settling nicely into her new life.

Laurel carefully packed the pieces for Joy to sell in boxes and placed them in her car. She was a bit nervous about her first pieces being displayed and for sale. What if no one wanted them? She pushed that thought aside and returned to the studio to grab the business cards and brochures Joy was going to display with Laurel's pottery. She looked around the studio to double-check she had everything she needed, then locked the studio door. Taking a deep breath, she walked to her car and drove to town.

She parked the car at the bookshop and walked in to find Joy before carrying everything inside.

"Good morning, Laurel." Joy's cheerful voice greeted her.

"Good morning." Laurel smiled as she hugged Joy.

"Let me show you where we'll be setting up your display first, then I'll help you bring the pieces in." Joy led the way to an empty table by one of the windows. "This is a high traffic area, but the table is situated in a way that it won't get bumped by people walking by. I thought the window would provide some natural light on the display and make your pieces visible to people walking by outside. What do you think?"

"Oh, Joy, this is perfect. Thank you so much! I hope people love my work. I'm so happy with how these pieces turned out. I'm excited to hear what people think."

"I think you'll be restocking this display soon." Joy put her arm around Laurel's shoulders and gave her a hug.

"I'll admit I'm nervous about all of this, but I'm sure that's normal, especially as this is my first display."

"We'll watch the space and make any adjustments to the display if we feel it's warranted. Now, let's go get your boxes and get this set up."

Twenty minutes later, they stood back and looked at the table. Laurel had to admit that it looked amazing. She took a few photos with her phone to share with Maggie and on her social media.

"Why don't you let me put these boxes in the back and let the staff know where they are when they need them for the sales?" Joy reached for the load in Laurel's arms. "Then we can have a cup of coffee before you leave."

"Sounds great." Laurel handed them over. "I'll wander around a bit. I have a few items I'd like to pick up while I'm here."

"Perfect. I'll see you in a few minutes, then." Joy took the boxes and disappeared into the storeroom.

Laurel looked around the bookshop and found a couple of books she wanted. She discreetly glanced over at her display as a few customers came into the store. She would love to see their reaction to her work. A couple of ladies stopped and chatted with each other as they picked up and returned several of the pieces.

Laurel realized she was standing there staring at them, so she took her books to the cashier and paid for them, then went off to find Joy.

On the way home, she stopped to run a couple of errands and pick up some groceries. As she was pulling into her garage, her phone pinged with a message from Joy.

Congratulations! You had your first sale today!

Laurel screamed, "*Woohoo!*" as she sent a text back and asked what the customer had purchased.

They bought the small vase and the dish for jewelry. Congratulations!

Thank you so much, Joy.

Laurel sent the text and unloaded her purchases from the car.

She couldn't help herself. Before she could put the groceries away, she dialed Maggie's number.

"Hey there, how are you?" Maggie answered the phone.

"*I did it*! I made my first sale today! I can't believe it! Joy and I set up the display this morning, and she just texted to tell me I made my first sale!"

"*Woohoo you*! I knew you could do this! Congratulations! I'm so proud of you, and your mom would be, too."

"Aw Maggie, thank you. That means so much to me. I know Mom is smiling down on me right now." Laurel wiped a tear from her cheek. "Thanks for all your encouragement and support. I really appreciate you."

"Any time."

They chatted for a few more minutes before hanging up. Laurel busied herself with stowing the groceries, then headed out to the studio for the afternoon.

LENA WAS COMING OVER THAT AFTERNOON TO HELP Laurel with the logistics of packing and shipping orders from her website. One of Lena's first implementations when she bought the winery was to sell their wines through their website. It took some organization and planning, but she had shown she had a knack for these things, and it was a great success. Lena told

Laurel she could help her organize an area for the packaging and shipping and get her set up with online accounts for delivery services.

Laurel didn't have any online sales yet, but she was doing some social media campaigns and wanted to be prepared when the sales eventually started coming in.

Cassie, without Laurel asking, had drawn up some designs for branded packaging. Although Cassie knew it was an overhead expense for Laurel that wasn't warranted yet, she said she wanted to show Laurel what was possible and something she could do in the future. In the meantime, Cassie had created various other marketing materials Laurel could use and include in her current shipping packages.

Laurel, with Lena's input, created a business plan and set measurable goals for herself. Laurel obviously needed to make a living from her pottery sales, but she wanted to be true to herself and not compromise how she wanted to live her life. She wanted to enjoy making her pottery and not have it become a chore over time—a chore that she would then regret doing. She wasn't looking to become rich. She didn't need to buy a bigger house, and she wasn't interested in filling her life with material things. She wanted to be an artist and live a simple—but fun and rewarding—life. That was what following her dream meant to her.

Lena arrived, and they went to work organizing a space for shipping in the corner of the two-car garage.

"I originally thought of setting this up in the studio," said Laurel, "but I don't want to lose any space. I only have one car, so this side of the garage is perfect for my shipping corner."

"I agree. This is perfect. You have plenty of room in here, and you already have the shelving where you can store the materials. Plus, this will also make it easier to load the boxes into your car when you're ready to ship them."

Lena explained how it was best to make sure things were organized in a particular way so that the process flowed. "It should work like an assembly line: put everything in the order you'll use it, so there's no back and forth in the process."

They created online accounts with a couple of different carriers, and Lena went over how to figure out the best carrier to ship with based on whatever region the item was going to. Within a short time, everything was set up and ready for those sales to happen.

"Lena, how can I ever thank you for all your help? I really appreciate it."

"No problem. Glad I could help. Listen, I've learned a few things over the years. Trial and error. I want to help you succeed. You might as well learn from all my mistakes." Lena smiled. "Believe me, I've made enough of them to share."

"Funny. Really, thanks so much. I'm hoping things start selling through my online store soon, and then I'll have some use for this stash of boxes and the functional setup we just finished."

"Don't worry, it will come. Just keep creating your beautiful work and sharing it on social media. You have your display at the bookshop now, right?"

"Yes, that should give me some exposure locally."

"Oh, it will. Everyone in town goes to the bookshop and café." Lena picked up her purse and phone. "Listen, I need to get going. I have a meeting at the winery. Oh, before I forget. The winery is hosting the next Chamber of Commerce mixer. I would love for you to come and meet some people. Also, I thought we could display some of your pieces around to showcase your work."

"Wow, really? That would be great. Thank you so much."

"Happy to do it. The chamber mixers are all about networking. There will be people you already know but more people to meet. It'll also involve food and our fabulous wines. It's on the twenty-third. You can bring your pottery by the day before. Sound good?" Lena climbed into her car.

"Sounds great. Thanks so much for everything. I really appreciate it."

"No problem. Talk to you soon."

"Yup. Talk soon."

As she closed the garage door, Laurel thought of someone else who should attend the mixer: Aiden. It would be a great way for him to meet more locals and promote his new remodeling business. She tried to convince herself that she was just being neighborly. It had nothing to do with the fact that they would get to spend more time together. She sent him a quick text and put her phone down.

Aiden replied immediately.

> Thank you for the invitation. Sounds like a great idea. Maybe we could drive together.

Laurel smiled and replied.

> Sure, that would be great.

> Have a great night. Hope to see you tomorrow.

Laurel's fingers paused above the phone. What was she supposed to say to that? She typed. She deleted it. Finally, she typed.

> Maybe we could do dinner again. Pasta?

> I would love that. I'll bring some wine. Oh, and the cutest puppy.

Laurel laughed out loud.

> Perfect. Have a good night.

> You too.

AIDEN PUT HIS PHONE DOWN ON THE TABLE. "WELL, what do you think about that, Sophie?"

Sophie cocked her head at the sound of her name.

"Our friend Laurel just asked us over for dinner tomorrow night."

Sophie wagged her tail and wandered over to sit in front of Aiden.

Aiden reached down and ruffled her ears. "You look as excited as I am. We like Laurel, don't we?"

Sophie wiggled and circled Aiden's legs.

"Okay, but we have to play it cooler than that. We don't want to scare her off."

With that, Sophie sat down and cocked her head again.

"Yes, girl. That's better. Okay, ready for some dinner?" Aiden filled up her bowl and returned to his work in the kitchen. He found it was easy to think about Laurel and still focus on the work at hand. He wanted to get to know her better. He knew about the recent breakup and starting her pottery business, but what about her family? Did she have brothers or sisters? Where did her parents live? She had mentioned fond family memories at the cabin, so he assumed she was close with her parents.

Okay, so maybe he couldn't focus completely on the work. He tried to put Laurel out of his mind while he finished sanding the hardwood floors in front of the stove.

His phone chimed as a text message came in. He'd look at it later, otherwise he'd never get this done. Turning up the music to give his mind a distraction, he worked for a couple more hours.

After using the shop vac on the dust and dirt from sanding, he grabbed a beer from the fridge in the garage and checked his messages. One each from his brother and sister and one from his mom. They were all checking on him since they hadn't heard from him in a while. *Ugh.* He knew he needed to come clean soon. He couldn't keep this from them much longer. To put them off a bit, he sent cheerful, quick messages to each of them with the promise that he would be in touch soon.

Laurel finished setting the table and turned down the burner under the pasta. Setting the timer, she quickly dashed to the mirror in the hallway for the second time to make sure she looked okay. *Why are you acting like this? He's just a neighbor—isn't that what you keep telling yourself? Calm down.*

Aiden and Sophie arrived at the back door as she was walking into the kitchen. She opened the door and promptly bent down to pet Sophie. Standing back up, she smiled at Aiden.

"Hi. Sorry about that. She looked like she needed some love. How are you?"

Aiden laughed. "Hi. Believe me, she's been getting plenty of love. Don't let her fool you." He followed Laurel into the kitchen. "Wow, it smells incredible in here. What magic are you cooking up now?"

"Pasta modelese. I hope you like it. It's another of my favorites."

"I'm sure I will. Shall I open this?" He set the wine on the counter.

"That would be great. Thanks. Everything is just about ready." Laurel strained the pasta into a colander in the sink. "So, how's the kitchen reno going?"

Aiden opened the wine and poured some into each of their glasses. Turning back to the kitchen, he sighed. "Well, it's going slowly, which kitchen renovations usually do. I might have been a bit too optimistic about the schedule, but it'll be amazing when I finish."

Laurel couldn't help laughing. "Didn't we have this conversation last time? Perhaps you enjoy my cooking too much."

Aiden shook his head as he joined in the laughter. "Um, in my defense, your cooking is incredible. I don't have a choice but to love it."

"Thank you. That's very sweet." She turned back to the stove and served the pasta, grating fresh parmesan cheese over each bowl, then mixing it in with the sauce.

Aiden sat down as Laurel placed the bowl in front of him. "Wow. This looks as amazing as it smells. What's in it?"

Laurel told him about how she had gone to a restaurant, and this was their menu special for the night. She'd asked the waiter if the chef might tell her the ingredients because she had enjoyed it so much. A few minutes later, the waiter returned with a hand-written recipe, complete with instructions from the chef.

"That's unheard of. Most restaurants won't share those details." Aiden took a bite of the chicken and pasta. "But I sure am glad they did. This might easily be my new favorite pasta dish. Wow."

"I'm glad you like it. Now you understand why I asked for the ingredients."

"Mmhmm," was all he could muster with another bite in his mouth.

"So, you said last time that you were making some changes in your life. What did you used to do for a living before moving here?" she asked as she took a sip of wine.

"I was a financial advisor for one of the largest global investment firms. I landed the job right out of university and climbed the ladder quickly."

"Did you like what you did?" Laurel asked.

"I loved it, actually."

Laurel looked at him quizzically. "But if you loved it, why did you leave?"

Aiden's smile showed a wariness Laurel hadn't seen in him before. "The million-dollar question. Although I was extremely good at my job, and at first, I really enjoyed it, the lifestyle that came along with it was the deciding factor."

"I don't understand."

"As I climbed the ladder, my lifestyle changed immensely." Aiden paused to take a bite of the pasta. "Because of the wealth some of our clients had, my life became an image. As my colleagues and I made more money for our clients and our firm, our wealth also increased. The bonuses alone were just crazy money."

"And this was bad?" Laurel tried to imagine what kind of money that might have been.

Aiden chuckled. "Well, money is great to have, but it isn't everything. The competition amongst my peers and so-called friends was just stupid. It was all about the latest toys and vacation destinations, and whose yacht we were spending the weekend on."

Laurel's eyes widened. "Yachts?"

Aiden sipped his wine. "Yes, yachts. For the record, I do not own a yacht. It sounds glamorous, but the people I was spending my time with were all so superficial. Stupidly, I thought that was the life I wanted. Money, toys, traveling. But, Laurel, in the end, none of that mattered. I wasn't being myself. I wasn't being the person my parents raised."

Laurel swallowed the last of her dinner and leaned back in her chair. "It's great that you recognized that—and made the decision to change it."

"Yes, it's the best decision I've ever made. I shocked everyone when I announced I was leaving my job and moving away from the city." Aiden shook his head. "I think a few of my so-called friends thought or still think I'm having a mental breakdown. But that couldn't be further from the truth. I don't miss that life at all."

"So-called friends? You mean those friendships didn't last?"

Aiden rolled his eyes. "Ha, not a chance. And that's a good thing. Believe me. They were people to party with, sure, but not people you could have a deep conversation like this with."

Laurel smiled. "Well, I'm glad you feel comfortable enough with me to say that."

"Y'know, I thought buying this house was wonderful, but the fact that I have you right next door is a huge bonus." He winked.

"And I'm not just saying that because of that amazing meal you just made for us."

Laurel stood and cleared the bowls away, turning her face to hide her blush. "I'm glad you moved next door. It's nice to have someone so easy to talk to."

She retreated to the kitchen with the bowls, and Aiden took the opportunity to take Sophie outside for a minute. When he came back, they sat in the living room, settling into opposite ends of the couch. "So, tell me about yourself. Do you have siblings? What are your parents like?"

Laurel sighed and sat back against the couch. "I am an only child. Um, sadly, both my parents are gone." Pausing to gather her thoughts, she continued. "I lost my dad to a massive heart attack ten years ago, and I just recently lost my mom to COPD." A few tears slid down her cheeks.

Aiden moved closer, gently reached over, and squeezed her hand. "I'm so sorry. My questions seem callous and heartless. I'm sorry, I had no idea."

His touch was unexpected, yet Laurel welcomed its warmth. "Thank you. It's okay. You had no way of knowing."

"It sounds like you've been through so much. Yet you seem to be one of the happiest people I've ever met."

Laurel smiled slightly. "Oh, I have my days, believe me. There are times when I'm coping okay and then *wham!* I'm a sobbing mess." Thoughts of her mom and dad made her smile even more. "My parents were my best friends. When we lost my dad, well, I grew up a lot. I had to be strong for my mom." She wiped a tear away. "We helped each other through it."

Aiden's thumb caressed her hand. "I can't imagine what you've been through—what you're still going through."

"I'll be honest. Some days it's hard for me to even explain it. But my parents wouldn't want me to wallow in grief or stop smiling and laughing because they aren't here anymore. My mom made that very clear." Laurel thought of the letters tucked neatly in the drawer of her bedside table. "My mom left me a couple of letters when she passed, encouraging me to live life to the fullest. It was her gentle push that gave me the courage to quit my job and get back to pottery."

"And to leave Graham?"

Laurel sighed. "Actually, that happened a couple days before my mom passed. She never really cared for Graham, but she had given up telling me he wasn't good enough for me. She was thrilled that I had left him."

"What about moving here?"

They both reached for their wineglasses with their spare hands. He smiled at her in a way that warmed her almost as much as his hand that still held hers.

"That was her suggestion—and the best decision ever. This place is so special to me. The memories we made here as a family are truthfully what sustain me now." Laurel looked around the room, conjuring up some of those memories.

Aiden squeezed her hand and smiled at her. "How wonderful to have those memories to anchor you."

Laurel's face lit up with a huge smile. "Wow. Anchors me. That is beautiful. That's exactly what it is." She stood and immediately regretted losing the touch of Aiden's hand on hers. "Listen, why don't we get a change of scenery and mood and go sit on the dock?"

Aiden whistled for Sophie as he stood. "Our dinners always get emotional, don't they? Sorry if my questions upset you."

She touched his arm and looked into his eyes. "Don't be sorry. I love talking about my parents. It's hard when you're grieving because people who know you don't want to bring it up, y'know, in case they upset you. Then no one talks about your loved ones, and that's exactly what you need to do. So, thank you."

"Anytime you want to talk about them, then, I'm here." Aiden smiled gently. "There's so much about you that I want to know."

As they sat on the end of the dock, Laurel sighed. "You're very easy to talk to. And I'm enjoying getting to know you."

"I feel the same."

As a sense of peace and warmth settled over her, Laurel suddenly felt the need to shift the conversation. She wasn't sure these new feelings for Aiden were a good idea right now. "So, about the chamber mixer. Have you ever been to one?"

"Not to a Chamber of Commerce mixer—but I've been to plenty of networking sessions like them. Have you?"

"No, but I've been involved in large conferences before, so I kind of understand the vibe. Although, I think this will be different as we're all locals, and we'll all be there to support each other. I'm not even nervous about displaying my pottery." Laurel shrugged. "I guess that could be because it's already at the book-shop, and everyone who will be there has probably already seen it."

Aiden nodded. "I'm looking forward to seeing the winery. You said a friend of yours owns it?"

"Yes, Lena. She's part of my group of girlfriends here. In fact, most of those friends will be at the mixer, so you'll get to meet them all. Oh, Brad and Bailey will be there too, so there'll be at least one guy that you already know."

"Phew. I was worried about that." Aiden grinned. "Just kidding. It'll be great to meet your friends."

"As a bonus, the wine and food will be amazing."

"Are you cool driving together? I don't mind driving us."

"Sure. It seems silly to take two cars when we live next door to each other."

"Great. So, will you be busy in the studio all weekend?"

"No. I'm going to go start cleaning out my parents' house in Addington. I need to get it done so I can put the house on the market."

"Ah. Not a fun task. Do you need any help?"

Laurel shook her head. "Thanks, but I think I need to do this on my own. It'll be quite emotional, I'm sure."

"I understand. Just scream if you need anything, okay?"

"Okay. Thanks."

They sat quietly for a few minutes, lost in their own thoughts, while they stared out across the lake. Light from the surrounding houses dappled the water. Laurel shivered as the breeze suddenly came off the lake.

"You're cold." Aiden glanced in her direction.

"Yeah, that breeze is really kicking up. It wasn't bad when we first came out here." At Laurel's prompting, they both stood and walked to the house.

Aiden stopped at the threshold and stuck his hands in his pockets. "It's getting late. Sophie and I thank you for another wonderful evening."

"Are you sure? I didn't mean to run you off." Had she said something wrong?

"You didn't run us off." He grinned. "Do you realize what time it is?"

Laurel looked at her watch and then back at Aiden. "Wow, I guess time really does fly when you're having fun. I had no idea it was this late."

"I've really enjoyed getting to know you better—and your wonderful cooking. Thank you again. I promise to repay you when my kitchen is done."

Laurel smirked. "Whenever that will be. I had a great time, too. You're good company."

"Good night, Laurel."

"Good night, Aiden." She ruffled Sophie's ears. "Good night, sweet girl."

Laurel locked up the house and cleaned the kitchen. Her every thought was of Aiden, remembering his touch. As she drifted off to sleep, she wondered what it would feel like to have him touch more than just her hand.

Eleven

Early the next morning, Laurel loaded her car with empty moving boxes, garbage bags, and other essentials, along with a cooler bag stocked with water and food.

As she drove around the lake and out of town, she turned on some upbeat music to keep her mind from dwelling on what she was about to do. She sang along, not caring if she was off-key or messing up the lyrics. She pulled onto the highway and set her cruise control. The drive was an easy one and traffic was light, so she made good time and pulled into the driveway an hour later.

She took a couple of deep breaths before getting out of the car and walking up the brick sidewalk to the front porch. It wasn't the first time she had been here since her mom passed away, but even the short passage of time had her looking at the house a bit differently.

Another deep breath. In and out. She put the key into the lock and turned the doorknob. What hit her immediately was the smell—a mix of flowers and cinnamon. Evidence of her mom's constant baking still lingered, even weeks after she was gone.

What struck her was how different the house felt. It was no longer her parents' home. She felt strange thinking that way, but it was devoid of life. It was eerily quiet and something else—sad. It was now just four walls that used to be a home full of love and laughter. She walked into the living room and slowly turned in a circle to look around the room. Her mom's recliner sat with her favorite throw blanket over the back. Her needlepoint pictures hung on the walls. But it didn't feel like her parents' home anymore.

Laurel walked through the house, opening the curtains and blinds to bring in the light and a couple of windows to get some fresh air inside. She walked back out to her car and unloaded the boxes and other stuff, then brought them into the house. She knew this was a big job, so she walked through each room and made a list of what she would keep, what would be donated, what items she would try to sell, and, of course, what would end up at the dump.

She turned on her mom's stereo and loaded five of her CDs, then pressed play and walked into the kitchen to start sorting. Even though the kitchen held the most stuff, there would be little she wanted to keep.

Laurel was pleased with herself when a couple of hours later she had cleared out the entire kitchen. She stacked the boxes for donation in the garage and went to work in the living room. After she finished that, she took a break for lunch while sitting on the back deck.

Looking out at the backyard, she thought about how excited her parents were when they bought the house. The yard was small and low maintenance, so they could spend more time enjoying life and taking trips to the cabin on the lake. Little did they know her dad would suffer a heart attack two years later and not live to see the next day. Laurel and her mom learned the hard way that tomorrow wasn't promised to anyone.

Laurel spent the afternoon working through the spare room, which tripled as an office and a library. All the shelves stacked with books were overwhelming. Her parents were avid readers like herself, and the range of subjects in this room was vast. Where to start?

An hour later, she found herself sitting in the middle of the floor going through each book, seeing if it was signed by a family member as a gift or by the author. Of course, she gave each book a shake upside down, just in case there were any notes or money tucked away by her parents. *Well, you never know.* She made a few piles: library, church, keep.

Late in the afternoon, she stood and stretched and looked around the room. The bookcases were empty, and the floor was covered in books—albeit in organized piles. She had accomplished a lot and decided it was time to take a break. She walked out to the dining room and opened the sliding door to the deck. She had always loved this view. Though the yard was small, it had some great old trees and some newer fruit trees her dad had planted. Lots of birds of various species enjoyed the yard. She noticed the irises and daffodils had finished blooming. She was happy that her mom had planted some at the cabin as well. It would be a nice reminder when they bloomed each spring.

She walked down the wooden steps and across the yard to the plum tree. She had always loved being here in spring to see the fruit trees in bloom, along with the many flowers scattered around the yard. Her mom had loved to cut some of the flowers and fill several vases around inside the house. That memory made Laurel think of the laundry room and the cabinet above the washer and dryer filled with vases. What was she going to do with all those?

She pulled herself back to focusing on the yard. The point of this break from sorting was just that: a break from fussing with what to do with all the contents of the house. The contents of her parents' life. That thought started the tears flowing. She stopped and pulled a tissue out of her sweater pocket. She dabbed the tears and wiped her nose, but she couldn't stop crying. Her entire life was now altered. Both her parents were gone. Neither one would see her fall in love, walk down the aisle, have children someday.

Neither one of them would be there when she needed them...like right now.

Her phone rang in her pocket as she tried to wipe away the tears again. She pulled her phone out and saw that it was Maggie. Of course. They were kindred spirits like that—in tune with each other at the most crucial times.

Laurel answered the phone while wiping her nose with a tissue.

"Hey, sweetie, how are you doing?" Maggie asked.

"Oh, me? I'm just great." Laurel did her best to hold the tears inside, but she didn't succeed.

"Hmmm. Sounds like it. I know how hard this all is. I wish I could take the pain away."

Sniffling, Laurel said, "I know you know exactly how hard all of this is. I'm not sure I understood when you went through it, but I certainly do now." Laurel blew her nose before she continued, "It just hit me, everything I would miss sharing with them. I thought I had come to terms with Dad never walking me down the aisle, but wow...it all just came crashing down on me, now that they're both gone."

"Oh, I know. I wish I could give you a big hug right now," Maggie said. "Listen, I called to tell you Tim is back from his trip, and he's heading your way."

"What? Really? Why is your dear, sweet brother heading my way?" The smile spread across her face. She hadn't seen Tim in a year, as he traveled so much for his job. He had always been a huge part of her life, and she would love to see him.

"Well, he's back stateside for a couple of months and feels awful that he hasn't been here for you. I told him you were cleaning out the house this weekend, and he wanted to help."

"Maggie, that really isn't necessary, even though I would love to see him."

"Well, he should be there in a few minutes. I just wanted to give you a heads up." Maggie sniffed.

"Oh, I do have the best friends in the world. Thank you."

As soon as he saw her, Tim swept Laurel into a huge bear hug and swung her around. This had been his greeting since they were kids.

She giggled as she looked up at him when he finally put her feet back on the ground. "Don't you think I'm a bit big for you to be doing that?"

"Never! You'll always be my extra baby sister!"

"And you, my big, dorky brother!"

This comment earned Laurel another big bear hug. "I was so sorry to hear about your mom. She was a such sweet lady, and I will miss her so much," Tim said. "She was a positive influence on my life when I was younger."

Laurel took his hand, and they walked into the kitchen. "Thank you. She loved you. She was very proud of you as well."

"Aw, that means a lot. I'm sorry I couldn't be here for her service, but it just wasn't possible."

"That's fine. I understood, really."

Tim looked around the kitchen. "I came to help you clean out the house, but it looks like I'm almost too late. Wow, you've been busy. I thought Maggie told me you were just starting this weekend."

"I did just start. I've gotten a lot done, though. Some of it was easy, like the kitchen, but other rooms...well, the contents trigger memories and tears."

Tim squeezed her hand. "I can understand that. It isn't easy. Well, I'm here to help, so what would you like me to start with?"

Laurel looked up at him and smiled. "Thank you. Just having you here helps. Well, if you can make up these empty boxes and bring them into the office, we can get all the books packed up and moved into the garage."

"Of course." Tim grabbed the tape gun and jumped to the task.

While packing the books in boxes, Laurel said, "I'm so happy to see you! It's been too long."

"Yes, it has been too long. Work has been crazy, but man, I do love it. I still love all the travel, even if it means living out of a suitcase."

"That's great, Tim. I always love the pictures you text me. I'm happy to hear you love your work so much."

"And Maggie tells me that you're finally following that dream of yours. The one you talked about constantly, years ago. Fill me in on how that's going."

Laurel told Tim everything she had accomplished so far: creating some great pieces, setting up her business, and having Cassie make the logo. She told him about her social media and what she was doing to grow an audience, and about selling her pottery at Lyman's bookshop.

"Oh Laurel, this sounds great. I'm so glad you're finally doing this. And, I will add, it's about time."

"I know, I know. I had a couple of detours, but I'm on track now. Don't worry."

"I'm glad to hear that. And you will not settle for any more losers, correct?"

"Correct."

"Good."

They moved the boxes into the garage, which was starting to fill up. After they worked for another hour, Laurel could tell from Tim's sidelong glances that he knew she was getting tired.

"Listen," he said at last, "you've been at this all day. Let me take you out to dinner, and then we can tackle the rest bright and early in the morning. What do you say?"

Laurel's eyes pricked with tears again at the thoughtfulness of his suggestion. "You're really coming back for more work tomorrow?"

"Yup, I'm here to help you get this big task done. Got it?"

"Oh Tim, thank you. Just having you here to talk to and laugh with has been great—not to mention the use of your muscles."

Flexing his biceps for effect, Tim laughed. "So, dinner?"

"Yes, that would be wonderful. Let me just wash my hands and grab my bag and a jacket."

"Perfect. I'll shut the windows and close the garage door. Where should we go?"

"I'm in need of comfort food, and tonight, that sounds like a burger, fries, and some wine."

"Sounds good to me. I'm craving a steak and a beer. How about we hit Johnny's on Third Street?"

"Perfect! I love that place!"

Over dinner, Tim filled Laurel in on his travels, and she talked about her studio and her pottery and how much she loved living in the cabin. They reminisced about their childhood summers spent on the lake and how close their families were at that time. Laurel knew that Tim and Maggie both understood what she was going through. Their support meant the world to her.

THE NEXT MORNING, TIM ARRIVED WITH COFFEE AND fresh pastries. While Laurel worked on more sorting, Tim loaded the boxes for donations into his truck and set off to the church, the library, and the secondhand store.

When he returned to the house, Laurel had more boxes ready for him. After he loaded those in the truck, they walked around each room and made notes of what still needed to be done, what furniture Laurel wanted to move to the cabin, and discussed what to do with the rest of the furniture.

Laurel was dead set against having a garage sale. It was too much work, and she just didn't think she could cope with people trying to barter down the prices of her parents' things.

They called a couple of places and decided that the local Habitat for Humanity ReStore would be the best place to donate to. Even better, Habitat would pick up the furniture the following afternoon. They were currently building ten new homes in the nearby town, so the timing seemed perfect.

While Laurel worked inside, Tim tackled the garage. It appeared that Laurel's mom hadn't had the heart to part with her husband's tools when he passed away. He had been a craftsman, and Tim knew the tools needed to go somewhere special. He made a few calls and found a local apprentice school that would gladly take any tools available. He got Laurel's approval and went to work sorting and boxing them up.

There were a couple of old woodworking tools that Tim thought Laurel might like to take to the cabin. Even if they were used as décor in the cabin or studio, they would bring happy memories of her father. Tim made a special box for these and wrote a note to tell Laurel what each tool was and what her dad would have done with it. He knew if he tried to tell her now, she wouldn't remember when she got back to the cabin and unpacked them. He taped up the box and marked it for the cabin and put it in the pile for Laurel's car.

They took a short break for lunch and then worked through the afternoon. There were times that Laurel broke down in tears. Tim was there to hand her a tissue and give her a hug. He listened as she talked about how much she missed her parents and wondered aloud how she could go on without them. He didn't offer any clichéd lines such as "They're in a better place," "It will get easier," or "I know how you feel." He just held her and let her grieve in the way she needed to at that moment. When the tears stopped, he hugged her tightly. She looked up at him and managed a smile.

"Thank you. Really. Sorry I'm such a mess."

"No thanks necessary. Really. Well, you are kind of a mess, but you always have been."

Laurel slugged his arm. "Hey!"

He laughed. "Joking. Just remember that you never have to apologize to me or anyone else for showing your emotions. Ever. Please remember that."

"Thanks. I know. It's been a bad habit for a while now. I'm working on it."

"Good to hear."

"Oh, and Tim, thank you for not saying all the things everyone else seems to say to me. Thanks for just letting me feel what I'm feeling."

"Even though I wish I could make your hurt go away, I know that isn't possible. All I can do is support you in whatever way you need me to," Tim said.

Laurel wrapped her arms around Tim and hugged him. "Thank you."

THEY FINISHED THE DAY BY DELIVERING THE REST OF the donations to various places in town, then Laurel packed up her car with the things she was taking back to the cabin. She would need to make a second trip to meet with the small moving company she contracted to deliver the several pieces of furniture and the rest of the boxes to the cabin. They were scheduled to come the following week.

The next day they cleaned the house, and Habitat for Humanity came to pick up the furniture she was donating.

Laurel walked from room to room, pausing in each doorway. As she came back into the living room, Tim held open his arms and she walked into one of his huge hugs.

"You did it, kiddo. I know this is so hard, but you've just checked off a huge task."

"Thanks Tim, for everything. I'm not sure how I would have done this without you."

"Absolutely, no problem. I'm glad my schedule allowed me to get back and help you."

"Me too. So, you're off again next Monday, right?"

"Yes, a quick trip this time. I was thinking I would come to the lake when I'm here for a few weeks. I'd love to see your studio and have a little R and R. Would that work for you?"

"Of course it will work."

Many hugs later, they said goodbye and Tim drove away. Laurel locked up the house and, with one last, deep breath, got in her car. As she drove home, she thought about all she had accomplished this weekend and how thankful she was that Tim was there. It would have been much more difficult without his words of encouragement and his comforting hugs.

She was looking forward to getting home—and to seeing Aiden. Had he been thinking about her as much as she'd been thinking about him?

LAUREL PARKED IN THE GARAGE AND UNLOADED THE boxes into a heap by the wall. She didn't have the energy to unpack them right now—neither the physical nor the mental energy, to be truthful. After a long hot shower, she took her journal and a glass of wine out to the deck. While the emotions of the weekend were still fresh, she wanted to capture them. She was surprised she didn't cry while writing it all down. Maybe she was finally coming to peace with letting the house go.

A sound caught her attention, and she turned to see Sophie running over to her. "Hey, I don't think you're supposed to be out on your own. Where's your dad?"

Aiden came jogging around the hedge that divided their properties, right on Sophie's tail. Climbing the deck stairs, he said, "Hi, welcome home. She shot through the door as soon as I opened it. Maybe she sensed you were back." He smiled. "How are you?"

"Hey. I'm good." She fingered her journal. "Just writing about it all."

"So, you're doing okay? I'm sure it couldn't have been easy."

"It was strange. The house just wasn't their home anymore. It was lifeless." She tilted her head as she looked at him. "I certainly cried some tears, but somehow, I got through it. Well, a friend surprised me by showing up to help. It was nice to reminisce about our parents together. Anyway, the task is done."

"I've not experienced that, but I can imagine it must be strange. Glad to have you back. You must be really noisy, because it was so quiet here while you were gone." He nudged her shoulder in jest.

"Ha ha. Thanks a lot." Laurel laughed, and it struck her that Aiden might've missed her.

They talked for a while longer, getting caught up on the house reno and having more stories of cleaning out the house in Addington. They alternated throwing the ball for Sophie until she finally gave up and plopped onto the ground.

"Tomorrow, I have to take the pottery over to the winery, so Lena has time to get it set up. Did you get business cards done?"

"I did, and I have my first two clients."

"What? That's wonderful. Congrats!"

"The first one is a small job in Jackson. My friend Geoff introduced me to this guy who needs some work done on his office." Aiden paused before continuing. "The second client is a bit special. It's a couple who were in a car accident. Both were injured, but the wife took the brunt of it. She's learning how to walk again."

"Oh, Aiden, how awful."

"Yes, but she's doing better than the doctors expected by this point, and she has the best attitude about it. Anyway, it's going to be a long road from wheelchair to walker to crutches to actual walking. So they need me to make the house more accessible for her."

"Wow, that's great. They picked the right guy."

"Thanks. That one is special, that's for sure. Just another reminder of how precious life is." Aiden looked out at the lake and then back at Laurel. "So, yes, I have my business cards and clients. I'm ready for the mixer."

"Great. I was thinking we should get there at about five. Does that work for you?"

They both stood, and Sophie gazed up at them. "Yes, that's perfect. I'm sure I'll see you before then." He looked down at Sophie. "Especially if she has anything to say about it. C'mon girl. Time to go home."

Laurel reached down and ruffled the fur behind Sophie's ears affectionately. "Sophie, you come visit anytime you want."

Twelve

L aurel spent the day working on glazing the latest batch of mugs. When three o'clock came around, she cleaned up the studio. Grabbing a stack of business cards, she flipped off the lights and locked the studio. She was eager for a refreshing shower.

While waiting for the water to get hot, she studied her reflection in the mirror. For several years, she didn't like to look at herself, as she only saw flaws. The curve of her hips made her figure a little fuller than the magazine models. She used to think her breasts could be bigger, but now she realized she never felt that way until Graham suggested a boob job. Amazing what a remark like that could do to someone's self-esteem. Just because that was his preference didn't mean there was anything wrong with her. They were in proportion to her build, and standing there while steam began to fog the glass, she liked them just fine.

She stepped into the hot shower and let the water wash over her, imagining her negative thoughts flowing down the drain.

After showering and wrapping herself in a towel, Laurel applied mascara, and leaning closer to the mirror, she looked at the freckles across her nose. Wrinkling her nose, she thought of all the years she had wished them away. She had especially hated them as a kid—but now she liked them. They seemed to have faded over the years, and she liked how they made her feel a bit carefree.

She wasn't sure how freckles could do that, but they made her think of summertime at the lake with her friends and family, her mom making sure she reapplied sunscreen after swimming. As a sarcastic teenager, she'd asked her mom if it would prevent her from getting more freckles. Before her mom could answer, her dad had scooped her up in a big bear hug and told her she was beautiful, and he loved her freckles because they came from him.

Thinking about that now made her miss her dad even more. So many things they were never able to share. She held tight to every memory of him.

Standing in front of her closet, she flipped through her clothes and chose a summery blue dress. She added a little bolero-like light sweater, thinking she might need it for the evening since the event was outside. The jewelry she chose was simple and fun. A silver necklace bore the word "dream" in cursive. Her silver earrings were etched with "do what you love/love what you do." And to complete the ensemble, her cuff bracelet said, "Well-behaved women rarely make history." The cuff was a gift from her mom many years ago.

She made a funny face as she took one last look in the mirror and smiled. Laurel stood a bit straighter and enjoyed the confidence she felt these days. She still had a long way to go with making her business a profitable endeavor, yet she knew it would happen.

When Aiden opened the car door for Laurel in her driveway, he said, "Hi. You look beautiful."

"Well, thank you. You scrub up pretty well yourself."

While waiting for Aiden to get in the car, Laurel realized suddenly that this felt more like a date. She told herself that it was just a business function, but the butterflies in her stomach tried to tell her differently.

As Aiden drove, they talked about their day and about

Sophie, of course, so Laurel was able to coax herself back to feeling normal by the time they arrived at the winery. They arrived just before five o'clock, and the parking lot was already filling up.

"Wow, looks like it's a popular event," Aiden said, pulling into a spot.

"Looks like it. I can see why, with this gorgeous setting."

They climbed out of the car and paused as they looked over the rolling hills of beautiful vines surrounding them.

"This place is gorgeous." Aiden smiled and put his hand on the small of Laurel's back as they walked together along the path and up the stairs to where the reception table was set up.

Laurel glanced around while she waited for the receptionist to finish with the people in line in front of them.

When she stepped up to the table, she was greeted by the smile of a twenty-something lady. "Hello! Welcome to Harvest Hills Vineyard. My name is Jenny, and I'm here to get you checked in. What's your name, please?"

"Hello, Jenny, a pleasure to meet you. My name is Laurel Hardiston."

Jenny stood quickly, almost knocking the table over. "Oh, are you the Laurel that made all of that gorgeous pottery?"

Giggling at the excitement in Jenny's voice, Laurel replied. "Ah, yes, that would be me. I take it you like the pieces?"

Jenny reached out her hand to shake Laurel's. "I love them! They are so beautiful. Gosh, I would love to be able to create something like that. You don't give lessons, do you?"

"Hmmm, no I don't. Never really thought about that. I just got back to pottery recently, so I've been busy getting my business going."

Jenny smiled and finally let go of Laurel's hand. "Sorry if I came across as some sort of crazy lady, but I love art. I appreciate when people create something uniquely their own. I would totally take lessons if you offered them." As Jenny handed Laurel her name tag, she also gave her a business card. "Please let me know if you decide to offer lessons."

Laurel took both and handed Jenny a business card of her own. "I certainly will." She looked behind her to see several people waiting. "Oh, I seem to have slowed down the line. Thank you, Jenny." Laurel stepped aside for Aiden.

He smirked and winked at her as he stepped up to the table. "Hi, I'm Aiden Bradford. Unfortunately, I'm not of star status like Laurel." He smiled at Jenny, who laughed.

"Mr. Bradford, everyone who visits us here is of star status in our books. Welcome. Here's your name tag. Enjoy the mixer." Jenny's warmth was just as welcoming for Aiden as it was for Laurel.

"Well, well," Aiden said, as they followed the signs to the event area. "You certainly made an impact on Jenny. I'm not surprised though—" He slowed slightly to lean over and whisper, "You've already made an impact on me."

Laurel smiled as she leaned over and whispered back, "You've made the same on me, Aiden."

They smiled at each other and again Aiden placed his hand on the small of Laurel's back as they walked along. The winery had a spacious room for gatherings or large tastings, which led to a deck that ran the length of the building and overlooked the vines. They stopped and looked around to find different tables set up along the outer walls where an array of food being offered. Before they could get any farther, a waiter arrived offering red, white, or sparkling wine.

"Sparkling, please," Laurel said.

"I'll have the same."

"Here you go, enjoy," replied the young man as he walked off to greet another visitor.

"There you are!" Lena pulled Laurel into a hug and then stood back. "I'm so glad you could make it. I love your dress."

Laurel smiled. "Thank you, it's one of my favorites. Lena, this is Aiden. Aiden, Lena."

Aiden smiled winningly and shook Lena's hand. "It's a pleasure to meet you, Lena. You have a gorgeous place here."

"Pleasure to meet you as well, Aiden. Welcome." Lena glanced around the room with contentment. "Thank you, it is pretty perfect. I'm glad you like it. We'll have to arrange a tour sometime."

"That would be great."

From the look on Lena's face, she was wondering what was going on between Laurel and Aiden. Laurel steered the conversation in a different direction. "Lena, thank you for the invitation and for showing some of my pieces. I really appreciate it."

Lena looked once more from Aiden to Laurel and then took the bait. "Of course. Oh, and I should tell you that they're getting some attention already."

"Really? Besides Jenny, who asked me if I give lessons—which is an interesting prospect."

"Jenny is a treasure and has an artistic flare she really wants to grow," Lena said. "You could totally give lessons."

"Hmm. I will give that some thought." Laurel smiled as she looked around the room full of people. "Someone else has noticed my pottery display? Where is it anyway?"

Lena led Laurel and Aiden through the throng of people. Lena greeted people as they weaved through the crowd. Lena somehow knew everyone by name as she thanked them for coming, all the while keeping their momentum.

Laurel was in awe, and several minutes later they made it across the room and in front of a stunning display of her pottery. "Oh, Lena. This looks amazing."

A silky silver tablecloth draped the round table. At the rear of the table was her twelve-inch-tall lavender vase filled with stunning lilacs, gladiolus, and hydrangeas. Shiny baubles of varying colors filled her oval bowl, glazed with a beautiful Tuscan yellow. One of her indigo place settings was displayed to the left.

Lena had included a bottle of her wine and one of the winery's stemmed glasses. Laurel's business card holder was set to the side and showed signs of depletion. She refilled it with the cards in her bag and turned to Lena.

"Thank you. The way you have paired things and the table-cloth, the flowers...it's stunning." Laurel gave Lena a side hug as they all looked at the table.

"Wow, Laurel, these are gorgeous." Aiden looked closely at the pieces, then back up at her. "You're very talented."

"Aw, thanks Aiden." Laurel beamed at the compliment as she caught the look on Lena's face.

"I'm so glad you like it, Laurel. Your pieces are the magic that makes it stunning," Lena said. "Your other pieces are scattered around on our serving tables, along with more of your business cards."

"Again, thank you so much."

"Now, I told you that your work was getting some attention. Well, there's someone who would like to meet you. Aiden, would you excuse us for a moment?"

"Of course. I see Brad has arrived. See you in a few minutes, Laurel." Aiden winked as he walked away.

Lena led Laurel out the door to the deck, scanning the crowd, and then waved. "Hettie, allow me to introduce you to Laurel. Laurel, this is Hettie. She owns the Rainbow's End B-and-B on Rainbow Drive." Lena stepped back as the two women shook hands.

"It is a pleasure to meet you, Hettie," Laurel said.

Hettie's smile lit up her face and welcomed Laurel as an old friend. "Oh, darling, the pleasure is all mine. Do you have a moment to chat?"

"Of course," Laurel said as Lena excused herself to go mingle. "There's an empty table over by the railing. Shall we have a seat?"

"Perfect." Hettie grabbed two fresh glasses of sparkling wine from a passing waiter.

They settled onto the high-backed bar stools and sighed almost in unison at the vineyard.

"What a beautiful view," Laurel said.

"It certainly is. I always love when they have the mixer here—or any event, for that matter."

Laurel tapped her fingers on the railing. "This is the first event I've attended. I just moved here, though I spent my childhood summers here, as well as lots of time off and on over the years. I've known Lena since we were kids."

"Yes, Lena told me that you had moved into your family's cabin on the lake." Hettie took a sip of her sparkling wine. "What a lovely place to call home."

Laurel swiveled her stool so she was facing Hettie. "Yes, it is, and it holds many happy memories as well."

Hettie placed her glass on the table and clasped her hands in her lap as she looked at Laurel. "So, you are probably wondering what I wanted to speak with you about?"

"Yes, I am a bit intrigued."

"Well, as Lena said, I own the Rainbow's End B-and-B. I've owned it for a couple of years and now I'm in the process of a complete renovation."

Laurel looked at her quizzically. "I'm sorry to say I've never been there. How do I fit in with your renovation?"

"Well, I'm changing the whole feel of the place. You know, new paint, redecorating the rooms, getting rid of, well, the old-lady vibe. When I bought it, I made a few changes, but I didn't have the money to renovate. Thankfully, business has been good, and I can now make it my place."

Laurel listened intently, but still didn't know what Hettie wanted from her.

Hettie smiled and leaned forward. "Now, I saw your lovely pieces today, and I want to hire you to make some pieces for the B-and-B."

A small knot of hope began to blossom in Laurel's chest. "Oh, of course, I would love to. What do you have in mind?"

"First, I would like a twelve-piece place setting like the one on the display inside. I would like them to be different colors, though not all the same. Also, I would like several of the tall vases, again in various colors." Hettie's hands flew around the air as her animated voice continued. "Then I want a special piece for each of the bedrooms. Now, I'm not quite sure what I mean by that, but I was thinking maybe you could come by and look around and help me figure out what we can do with the rooms."

Laurel hoped her face wasn't giving away how surprised she was—let alone how excited. *Act professional. You can jump up and down and scream later.*

Hettie continued, "I originally thought a taper candle holder in each room would be nice, but it's not a good idea to equip each room with a fire hazard. So, maybe between the two of us, we can figure something out. What do you think?"

Laurel couldn't believe what she was hearing. "Hettie, I'm flattered, and I would love to work with you on making some special pieces for your place. Thank you."

Hettie reached over the table, grabbed Laurel's hand, and squeezed it. Her smile was so bright that it sparkled in her eyes. "Oh, dear, I'm so happy you are interested. I just fell in love with your creations, and Lena was right—you are a very special soul."

Laurel could feel her cheeks flushing in response to Hettie's compliments. "Why thank you. That is so sweet of you to say. When would you like me to come by to look around?"

"Gosh, is tomorrow afternoon too soon?" Hettie's excitement was contagious.

"Of course not. That would be great. What time works for you?"

"Shall we say three o'clock?"

"Perfect. I will be there. Again, thank you so much. I look forward to it."

"Great. Okay, well, I've taken up enough of your time. You must go mingle. I will see you tomorrow. Thank you, dear." Hettie touched Laurel's arm as she said goodbye and walked away to speak to the mayor.

Laurel took a sip of her wine and tried to keep her hand from shaking. She couldn't believe what had just happened. Her cheeks were starting to hurt from smiling so much. She knew this was a huge break for her. The B-and-B had visitors from all over. Her work would be seen by a lot of people. This could be the break she needed.

She scanned the deck and saw Lena looking over at her. Although engaged in a conversation with Hank the winemaker, she gave Laurel a thumbs-up. Laurel returned the thumbs-up and nodded.

The view from the deck was spectacular: rolling hills lined with rows and rows of vines. The vineyard was a landscape of lush green leaves and new clusters of grapes. Laurel could certainly understand why Lena loved this place so much.

Looking around, Laurel saw Cassie with a man she didn't know. They were standing by the railing a ways off, looking at the vines and talking. Perhaps it was Cassie's client at Brady Tech. Cassie said something that made the man laugh. Laurel smiled, watching her friend. Then the man leaned over and said something close to Cassie's ear, which made them both laugh. Laurel walked away to mingle.

The conversation with Hettie had given her the boost in confidence to be a bit braver and to introduce herself to people. Meeting with several of the town's folk and making new connections kept her busy for the next hour. She passed out half of the business cards she had brought with her. Several people had seen the displays of her pottery and commented on how much they liked them.

Laurel was saying goodbye to a friend of her mother's when Aiden, Brad, and Bailey walked onto the deck. Laurel hugged Brad and Bailey. "Hi guys! Having fun?"

Bailey looked at Aiden. "Yes, we are. It's great to meet Aiden. Are you making lots of connections, Laurel?"

Laurel bounced a little as a smile lit up her face. "You are never going to believe what happened. Hettie from Rainbow's End B-and-B wants to hire me. I'm meeting with her tomorrow afternoon. She's already told me about several pieces she wants, but she also wants me to walk through the B-and-B with her so we can think of some other pottery for individual rooms. I can't believe it!"

Aiden was the first to hug her, much to Laurel's surprise. "That's incredible! Congratulations!"

Bailey and Brad both hugged her as well. "Congratulations! You deserve this," Bailey said.

Brad hugged her again. "I'm so happy for you. Congratulations!"

"Thanks guys! I appreciate you all so much. Now—" Laurel lifted her empty glass. "—how about some bubbly to celebrate?"

It wasn't until the crowd started to thin out that she saw Cassie again. Laurel waved to her, and Cassie walked over, accompanied by the man from earlier. "Hi, I was hoping you were still here." Cassie gave Laurel a hug. "Hi guys." She hugged Brad and Bailey.

"Hi. This is Aiden Bradford, my next-door neighbor and—" Laurel looked up at him, and they smiled at each other. "—my friend. He's a carpenter. Aiden, this is Cassie."

"Hi Aiden, nice to meet you." A knowing look passed between Cassie and Bailey.

"It's nice to meet you as well, Cassie," Aiden said.

"I want to introduce all of you to Sean Brady of Brady Tech. Sean, this is Laurel of Blue Heron Pottery, and Bailey is an architect. I've known them both since we were little girls. This is Brad. He owns Hole-in-the-Water Boat Works." Cassie smiled. "And this is Aiden."

Sean smiled as he greeted everyone. "It's a pleasure to meet you all. Cassie has told me a lot about you—well, except for you, Aiden."

Aiden shook his hand. "Pleasure to meet you."

"Pleasure to meet you, Sean." Laurel smiled. "Your company is new to the area. Are you enjoying our town?"

"Very much so. It's been a good move for our company. We're happy with the location, and our employees that relocated with us really love it here."

Cassie stood there, beaming. Her smile lit up the room. Something was up with her, and Laurel couldn't wait to talk to her about it later.

Brad and Bailey excused themselves to mingle with some other attendees.

"I'm trying to convince Sean that he needs to try paddle boarding. He's a big chicken, though." Cassie looked at Sean for his reaction.

Laughing as he had in the vineyard, Sean said, "I am not a chicken. I just don't think I have the balance for that."

"Chicken...*bok, bok, bok*." Cassie laughed.

Laughing along, Laurel said, "It's not as difficult as it looks. Cassie taught me. I'm sure she would show you."

"I would if he wasn't a chicken," she fired back.

Laurel could tell this conversation had been ongoing between them.

Sean put on a mock pout. "I am not a chicken."

"Then prove it. This Saturday. Eleven o'clock," Cassie teased him.

"Sean, if I were you, I would just give in," Laurel advised. "She's relentless when she gets an idea in her head. I mean that as a compliment."

"Oh, I know how relentless Cassie is! Fine. I'll do it. Saturday, eleven o'clock. Where?"

"My dock," Laurel said, at the same time Cassie said, "Laurel's dock."

"Laurel, are you in on this with Cassie?" Sean asked, eyeing them as Aiden just shrugged and smiled at him.

"Well, I wasn't until now." She winked at Cassie.

"Okay, you both win. But why just pick on me? What about Aiden here?"

Laurel and Cassie turned to Aiden and a conspiring look passed between them.

"Sean, what did I ever do to you, man? I was just minding my own business over here." Aiden shifted his feet nervously.

"Hey, I just thought you might like to be embarrassed as well." Sean laughed good-naturedly. "The more the merrier, they say."

"Great idea, Sean. C'mon, Aiden. It'll be fun." Laurel winked at Cassie. "Looks like we have another victim—I mean—"

"No, I think victim is the right word," Aiden said, but he was smiling too.

"Sean and Aiden, we promise you won't be sorry. It'll be a lot of fun," Cassie said.

Before they could answer, Lena approached and joined their conversation. Cassie introduced Sean to Lena.

After speaking with Sean for a few minutes, Lena turned to Laurel and asked, "So, Laurel, tell me about your chat with Hettie. Did she place a large order?"

"What large order? Laurel, tell us! How exciting!" Cassie said.

Laurel recounted the conversation with Hettie. She was so excited about this opportunity, and she knew her friends loved seeing her so animated as she spoke. "So, I'm meeting her at the B-and-B tomorrow afternoon at three o'clock. I can't tell you how excited I am."

Lena wrapped her arm around Laurel's shoulder and gave her a hug. "Honey, we can see how excited you are. We're so thrilled for you."

"Yes, we are!" Cassie joined in the hug.

Sean, smiling, pulled out his phone and snapped a photo before any of them could say no. "This moment needed to be captured. Congratulations, Laurel!" He looked down at his phone and typed a quick message, then looked up at Cassie. "I've just sent it to you, Cassie."

"Aw, thank you so much." Cassie pulled out her phone and showed the photo to Lena and Laurel.

"Love it! Thank you!" Laurel said.

Lena glanced around; they were the last ones there, and the caterers were starting to pack things up. "Hey, did you all get enough to eat?" Lena asked. "They're clearing up, but there's so much food left over..."

"Food? Nope, never had a chance. I was so busy talking with people that I never made it over to that incredible spread." Laurel eyed the long food table.

"C'mon, let's all grab a plate before they take it away. I'll grab a bottle of wine," Lena said.

No one needed to be told twice. They all headed toward the food and then, with full plates, went over to the table in the corner to get out of the way of the catering team.

Lena returned with Hank and introduced him to Sean and Aiden, the only ones he hadn't met before. "Hank, let's grab some food, and then you can open this incredible bottle of wine and tell us how you make the magic happen." Lena lead the way to the food table once more.

When they returned, Hank poured them each a glass of wine as he told them about the blend of grapes, explaining the hints of pepper and black cherries they might taste. Watching him, Laurel could tell he was in his element. He loved what he did.

Raising his glass, Sean said, "To Hank. You're one helluva wine maker! This is excellent. Am I also getting a hint of chocolate in this blend?"

Hank's lips quirked in a bit of a smirk. "You, sir, are no wine slouch. You know wines very well, I suspect. Yes, not everyone notices the chocolate."

Sean swirled his glass, then held it to the light to examine the deep color. "It has great legs, and the rich color is amazing. Yes, I may know a thing or two about wine, but the most important thing I know is what I like. And this is an excellent bottle of wine. Thank you for sharing."

While this conversation was taking place, Laurel noticed the way her two friends watched the men. They both had smiles that lit up their eyes. If Laurel were to hazard a guess, she would say they were both smitten. Oh, she was going to love telling them what she observed when the three of them were alone. She would love to see both her friends find love. Perhaps these would be the two men to make that happen.

Then her eyes traveled to Aiden—who was looking straight at her. His eyes lit up as he smiled at her. *Perhaps he's the one for me.*

They enjoyed the food and wine and lively conversation. Laurel could see why Cassie liked Sean. He was so down-to-earth and unpretentious. Oh, and funny. Between the three guys, they were all laughing so much it was hard to breathe. After having coffee, they took a tour of the wine cellar, and Sean bought a couple of cases of wine before they all called it a night.

Aiden and Laurel talked about the evening on the way home.

"I know this may sound strange, but I'm proud of you. Life has knocked you down, but you came back, and look at all you've done. Congratulations." Aiden glanced over at her.

"Aw, thanks Aiden. I appreciate that. What a whirlwind it's been—and now it's getting serious with this order from Hettie."

Aiden pulled into Laurel's driveway and walked around to open the car door.

They walked to her door in silence. Laurel wondered what it would be like to kiss him, but it was too soon for that. There was no intelligent reason to think that way.

"Thank you for inviting me," Aiden said at last. "I enjoyed meeting your friends and made some great connections."

"I had a great time. Thanks for driving." For an instant, she really considered kissing him—but in the end, she chickened out. "Good night."

Aiden's green eyes sparkled as he looked at her. "Good night, Laurel. Sleep well."

Closing the door, she leaned against it and sighed. *I think I'm falling in love with him.*

Thirteen

L aurel had trouble sleeping that night; she was just so excited about her meeting with Hettie. It felt like a door had been opened, and all she had to do was walk through it and the next stepping stone toward her future would appear.

After breakfast, she brainstormed a bit on unique pieces that would be a good fit for the B-and-B. She sketched some rough ideas out in her notepad while she finished her coffee. She worked in the studio and had so much energy from the anticipation of the meeting that she was able to get several pieces done and placed on the drying rack before it was time to go.

Laurel arrived at the B-and-B and, as she walked up the steps to the front porch, Hettie opened the door with that huge, infectious smile lighting up her face.

"Oh Laurel, welcome! I'm so excited to have you here. Please come in."

"Hettie, how are you? Believe me, I'm just as excited to be here."

Laurel followed Hettie into the foyer and glanced around at the entryway. The Victorian-style house was beautiful, but in need of redecorating and updating. Hettie started by giving her a tour of the entire place so she could get a feel for it all before they discussed ideas.

Some of the rooms had been repainted already, and in the others, Hettie had placed paint strips in them so Laurel could see what the colors would be. There were six bedrooms, each with its own bathroom. Downstairs there was a living room, a library, a dining room, a kitchen, and a sunroom overlooking the back garden.

They finished the tour and began again with the bedrooms. They discussed different pieces for each room, and Hettie decided each bathroom needed a matching soap dish and toothbrush holder. Laurel suggested small, shallow bowls for jewelry, coins, and keys in each room. Hettie also wanted each room to have a medium-sized vase for fresh-cut flowers from the garden.

Downstairs, they agreed on various decorative bowls, small vases, and small butter-keeper crocks for the breakfast tables. When they had finished the walk-through, Hettie brought them iced tea, and they sat in the sunroom to review the list they had created. Along with the items Hettie had requested the previous night, this was turning out to be a huge order for Laurel. They talked about timing and what Laurel thought was possible. Laurel promised to put together a proposal—which would include rough sketches of the pieces and pricing for each—and have it to Hettie in a couple of days.

It was difficult to tell which of them was more excited. Hettie's energy was palpable, and Laurel still couldn't quite believe this was all happening. It was a huge break for her, and she felt so lucky to have this opportunity.

She drove home with a big smile on her face and her head spinning with ideas. When she arrived home, she grabbed her sketch pad and her colored pencils and sat at the table on the deck. Holding the pencil, she felt that as soon as she touched the paper, the pencil took off on its own. A rough sketch of a bowl, a plate, a vase, and a soap dish all just flowed onto the paper. She reviewed the photos that she had taken of each room and sketched them in the colors they would be painted. Then she added her pottery to the room sketches.

As she looked at her photos, she suddenly had a thought—a new piece that she had never thought to create. A wall plate! She remembered that she and her mom had bought a couple for her house years ago. Laurel worked to add those to each room sketch.

Once she finished, she looked through each sketch and made a list of pieces she needed to price for Hettie. She wrote it out by hand first, as that was always the best way for her to start. Then she would create the proposal on her laptop and email it to Hettie. She knew she told Hettie that she would have the proposal to her in a couple of days, but she really wanted to send it to her tomorrow. Laurel didn't want to look too eager, but she also felt that it was the best way to work with clients: under promise and over deliver.

Once she finished writing the proposal, she stopped and stood. Stiff from sitting, she bent over and touched her toes. Straightening up, stretched her arms over her and rolled her head from side to side to stretch her neck.

Looking down at the table, she couldn't help but smile. Today's meeting with Hettie had been a rush for Laurel. She seriously couldn't believe how her life had changed. Two awful events had sent her entire world into a tailspin—yet somehow, she had picked herself up and taken control of her life. *Finally*. Laurel wished her mom was still here to watch this dream unfold. Her heart ached thinking about how much she missed her mom. She missed their daily conversations, their shopping trips, and she missed her mom's hugs.

THE NEXT MORNING, LAUREL PREPARED THE PROPOSAL for Hettie, double- and triple-checking it to make sure it was professional, clear, and concise. She included sketches of the pieces and detailed dimensions so Hettie would understand exactly what Laurel was creating. At two o'clock that afternoon, she hit send on the email and let out a breath she hadn't realized she had been holding in.

Laurel decided she needed to get away from her computer or she would stare at it, waiting for Hettie to reply, so she filled her water bottle and walked down to the dock. Taking off her shoes, she dangled her feet over the edge. Something about the water calmed her. The ocean, the lake, a river—heck, she and her mom were always splashing in puddles, being silly together.

The water was still high enough that, bending her toes a little, she could splash in the water. As she kicked her feet up in the air, the water droplets sprayed out in front of her. The sun felt warm on her face, and she closed her eyes and enjoyed the moment.

Being still, Laurel listened to the sounds of nature around her. A few ducks quacked nearby. Somewhere down the lake, a fish jumped out and splashed back into the water. The soft breeze whispered through the pine trees. The lake gently lapped at the shore. Her breathing slowed, and she realized that she had been quite anxious putting the proposal together.

Feeling more relaxed, she stood and made her way back to her studio. Having been on the dock for only thirty minutes, she thought it was too early to hear back from Hettie. She was surprised when she saw Hettie's reply waiting for her. Slightly afraid that Hettie might have changed her mind, she crossed her fingers and clicked on the email.

Laurel, thank you so much for getting the proposal to me so quickly. I love the wall plates! What a fantastic idea! I have signed the proposal, and you will find it attached. I am so excited! Look forward to seeing these beautiful pieces throughout our rooms.

Must run. I am in the middle of painting rooms today and must keep going. Talk soon.

Thanks again. Hettie.

Breathe in and breathe out. Unable to contain herself after a shaky breath, Laurel screamed, "WOOHOO!" and sent a group text to her friends telling them her exciting news. *Breathe in and breathe out.*

Grabbing her notepad, she reviewed the materials list that she had created. Laurel double-checked the studio's supplies and then locked its doors before heading to Willow to hit the art store.

Laurel slowed the car as she joined the line of traffic ahead. Flashing lights met her, along with detour signs. *Great, a detour. Just what she needed.* She was hoping this would be a quick trip. She turned to follow the detour. Traffic crawled in front of her, as this was a twisty road and not often traveled. In the end, it took another thirty minutes to reach the store. Reaching for a shopping cart, she had to fight to get it to detach from the other carts. *C'mon, I just want to do my shopping.* Why was everything fighting her? Pushing the cart to one side, she stopped herself. *Stop with the bad mood. It was just a detour and a stuck cart. Don't let it ruin your day.*

With the internal lecture over, she made her way up and down each aisle, picking up the items that she needed. Laurel lingered over a few displays of new glazes and paints and decided to treat herself to a couple as a reward for her new contract.

As she was loading her car, her phone buzzed as her friends all replied to her message. Words of congratulations and encouragement, along with plenty of emojis, made Laurel smile. Choosing a different route home, she turned on the radio and sang along as she drove back to Lake Benton.

AFTER DINNER, SHE WROTE A DETAILED PLAN AND schedule for Hettie's order. She planned to start early the next morning. Lena, Maggie, and Cassie all called that evening and were so excited for Laurel. Their support and encouragement, along with her own excitement, made her giddy.

For the rest of the evening, text messages flew back and forth within the group. As they were all entrepreneurs, they told her they knew all too well what the first big contract meant—not only for the bank account but, possibly more importantly, what it meant mentally. They had all been there, starting a dream and waiting for the rest of the world to get on board with it. All of them, regardless of what strong women they were, had periods of self-doubt. They'd had many conversations over the years about those doubts and when, early on, they had questioned whether their dreams would become a reality. They knew this was huge for Laurel, especially since she had struggled for so long to even start this journey.

Fourteen

L aurel practically fell asleep as soon as her head touched the pillow. The overthinking and work she put into the proposal, along with the sheer excitement, had exhausted her. She awoke so refreshed and eager to get out to the studio that she had to force herself to slow down while eating her breakfast.

The hours flew by while she sat at the pottery wheel. Her playlist was blasting upbeat music, and she sang along as her hands worked their magic with the clay. She took a break for lunch and then spent the rest of the afternoon throwing plates, soap dishes, and all sorts of other things. At the end of the day, she stood and looked at the drying rack that held the day's work.

The next morning, she awoke to the sound of rain pounding against the window. Laurel sat up and unplugged her phone from the charger on the bedside table. Usually one to check the upcoming weather, she realized that she hadn't looked at the app in several days. What greeted her was not good news. Heavy rain was expected over the next forty-eight hours and localized flooding was expected. Some storms were predicted to be severe.

Groaning, she put her phone back on the table and made her way into the bathroom to get ready for the day. She didn't mind the rain, and they needed it, but two days of heavy rain didn't sound fun.

While she was eating breakfast, Aiden sent a text.

> Good morning. Just wanted you to know I've got to go out of town for a couple of days. Geoff needs some help with a project, so I'm going to go help him before I start my other two jobs. Didn't want you to think Sophie and I were missing.

> Good morning. Thanks for letting me know. I would have been curious. Drive safe; this weather looks like it's going to cause a mess.

> Will do. Stay dry.

Well, that was interesting. Why would he feel the need to tell her if they were just neighbors? Her mind wandered with all kinds of thoughts about Aiden. Aiden and her. She knew she really enjoyed spending time with him. He seemed to feel the same way. Maybe this was leading somewhere. *Okay, enough. You have a busy day ahead. Focus.*

After breakfast, she made a pot of tea and poured it into a thermos. She also grabbed a couple of healthy snacks to take with her. Running back and forth in the rain wouldn't be ideal, so she put everything she thought she might need into a bag and slid into her raincoat. Peering outside, she opened her umbrella and made a run for the studio.

The storm was relentless all day, and Laurel couldn't remember a day when it had rained so much. When she rushed back to the house for lunch, the lake was already rising with the amount of rain that had fallen. The backyard had large puddles that would soon merge if the rain didn't let up. She checked the weather again while she ate lunch. The forecast still showed heavy rain over the next twenty-four to thirty-six hours.

She took a few moments to walk around the house and check

for leaks, examining mostly around the windows since the rain was coming sideways at times. Everything seemed okay, thankfully, so she went back down to the kitchen and washed up her lunch dishes.

Laurel made another pot of tea and refilled her thermos. Putting her raincoat back on, she opened the door and tried to open the umbrella, but a wind gust made that impossible. She gave up and made a run for the studio. Inside, she took off her raincoat and grabbed a towel to dry off her hands and face.

The afternoon hours disappeared as Laurel created piece after piece for Hettie. At the end of the day, the drying rack was loaded with a good portion of the order. Laurel stood and looked at what she had accomplished and couldn't help but be pleased. Oh, she knew there was a lot of work still to be done, but she was happy with her day's work. After she cleaned up the studio, she loaded her laptop, notebooks, phone, and charger into one bag and the thermos and snack container into the other bag. Putting on her raincoat again, she peered outside and decided against fighting with the umbrella. Pulling her hood up, she glanced around to make sure she had what she needed. One, two, three. She opened the door, stood still long enough to lock it, and then ran up the stepping stones to the deck. She was drenched by the time she made it inside the house.

"Ugh, what a miserable day," she mumbled as she took off her shoes and raincoat.

Upstairs, she changed into a pair of yoga pants and a long-sleeved shirt. Although it was early evening, it was very dark outside. She turned on a few battery-operated candles before going downstairs. Laurel walked around the living and dining rooms, turning on more battery-operated candles. At least she would have some candlelight if the power went out.

Pouring a glass of wine, she set about the kitchen making dinner. In need of comfort food because of the weather and being tired from working, she decided on chicken alfredo pasta. That would also mean she would have some leftovers for tomorrow.

The news was on in the background, and she listened to the many reports of flooding, trees down, and even a few power outages. While she ate dinner, Laurel sent a group text to check on her friends. Thankfully, everyone was fine. No one had suffered any flooding or storm damage so far.

Cassie joked that if the rain didn't stop soon, she would finally have lakefront property. They promised to check in later and let each other know if they needed anything.

Laurel finished her dinner and cleaned up the kitchen, then took her laptop and notebook and settled on the couch. She put her phone on to charge, as she wanted to be sure it was fully charged if she lost power.

In her clay notebook, she updated which pieces she had thrown today, making notes of the type of clay she used and various other details. She would go back to add the glaze and paint details once they were done. Reviewing what she had accomplished today, she was pleased. One more full day of throwing tomorrow, and she could move on to the next stage.

Rain beat on the windows and gusts of wind seemed to rattle the house. The news was displaying the latest doppler radar, and a strong line of storms was moving across the area.

As Laurel worked, the lights flickered once or twice, but thankfully the power stayed on. The large, floor-to-ceiling windows gave her a bird's-eye view of the backyard and the lake. The wind had picked up, causing the rain to blow sideways again. Thunder rumbled in the distance, and flashes of lightning lit the sky across the lake.

As a child, Laurel wasn't a fan of storms. Now, she couldn't remember why that was. She found herself mesmerized watching the rain hit the window. The lights flickered on and off and on again. A flash of lightning. A crack of thunder—and power went out.

The candles scattered around provided a perfect glow and enough light. She turned off her laptop and set her clay notebook on the table. Then she reached over, filled up her wineglass, and picked up her Kindle.

"Guess someone is telling me it is time to stop working for the night," Laurel said to no one. She adjusted the pillows behind her and spent the next hour or so reading her latest book. The storm was relentless, and several claps of thunder made her jump.

The power was still out a couple of hours later when she climbed the stairs, happily exhausted and ready for bed. A good night's sleep and she would be ready for tomorrow. Hoping for the power to come back on, she fought for sleep as the storm continued.

SHE AWOKE BEFORE HER ALARM AND WAS GREETED BY AN overcast sky. And power, thankfully. No rain was currently falling, but it was obvious more was on the way. Laurel decided to wander outside to see how the yard had survived. What she found upon stepping onto the deck was, quite honestly, a mess. The yard had standing water in places; leaves and branches were scattered everywhere. The flowerpots were full of rainwater, and some had tipped over with the weight. She poured the water out and straightened the pots. The birdseed in the feeders was wet, but she shook the feeders to make it easier for the birds to get the seed. She would need to replace the wet seed, but there was no reason to do that until the rain had finished.

Laurel wandered through the yard, picking up branches. Down at the dock, she saw just how high the lake had risen. Thankfully, it wasn't a threat to cause further damage to the yard —yet. Slopping back up to the deck, she wiped off her feet and went inside to have some breakfast.

The rain started again late in the morning, when Laurel was busy working in the studio. At least there were no thunderstorms and wind—just a very steady rain all day. Laurel finished most of the pieces for Hettie, and at the end of the day the drying rack was stacked. Everything had gone well, and she felt so accomplished. Exhaustion was setting in as she cleaned up the studio and took her laptop and notebook to the house.

Her back and shoulders were aching from being at the wheel all day, so she poured a glass of wine and went upstairs to take a shower. As she stood in the shower, she let the hot water run over her shoulders and down her back as she rotated her neck in a stretch. When she stepped out of the shower, she was amazed at how much better she felt. She towel-dried her hair and lathered on a luxurious body cream before putting on a pair of yoga pants and a blue, long-sleeved T-shirt.

Back downstairs, she put on some music as she heated up leftovers for dinner. The rain was still pouring when she sat down to eat.

An hour later, she was situated comfortably on the couch, updating her clay notebook with today's work. She looked out the windows and noticed that the rain had let up and there appeared to be a break in the clouds. A light breeze was blowing and would hopefully dry things out. Admittedly, she was looking forward to seeing the sun once again. Having finished her work, she set the notebook on the coffee table and switched from music to a movie on TV.

A strange creaking noise suddenly came to Laurel's attention, and she stood as she tried to figure out where it was coming from. Looking around the living room and dining room, she didn't see anything amiss. Laurel opened the French doors just in time to see the large oak tree leaning precariously.

"No, no, no, no, no...please don't—"

THE TOP OF THE LARGE TREE CRASHED INTO THE SIDE of the studio with the most excruciating sound—or perhaps that was that Laurel's scream. She stood there in shock, staring at the gaping hole the tree had carved into her sanctuary. All she could think about was all her new pieces, stacked on the drying board—but now certainly smashed beneath the weight of the tree.

Aiden was suddenly standing next to her, saying her name. "Laurel, are you okay? Are you hurt? Please tell me you're okay." Aiden pleaded with her, his face full of concern.

"What?" Laurel asked slowly, coming out of a daze.

"Are you hurt?" Aiden asked again.

"What? No, I had just opened the door when—" Laurel put her hands over her mouth. "Oh my—my studio. All my hard work is ruined. I just spent two days creating all these new pieces for a Hettie, and surely they're all smashed now."

Aiden pulled her into a hug as the tears started to flow, but Laurel tried to pull away from him.

"I have to get in there. I have to see if there is anything left." Laurel pulled away and rushed toward the studio.

Aiden grabbed her arm just as they both heard sirens.

"What's that?" Laurel asked.

"That'll be the fire department. I called 911 when I saw the tree down. I didn't know if you were inside the studio. I had just gotten home." Aiden put his arm around her shoulder to keep her from going near the studio.

The firefighters and paramedics came around the house and talked to Aiden and Laurel as they assessed the situation. Once it was clear that no one was inside, the paramedics left. The fire crew checked the building and talked to Laurel and Aiden about getting a tree service out to remove the tree from the studio.

"I just need to look inside," Laurel pleaded. "I need to know how bad it is."

"I'm sorry, ma'am, but you can't go in until the tree is removed. It just isn't safe," the fire captain explained.

"But—" Laurel started.

"Laurel, listen, I will get this taken care of. Let's let the guys go, as I'm sure they have a lot of calls right now. I will get on the phone, and we'll get the tree removed. Okay?" He held Laurel's shoulders and tried to get her to focus on what he was saying.

Laurel's shoulders sagged. "Okay, okay. Thank you, Captain Marshall, for coming out. I appreciate you and your crew being so kind." She shook the captain's hand and waved the crew goodbye.

When they had gone, Laurel went inside, found her insurance information, and called the after-hours number. She poured a glass of wine each for herself and Aiden and walked back outside.

Aiden was on his cell phone, just finishing a call. "Okay, perfect, Brad, thanks so much. We'll see you shortly."

Laurel handed Aiden the glass of wine. "Brad? What's Brad going to do?"

"Well, Brad's brother owns a tree service. Brad helps him out whenever he gets a lot of calls. They just finished another job and are on their way here now."

"What? That's great! Thank you. Listen, I talked to my insurance company. They are obviously busy, and I told them that we need to remove the tree now. They asked me to take photos from all different angles and then an assessor will be out first thing in the morning. Can we do that?"

"Of course we can. Let's take a few now before Brad and his brother get here, and then we can have them take others once they have their equipment set up. They'll be able to get photos from above, okay?"

"Yes, thank you. That's good. Thank you so much for your help."

"You're welcome." Aiden's eyes met Laurel's, and she could see the emotion shining in them. "I'm so relieved that you weren't in there when the tree came down. I was so worried when I looked out my window."

"Me too. I think it's just now hitting me, pun intended, that the tree could have come down any time in the past two days when I was in there working." Laurel's voice shook a little as she looked at the studio again.

Fifteen minutes later, Brad and his brother, Sam, arrived, and with Aiden's help, they completely took charge of the situation.

Laurel tried to help, but Aiden was able to convince her to

watch from the deck. Even in the state she was in, Aiden didn't treat her like she was helpless. He treated her with respect and compassion.

The guys took the photos she needed for the insurance adjuster and then set about removing the tree from the studio. They worked methodically and finished a short time later. Once it was safe, Aiden told Laurel they could look inside to see the damage.

With Aiden standing next to her, she unlocked the door. She took a deep breath and looked inside. The tree had landed where Laurel had feared: right on top of the drying rack. Everything she had created in the past two days was destroyed. Small branches, twigs, and wet leaves were mixed with broken pieces of pottery. The tree had also knocked down one of the shelves that held her completed products.

A gasp escaped her lips as she took it all in. "Oh. Wow. It's all destroyed."

Aiden put his arm around her shoulder to steady her on her feet. "We can fix it," Aiden said.

"How? Look at this mess. I can't believe I thought I could make this work. This stupid dream of mine."

"Laurel, look at me." Aiden held her shoulders and turned her toward him. "Laurel, your dream is not stupid. We can fix this. I can fix this. We'll have you back up and running in no time."

A tear escaped Laurel's eye and slid down her cheek. "I just don't know if I can do this."

Aiden touched her face and brushed the tear away with his thumb. "And I know you can. I know it looks bad right now, but I'll help you."

Laurel walked over to the wheel and was relieved to see it remained unscathed. She turned to Aiden and looked around the studio again. "You really think we can fix this?"

"I don't think we can. I know we can."

"Okay. I don't even know where to start, though."

"Well, first Brad and Sam are going to secure tarps to get it through until the morning. We should be done with the rain now, so that's a positive. I've assessed what supplies I will need. I'll grab my tape measure and make a list. Then, first thing in the morning, we'll get started. Sound good?"

Still, Laurel felt unsure. But, taking a deep breath, she nodded her head. "Okay, sounds good."

Brad came to the door then and led them outside. "We're going to get the tarps on and then head out. Sounds like we have a lot more work around town to take care of. Laurel, the tree fell due to two reasons. First, the ground is just saturated because of all the rain, but if you look here." Brad showed her the tree where the center was almost hollow from insects and rot. "Second, it needed to come down due to its condition. I'm sorry it happened the way it did. Are you doing okay?"

"Oh Brad. You, Sam, and Aiden have been wonderful. What would I have done without you?" Laurel hugged herself to keep her hands from visibly shaking. "I'm still in a bit of shock, to be honest. Thankful I wasn't inside. Aiden assures me that we can fix it and I can start over. Thank you all so much."

"We're all thankful that you weren't in the studio. Aiden is right. It is fixable, and if anyone can do that, it's Aiden. I'm going to help Sam get the tarps up."

Laurel looked up at Sam on a ladder as he started to spread the tarp out. Brad and Aiden went to help him. When they had secured the tarps, Laurel thanked Brad and Sam again as they all walked out front to their truck and said goodbye.

As she and Aiden returned to the backyard, he asked, "Are you doing okay?"

"Oh Aiden, how can I ever thank you for your take-charge attitude tonight? I really appreciate everything you've done."

Aiden smiled. "You could repay me by making your incredible au gratin potatoes again."

Laurel chuckled. "Seriously, that is easily done. No problem. Why don't you come inside and have another glass of wine? We can make a plan for tomorrow."

She closed and locked the studio door, even though that was laughable with only tarps securing the roof and siding.

Once inside, Laurel picked up the bottle of wine and brought their glasses into the living room. She returned to the kitchen and put some cheese and crackers on a tray and carried it to the coffee table.

Aiden had his notebook out and was jotting down a list. He raised his eyes to meet hers and smiled. She poured a glass of wine and handed it to him.

"So, I'll need to measure a couple of things when we have more light in the morning. I'll do that first thing and then go get the materials needed. Did the insurance company give you a time that the assessor will be here?"

"They said he will be here at eight o'clock. I'll upload the damage photos to my online portal on their website. Then hopefully once he comes, we can start."

"Tomorrow, he will write up his report, but we don't need to wait for an insurance check to arrive. As soon as he's done with his assessment, we can get started. We want to get you back to work as soon as we can." Aiden sipped his wine and reached for a piece of cheese and a cracker.

"That's true. I wasn't thinking about it the right way. I just need him to see it before we start. Do you have any idea how much the materials will cost?" Laurel asked.

Aiden looked at his list, seeming to calculate in his head, and then wrote something on the bottom of the list. He turned the page to show Laurel.

Laurel read it and laughed. "A dish or two of Laurel's au gratin potatoes."

Aiden smirked. "Well, I can't be certain whether it is one or two, but we can negotiate that as need be."

"Hmmm, well...I guess if that's what it will take, then that's what the payment should be." Laurel smiled. "But I'm still going to pay for the materials and your time."

Aiden shook his head. "No. Absolutely not. Friends help

friends. Neighbors help neighbors. That's how life works."

"Aiden, I'm not going to—"

"Laurel, I insist, okay? Please let me do this. You have a lot on your plate right now, and that includes making more plates," Aiden said. "Potatoes will be payment enough."

"Okay, okay. I can see I'm not going to win this argument. Let's agree to a couple of dinners which include au gratin potatoes. Deal?" Laurel held out her hand to shake on the deal.

Aiden took her hand and shook it as a smile lit up his face. "I think this is the best payment I have ever received for my work."

They both noticed that they were still holding hands after the shake, and both pulled away at the same time.

"I don't suppose you have a chainsaw, do you?" Laurel asked. "I still have a tree in the yard that I need to get cut up."

"As a matter of fact, I do. How about we plan that for this weekend? We can get it cut up and stacked, and you'll have some firewood come winter."

"Perfect. Thank you. I really do appreciate all your help."

"Glad I can be of service."

Laurel's phone started beeping with text messages. She picked it up and found a group text, started by Bailey.

> Are you okay? Brad just texted and told me a tree fell on your studio.

"Sorry, Aiden. I'll just be a moment." She started to type her reply.

"No problem at all. I'm sure they are all worried about you." He grabbed another piece of cheese and a cracker.

Laurel texted back.

> Hi, yes, I am okay. Thankfully, I wasn't in the studio when the tree came down. Aiden phoned Brad, and he and Sam removed the tree and covered the studio with a tarp. Aiden and I are sitting here planning for the repairs and cleanup tomorrow after the insurance adjuster comes.

A flurry of concerned responses flooded her phone. It was funny to Laurel that those were followed by several remarks of, "Aiden?!?"

She asked if everyone else was okay and ignored the Aiden-related questions.

Everyone else was okay, they replied, and Lena said that the rain at this time of year was good for the vines. A few more "Aiden?!?!" messages came through before Laurel replied.

> Glad you are all okay. Thanks for checking on me. I'll let you know how things go tomorrow. Everything I created for Hettie is destroyed, so I have a lot of work ahead of me once we get the studio workable again. Back to planning. Love you all.

She put her phone on silent before she placed it back on the table. She knew they would continue asking the Aiden question —and speculating since she wasn't replying.

"Is everyone okay?" Aiden asked.

"Yes, thankfully." She took a sip of wine and took a deep breath. *In and out.*

"How are you doing?" Aiden watched her closely.

"Better, I guess. The shock has worn off. I need to let Hettie know there will be a slight delay in my delivering her order. Now my focus needs to just be on cleaning up the mess and getting back to work." Laurel paused and noticed Aiden watching her. "What? Why are you looking at me like that?"

"Like what? I'm just making sure you're okay. It's been a rough night."

"Thanks to you, I'm getting through it. I'm not sure what I would have done without your help—which will continue tomorrow and on the weekend." Laurel met his eyes. "Thank you so much, Aiden."

"You're welcome." Aiden took the last sip of his wine and stood. "Thank you for the wine. You should get some sleep. It's been a long day. We have a lot to do tomorrow. Okay if I come by at seven a.m. to take the measurements?"

"Yes, of course. That will be fine."

They walked to the door, and Laurel wasn't sure if Aiden noticed, but she felt a shift in their friendship. She wasn't supposed to be falling for a guy right now, but he was so different. They were so at ease with each other. Standing in the open door, they both lingered.

Aiden looked as if he wanted to say something. Finally, he just reached out and touched Laurel's arm. "Get some sleep. I'll see you in the morning." He turned and walked out the door.

"Good night," Laurel said, and she closed the door and leaned against it with a sigh. *What were you expecting him to do? Kiss you? You aren't looking for a relationship, remember?* That was the last thing she needed right now. Sighing, she walked back into the living room and picked up the wineglasses and tray.

She straightened up the kitchen and took one last look out the door at her studio. She picked up her phone and turned out the lights before walking upstairs to bed. She plugged her phone into the charger without checking the messages and practically collapsed into bed. Suddenly, the emotions of the night caught up with her and she was asleep just as her head hit the pillow.

Fifteen

As exhausted as she was, Laurel's dreams were anything but sleepy. They were focused on a certain good-looking neighbor. Aiden kissing her, touching her in ways no man had ever touched her. In her dreams, they appeared to be very much in love with each other. It wasn't just lovemaking that she dreamed about—it was she and Aiden as loving partners, laughing and having fun together—in the forefront of her vivid dreams.

The alarm woke her from a dream she never wanted to wake up from. Laurel slowly opened her eyes and let out a sigh. "Stupid alarm. Couldn't you have waited a little longer to wake me?"

She showered and dressed in jeans and a long sleeve T-shirt. She thought about putting on makeup, but that seemed silly since she was going to spend the day cleaning up the mess in the studio. Still, she opted for a bit of mascara and a dusting of blush on her cheeks. With one last look in the mirror, she grabbed her phone and went downstairs.

In the kitchen, she flipped on the kettle for tea. After pouring herself a glass of orange juice, she lined a basket with a towel and filled it with a few of the blueberry muffins she had made the other day. She ate a bowl of yogurt with some fresh fruit and drank her juice and tea.

Aiden arrived at the door at seven o'clock sharp. Laurel jumped when the doorbell rang, even though she was expecting him. Suddenly, she was a bundle of nerves, telling herself nothing had changed between them in real life, that it was just her silly dreams. But even after telling herself that, she still stopped to look in the hall mirror before opening the door.

"Good morning, Laurel." Aiden walked in the door. "You look like you got a good night's sleep. How are you this morning?"

"Good morning. Yes, I slept...um...very well." Laurel found herself flustered just remembering the dreams she had. "I'm good. I'm ready to tackle the cleanup and get my studio fixed."

"Great. Well, let's go get things measured, shall we?" Aiden asked.

"Yes, of course. Listen, do you want some coffee first? And I have homemade blueberry muffins, if you like." Laurel offered.

"Thank you. Yes to both, but let me get the measurements first, otherwise I might just sit here and eat that entire basket of muffins." Aiden winked at her.

"Okay, okay. We wouldn't want to keep you from your work today. Especially since it's my studio." Laurel opened the French doors to the back deck.

The blue sky and sun that greeted them made them both stop and look up.

"There's nothing like the first sunny day after days of rain to make you smile." Laurel took a deep breath of the fresh air.

"I agree. What a beautiful day it is!"

Laurel led the way to the studio and tried to keep her positive attitude as she unlocked the door and walked inside. Looking around, she sighed before taking another deep breath. "Okay, what can I help you with on the measurements?"

Aiden took out his tape measure and notebook and showed Laurel where to hold the end of the tape measure. He worked with ease as he measured, jotting things down in his notebook and explaining to Laurel what needed to be done. A short time later, they were done and walked back into the kitchen.

As they each enjoyed a muffin and coffee, they discussed the plan for getting the studio fixed. Aiden explained what he needed to purchase and how quickly he thought he could complete it. Once the adjuster had visited and before Aiden started the work, Laurel said she would start cleaning up the broken pottery.

They were interrupted by the doorbell. It seemed too early for the adjuster. Laurel went to the door and answered it.

"Hi, Laurel Hardiston?" the man at the door asked.

"Hi, yes, I'm Laurel."

"Ted Jones from Acme Insurance Company. I'm here to look at—" he paused and reviewed his clipboard, "—your studio."

"Oh, great. You're early. How wonderful! Please come in." Laurel led him into the kitchen.

Aiden stood.

"Mr. Jones, this is Aiden, my neighbor...and friend. He's been a godsend and is going to do the repairs to my studio."

"Please, call me Ted. Nice to meet you, Aiden." He turned his attention back to Laurel. "I hope you don't mind that I'm early. I have quite a long list of appointments today and thought I would get started as soon as possible."

"No, we don't mind at all," Laurel answered. "We were just discussing our repair and cleanup strategy. Would you like some coffee and a blueberry muffin?"

"Thank you, but no. If I stop now, I won't get through my appointments. This shouldn't take too long."

Laurel opened the door to the deck. "Of course, no problem. We'll show you the studio. Right this way."

Ted first walked around the studio and then walked inside, all the while making notes on his clipboard. He snapped a few photos and made more notes.

"I uploaded photos to my account this morning. They show

the tree still in the studio. That tree over there." Laurel pointed to the tree on the ground. *Talk about stating the obvious.*

"Yes, we got the photos. Thank you. That does make the process quicker and easier. Sometimes, technology is very helpful. This is all straightforward. I'll upload my report and you should hear back from the office shortly. Your policy covers this sort of issue, so we will get you taken care of quickly."

"Wow, thank you so much. That is great news. I really appreciate the quick response. This is my pottery business, and I have a big contract that I now need to recreate most of the pieces for."

Ted smiled. "Glad to help. That was some rough weather we had. I'm sorry about the tree." He paused and looked like he was searching for a memory. "Are you related to John Hardiston?"

Laurel was a bit startled to hear her dad's name. "Yes, John is my father. He passed away many years ago now. Did you know him?"

"I'm sorry for your loss. I remember when he passed away. I went to school with your dad. He was two years in front of me. I made it on the junior cross-country team, and your dad was a great mentor to me. Always giving me tips and pointers to improve. I really appreciated his help. Nice guy. Again, I'm sorry for your loss."

"Aw, thank you for telling me that story." Laurel smiled. "That sounds exactly like something he would've done. He was a great man. I miss him terribly."

They walked around the deck to the driveway. Ted shook her hand and then patted it, looking into her eyes. "Take care now." With that, he got into his car and drove off.

"That must be the nicest person I've ever met from an insurance company," Aiden said. "What a nice story about your dad, huh?"

Laurel smiled up at him. "I agree. That was a great experience. And wow...he knew my dad. How cool is that?"

Aiden appeared to consider her for a moment. "That smile

looks good on you. You've had a rough time, and your smile still shines so brightly."

Feeling herself blush, Laurel looked at Aiden. "Thank you. I hate being sad or wallowing in self-pity. I just keep trying to be positive. Surrounding myself with great friends helps—that means you."

"I'm honored to be included in that group. I'm lucky I bought that house next door. I met you, and life is brighter already." Aiden said, before he shifted the conversation on to their day ahead. "Okay, we have a busy day, so I better get to the hardware store. Do you need anything while I am out?"

"Yes, yes, you're right. Um...no, I don't need anything. I'll get started on cleaning up the broken pottery while you are gone. Thanks, Aiden."

Aiden walked next door to his truck and left. Laurel went inside and topped up her coffee cup before grabbing a few cleaning supplies and walking back out to the studio.

Before she got started, she sent a text to Hettie.

> Good morning. I hope you made it through all that rain without any issues. I wish I could say I did, but after working on your order for the past two days...well, a tree fell on my studio and hit the drying rack where all your pieces were sitting. Don't worry. I'm getting the studio fixed today and hopefully will be back at the wheel again tomorrow. So, just a slight delay. I apologize, but I'm finding that life can just throw punches when you least need them. I'll let you know when I am back up and running.

The messaging app showed that Hettie was typing straight away, so Laurel held her phone, waiting for the reply, silently saying a prayer that Hettie would be understanding.

Oh dear, I am just so glad that you are okay.
How scary. Please don't fret. Take all the time
you need. Hugs.

The "hugs" sign-off brought a smile to Laurel's face. Hettie was a special soul. She replied with a couple of emojis.

Knowing that she needed some uplifting music to keep her spirits up while she was cleaning the mess, Laurel turned on some classic rock. After a deep breath and a good long look around the studio, she got to work.

She worked at picking up the larger pieces of pottery and was surprised that a few pieces looked to be salvageable. She put them aside and then swept up the rest of the pieces. She had brought in an empty five-gallon bucket and soon found it wasn't enough, so she went into the garage and grabbed a large garbage bin and took it around to the studio.

She knew it was a fruitless task to deep clean the studio before Aiden was done with the repairs, but she made progress before he returned.

An hour later, Aiden returned and backed his truck into her driveway. He greeted her as he carried the first of the load to the side of the studio. "Excellent choice in music, if you don't mind me saying." He sang every word of Hotel California on the trip to his truck and back again.

When he returned with the second load of materials, Laurel joined him in singing and they laughed together when one of them sang the wrong lyrics. There was quite a debate as to which of them was wrong, but the laughter they shared made sure it was all in fun.

The hours passed quickly as they worked together to replace the roofing and siding the tree had demolished. They stopped for lunch, and Laurel brought out sandwiches, salad, and chips. They ate on the deck, and Aiden told Laurel stories about his dad and what an incredible craftsman he was. The way Aiden spoke of him showed how much he admired his dad. She could understand why he had changed his path in life and followed what his father had taught him. Aiden clearly shared the love of carpentry with his dad.

By late afternoon, the roof and side of the studio were repaired. Aiden and Laurel removed the drop cloths inside the studio and finished cleaning up the remnants of the mess. They even moved the shelf back in place.

Laurel sighed and looked around the studio. It looked almost back to what it had been before the tree had crashed onto it. She knew she could pick up the pieces, so to speak, and carry on—thanks to Aiden.

"How can I possibly thank you for all your hard work? I would be in such a mess if you hadn't had been here to fix this."

"Hey, we already agreed on payment—your au gratin potatoes!" Aiden winked at Laurel.

"Yes, of course we have. But seriously, thank you so much. I really appreciate you and everything you've done for me."

"You're very welcome, Laurel. I'm glad I was here to help. Truthfully, this just reinforced my desire to do this for a living. Tomorrow, I'll get the siding painted and then this weekend we can cut up the tree for firewood."

"Sounds great." Laurel tried to remind herself not to stare at Aiden. "Are you hungry? I was thinking of ordering pizza."

"I'm starving. How about I feed Sophie, grab a shower, and meet you back here?"

"Okay, I probably should take a shower, too, and then order the pizza. That will give us time."

An hour later, they sat on the deck eating pizza and sharing a bottle of red wine. The sun was low in the sky, casting long shadows across the yard. They could hear a couple of ducks quacking about on the lake. Although Sophie had eaten her dinner, she sat between the two of them, clearly hoping they would drop some pizza for her. She didn't beg, but occasionally she looked up at each of them with her big, puppy-dog eyes, hoping to guilt them into dropping some food.

"I don't know how you don't cave every time she looks at you like that." Laurel fought the urge to give in to Sophie.

"Oh, believe me, the struggle is real...every day."

When they had finished the entire pizza, Laurel took the plates and empty pizza box inside. She came back outside to find Aiden throwing a ball for Sophie. She was a bit better at the "drop" command, but sometimes it took Aiden saying it a few times before she dropped the ball. The game continued for a few more minutes before Sophie decided to explore around the boat shed.

Aiden and Laurel talked as they watched Sophie sniffing around the shed. She seemed focused on one area and wouldn't come when Aiden called her.

"I'd better go see what she has found, just in case it's a snake or something," Aiden got up to walk down to the shed.

"I hope it isn't a snake," said Laurel. "Ick."

Aiden talked to Sophie as he approached her. "Whatcha found, girl? Let me see." Sophie didn't want to let Aiden get between her and whatever she had found. Aiden got down on his knees so he could see what Sophie was so excited about.

"Laurel, you need to come see this," Aiden called over his shoulder.

"If it's a snake, then I don't need to see it," Laurel said, even as she was walking down to the shed.

"Don't worry, it isn't a snake." Aiden reached under a bush and gently tried to retrieve whatever Sophie had found.

Laurel stood next to him and tried to see what was under the bush. Aiden held up a small, very frightened kitten.

"Aw, it's so tiny. Is it okay?" Laurel dropped to her knees to get a better look.

Aiden carefully checked over the black-and-white fluff of fur. The kitten mewed and mewed as Aiden held it. "She seems to be okay. No visible injuries. I think she's just scared and hungry."

Sophie stuck her nose straight in the kitten's face, sniffing. "Sophie, come on now, give her some room," Aiden said as he got to his feet. Sophie circled his feet as if saying, "Hey, I found it. It's mine."

Aiden handed the kitten to Laurel, and she absolutely turned to mush. "It's okay, don't be scared. We're not going to hurt you. I bet you're hungry, aren't you?" Laurel placed a gentle kiss on the kitten's head. "Look at how cute she is. Did you see her paws?" She held up the kitten to Aiden. The front left paw and back right paw were white, like little socks.

Aiden gently rubbed the kitten's head. "You are such a cutie, aren't you?"

As they walked up to the deck with Sophie still circling their legs, they tried to guess how old the kitten might be. Neither one of them had any idea, and they didn't want to feed it anything it shouldn't have.

"I think we should give her some water to start, and I'll call the vet hospital to see if we can bring her in this evening." She walked into the kitchen and grabbed a bowl with one hand while holding the kitten in the other.

Aiden took the bowl and filled it with water. They set the bowl and the kitten on the counter and watched as the kitten sniffed the water and immediately started lapping it up. Aiden rang the vet hospital and was told they could bring her right in.

While Laurel watched the kitten drink more water, Aiden got Sophie's leash and drove his truck over to Laurel's driveway. Laurel wrapped the kitten in a towel and climbed into the truck. Sophie sat between them and sniffed at the kitten so sweetly.

"Will you keep her if the vet says everything is fine with her?" Aiden asked as they drove into the parking lot.

"Definitely!" Laurel said.

The vet examined the kitten and determined it was probably eleven-to-twelve weeks old—old enough to be weaned from its mother. The kitten was in good health overall and wasn't suffering from any ailments. The vet gently bathed the kitten and dried her while she discussed Laurel's options.

"Oh, I'm going to keep her," Laurel assured her. "There's no way I'm going to put her up for adoption."

"That's wonderful to hear. She is a sweetie. I'm happy she'll have a good home." The vet handed the now-dry kitten over to Laurel.

As Laurel paid at the front desk, Aiden and Sophie walked in the door. "Where have you two been?"

"Sophie thought that if you were going to keep the kitten that we had better run to the pet store and get you some supplies." Aiden smiled and pet Sophie. Sophie sat and looked up at Laurel and seemed to be smiling like she knew Aiden was speaking about her.

"Aw, Sophie, that is so sweet of you. You, too, Aiden. Thank you. The vet said she's healthy."

"That's great news. Let's get you home." Aiden petted the little fluffy head that stuck out of the towel in Laurel's arms.

When they arrived at Laurel's house, she looked in the truck and realized just how much Aiden had bought at the pet store. "You don't think you bought a little too much?"

"Don't blame me. Sophie was in charge. She chose everything except the food. She only wanted me to buy *her* favorite food."

Between the two of them, they carried everything into the house. Laurel put one of the three cat beds down in the living room and gently placed the kitten in it while she looked through everything else Aiden and Sophie had bought.

Aiden helped her set up the litter box and put the food away. When they returned to the living room, they found Sophie lying half on the bed; the kitten was tucked up against her, sound asleep. Sophie looked up at them and gave the kitten a gentle lick.

"Well, I guess we know how Sophie feels about *her* kitten. How sweet." Laurel said.

"Wow. Would you look at that? Looks like they may be the best of friends."

"That is so precious."

"Now, somehow, I have to get Sophie to go home. It's late."

Aiden walked over to Sophie and leaned down, talking to her. He reassured her that she would see *her* kitten tomorrow. Sophie seemed to understand and gently stood. She leaned down and gave the kitten a good sniff before letting Aiden lead her to the door.

"Thank you. See you in the morning." Laurel held the door open.

"Sleep well, Laurel," Aiden said, as he walked Sophie to the truck.

Laurel stood and watched them back out of the driveway and drive next door, disappearing behind the tree line that separated their two properties. She closed and locked the door, then went to look in on the kitten. She had woken up and mewed as she looked at Laurel.

Laurel lifted the kitten and showed her where the litter box was set up and then showed her where her bowls of food and water were.

The kitten scarfed down the entire can of food before taking a drink or two of water. She sat and looked up at Laurel.

"Welcome home, little one. We need to give you a name, don't we?"

The kitten mewed in response.

Laurel sat up for a while longer until the kitten used the litter box. Then she picked her up and carried her upstairs to her bed.

The next morning, she awoke to find the kitten sound asleep on the pillow next to her. As soon as Laurel moved, the kitten woke up and mewed. They walked downstairs and Laurel fed her, and then she went back upstairs to get ready for the day.

Aiden and Sophie arrived a short time later, and Sophie immediately sought out the kitten. The reunion was a sight to see as they circled and sniffed each other. Sophie plopped down, and the kitten nuzzled up against her.

"We need a name for the little bundle of fur," Laurel said. "Socks is what comes to mind, but I don't know. What do you think?"

Aiden grinned. "I love it. It fits...just like a sock."

Socks mewed, and Sophie barked their approval.

"Well, that's decided. Let's get some work done." Aiden said, as he walked out the French doors. Sophie followed, and then Socks, and then Laurel.

Laurel worked inside the studio while Aiden painted the siding. Sophie and Socks played and eventually fell asleep together on the deck.

Aiden finished the painting a couple of hours later. When he appeared at the studio door, Laurel was completely focused on the clay she was forming on the wheel. Sensing she was being watched, though, she looked up and smiled at Aiden before turning her eyes back to the clay.

"Are you finished already?" She dipped the sponge in water and wet the clay as she effortlessly manipulated it between her fingers, not looking up.

"Yes, all finished. I'm going to head home and—" There was a pause before he said, "Get that shag run installed."

Laurel burst out laughing as she stopped the wheel and deftly cut the bowl from the wheel. She stood and placed it on the drying rack, then turned back to Aiden. "I thought we had talked about this, and you understood that you should leave the decorating to someone who has some taste."

Aiden laughed. "I just wanted to see if you were listening while you were so entranced in your creation."

"Oh, I was listening, and I'm glad I was—so I could steer you clear of that damn shag rug obsession you seem to have."

"What would I do without you keeping me from making a bad decorating decision?" Aiden smiled as he leaned against the door frame.

"I don't think we want to find out." Laurel winked. "Thanks again for everything, Aiden. I really appreciate it. Let me know when you want to have dinner with your hard-earned au gratin potatoes."

"You're welcome, Laurel. My schedule is pretty free. What do you think about Saturday, after we cut up that tree? If that works for you."

"That works perfectly for me. I'll pick up some chicken to grill, okay?"

"Great. Okay, I had better go pull Sophie away from her new best friend and head home. Talk to you later."

Laurel followed Aiden outside and up to the deck. There they found Sophie and Socks still curled up together, awake and watching the humans.

"Let's go, Sophie."

Although reluctant, the little lab stood and bounded over to Aiden.

"Good girl, Sophie. We'll come see Laurel and Socks soon."

Laurel picked up Socks and waved as she watched Aiden and Sophie walk around the house and into their yard.

Socks could have been named Shadow because she soon followed Laurel everywhere. She seemed to be comfortable curled up on Laurel's desk in the studio, sitting on a dining room chair while Laurel made any meal, snuggled on the couch at the end of a long day, or curled up on Laurel's bed throughout the night. If Laurel was outside, Socks would be there with her. She would explore the yard but always seemed to keep an eye on Laurel's whereabouts.

But as soon as Aiden let Sophie out in his backyard, Socks and Sophie sought each other out—circling and sniffing each other, chasing each other across both yards. It was as if Socks knew Sophie saved her that night. It didn't matter that dogs and cats weren't supposed to get along; those two did.

Laurel worked long hours over the next few days as she recreated Hettie's pieces. She had to admit that some of the pieces were better the second time around. She loaded the kiln several times and became more excited once she pulled them out and saw how beautiful they were. She still had painting and glazing to do, but by the end of that long week, she felt back on track.

Friday afternoon, she took a break and went to the grocery

store for potatoes, chicken, and all the fixings for Saturday's dinner with Aiden. She decided to make a double batch of au gratin potatoes so Aiden could take some home. She made the potatoes that night so she could just put them in the oven tomorrow. She marinated the chicken with rosemary, lemon, and extra-virgin olive oil. Laurel loved this Tuscan Lemon chicken recipe and hoped that Aiden would as well.

Cassie called Laurel later that night to let her know she and Sean would be over Saturday around noon. The weather last weekend had delayed Cassie in giving Sean a paddle boarding lesson. Laurel told her that she and Aiden would be around, as they were cutting up the tree tomorrow.

"Hey, I'm making dinner for Aiden tomorrow night as a thank-you for fixing my studio. Why don't you and Sean join us?"

Cassie's hesitation was evident in her tone. "Oh, I don't know. We're just business associates. I don't want Sean to think I'm forcing couple activities on him."

"Cassie, that's silly. Aiden and I aren't a couple either. We're just friends and neighbors. Everyone needs to eat, y'know. At least think about it."

"I'll think about it. Tomorrow is the first non-work function Sean and I have done, so I'm already a bit nervous."

"Try not to overthink it," Laurel said, even though she knew she would be doing the same thing.

"I'm trying, believe me. Okay, must run. I'll see you tomorrow."

"See you tomorrow."

AIDEN AND SOPHIE ARRIVED THE NEXT MORNING, READY to get to work on the downed tree. Well, Aiden was ready. Sophie searched for Socks, and the two of them played outside while Aiden and Laurel prepared their tools. Then they took Sophie and Socks inside so they would be out of harm's way while the tree was cut up.

While Aiden used the chainsaw, Laurel loaded the wood into the wheelbarrow and stacked it on the woodpile. It seemed a bit strange to be in shorts stacking firewood in the heat, but Laurel knew she would appreciate the firewood come winter.

Laurel and Aiden made a good team. There was an ebb and flow to them. Laurel noticed it when they were cleaning up the studio. Aiden somehow knew exactly where Laurel wanted some pottery moved to when she handed it to him. She'd stood there with her mouth open, ready to tell him, and ended up closing it and smiling at how nice it was to have him there.

Aiden and Laurel finished cutting and stacking the wood when the sun was high in the sky and the temperature was soaring. Laurel wiped the sweat from her face and shaded her eyes with her hand. The tree's sudden departure, although not a fun ordeal, had opened the view of the lake.

Laurel opened the door, and Sophie and Socks greeted her. Both circled her legs, vying for affection. Aiden called for Sophie, and she bounded out the open door. Socks followed Laurel into the kitchen. She put some treats down for her before getting some refreshments for Aiden and herself.

Laurel carried the tray outside with lemonade and some sliced apples and cheese. They sat at the table in the shade and chatted while they drank the lemonade and munched on the cheese and apples.

A short time later, they heard a car drive up.

"That will be Cassie and Sean." Laurel got up to greet them.

The conversation and laughter that preceded Cassie and Sean made Laurel smile. The two of them clearly shared a mutual admiration. Something Sean said sent Cassie into a fit of giggles as they came around the deck. It was so much that it took Cassie a minute or two to stop giggling.

"Hi, Laurel," Cassie said as she hugged her.

Aiden came up behind Laurel and greeted Sean first, then Cassie.

"Should we ask what was so funny?" Aiden eyed the two of them.

Sean and Cassie looked at each other, which sent them both into fits of laughter again. When they finally stopped, Sean shook his head. "No, it's kind of an inside joke."

Cassie added, "Yeah, you had to be there," while stifling her giggles.

"Okay, well, we won't ask then." Laurel led them to the table. "Can I get you two something to drink?"

"Some lemonade would be great," Cassie said, and Sean agreed.

They talked about the tree damaging the studio and how Laurel and Aiden worked together to repair it. Aiden told them that they had just finished cutting up the tree and stacking the now firewood.

"Sounds like you guys could use a swim to cool off," Cassie said.

"Yes, we do. Let me go throw on swim trunks."

Laurel smiled. "Great, I'll go change as well. Be right back."

A few minutes later, they were all down at the boat shed. Laurel and Cassie carried the paddleboards out to the water's edge.

Cassie turned to Sean, smiling. "Are you ready?"

"To make a fool of myself?" he fired back. "Sure, why not?"

"You'll be fine. The water is pretty calm, so that will help." Cassie carried her paddleboard into the lake.

Sean followed with one more look over his shoulder at Aiden and Laurel.

Cassie was a calm, patient teacher. She showed Sean how to mount the board and then kneel, making sure he was evenly over the center before encouraging him to slowly stand.

Sean stood, arms flailing a bit, before *SPLASH!*

Cassie walked him through the lesson again, and the second

time Sean stood, he lasted a bit longer before falling into the water again.

"Sean, stop thinking so much." Cassie tried to stifle her laughter. "Just center yourself, stand, and use the paddle to help balance."

Sean laughed as he reached for the board again. "Oh, is that all I have to do?"

Cassie slowly encouraged Sean again as he tried one more time, and this time he stayed upright.

"Third time's a charm. Look at you." Cassie mounted her board and paddled next to Sean. She continued with encouraging words as she showed him how to stay upright while slowly paddling around.

It didn't take Sean long to feel confident. "Okay, Aiden. Next victim. Your turn."

Aiden and Laurel laughed as they carried their boards into the water. Aiden tried to stand way too quickly and immediately fell off the board.

Sean laughed and mimicked Cassie and Laurel's instructions while Aiden tried once again. He fell two more times before finally finding an evenly centered position, and that was it. He had it down.

"Wow, this is easy." Aiden steered his paddleboard around.

"And here we thought it was difficult. Look at us now." Sean followed Aiden out farther into the lake.

Laurel and Cassie laughed as they paddled behind them.

The four of them paddled about as the sun warmed their skin. A light breeze helped to keep them gliding along without much paddling at times. A wave from a passing boat caused both Aiden and Sean to fall off their boards. That sent Laurel and Cassie into a fit of giggles; they were skilled enough to stay upright.

That, of course, frustrated the guys while they were trying to get back up on their boards. Every time either of them got up on the board and tried to stand, the other one wobbled their paddleboard and caused a wave to knock the first off.

Laurel and Cassie finally sat on their own boards and just watched the guys messing about. They attempted to give instructions, but their laughter stopped them from being much help. A good five minutes later, both Aiden and Sean were back up on their boards, and they all continued exploring the coves nearby.

"I have to admit, I'm really enjoying this," Sean said, as he and Cassie led the way deeper into a cove.

"I'm glad. I thought you would. I find it very relaxing, especially after a long day sitting in front of a computer," Cassie said.

"Yes, I can see it would be. A way to stretch some muscles and clear the mind."

Cassie smiled and looked over at Sean.

He caught her looking and smiled back. "What? What's that smile for?" Sean asked.

"I'm just really enjoying the day. I'm glad you agreed to come out today."

"Cassie, thank you for asking me and for insisting I needed a break. I haven't had this much fun in way too long. And I'm especially enjoying spending time with you."

Cassie slowed down and looked over at Sean. "I'm enjoying spending time with you too."

"Good. Maybe we should do more of this then," Sean said, smiling at Cassie.

"I would like that very much," Cassie said. "Now, how about we race back to the entrance of this cove?"

Laurel smiled to herself at the sweet conversation she had just overheard.

Cassie expertly turned her board and paddled as fast as she could.

Sean was caught off-guard, and when he tried to turn his board around, he leaned too far and fell into the water.

Cassie was just passing Aiden and Laurel when Sean fell into the water.

"Um, I think you can stop paddling. Sean is in the water," Aiden said.

Cassie slowed and turned around. She held up her paddle triumphantly with both hands. "I think we'll just say that I won that race, right Sean?"

Sean had just climbed up on his paddleboard but had yet to stand. He was laughing so much that he could barely stay kneeling on the board. "Hey, I wasn't ready."

"Not the correct answer."

Sean bowed slowly, wobbling a bit. "Yes, Cassie, you *won!*"

Cassie laughed. "*Yes!*"

Sean looked to Laurel. "Is she always this competitive?"

Laurel shook her head. "No, you must bring it out in her." She tried to keep a straight face.

Aiden said, "Sean, if you can stand back up, we might actually be able to challenge these two beautiful ladies to a race."

"I think we should make it a little easier for you guys. How about you and me against Cassie and Sean?" Laurel asked.

Aiden laughed. "Okay, let's do this."

They waited until Sean stood again, and then the four of them started racing, each paddling as fast as they could, which of course caused waves or a wake for the others. They were all laughing so hard when Laurel and Aiden reached the opening of the cove first. Cassie and Sean came in a very close second.

Laurel reached over to high-five Aiden, and when he moved to slap her hand, they both lost their balance.

Aiden grabbed onto Laurel as they fell into the water. Holding onto her as they emerged above the water, Aiden pulled Laurel close and looked at her. Laurel was sure he was about to kiss her when a large splash caused them both to look toward the sound.

The splash was Cassie pushing Sean into the water, and that set all of them to laughing once again. The moment between Aiden and Laurel had passed.

They paddled back to Laurel's dock. The afternoon sunlight was slowly dipping behind the old trees, casting long shadows across the yard. They stored the paddleboards back in the shed and chatted as they walked up to the deck.

"Listen, I've planned a feast as a thank-you to Aiden for repairing my studio. There's more than enough food. Why don't the two of you join us?" Laurel asked.

"Oh, I don't know." Cassie looked to Sean.

Sean looked back at Cassie and smiled. "If you don't have any other plans, I would love to stay for dinner. It would be the perfect end to a great day. Are you free, Cassie?"

"I don't have any plans." She turned to Laurel, "Thanks Laurel, we would love to stay for dinner."

"Great! But I should warn you that the au gratin potatoes will not be shared." Aiden smiled at Laurel.

She reached over and patted his arm. "Don't worry, I made a double batch just in case Cassie and Sean joined us."

Aiden winked at Laurel. "I knew I could count on you to look out for me. Thanks."

"It's only fair," Laurel replied. "You seem to have been looking out for me since you moved in. I appreciate you. Thank you."

Aiden put his arm over Laurel's shoulder and hugged her. "Any time."

"Okay, shower time," Cassie said. The look she gave Laurel made it clear she was sensing that she and Sean really should have left Laurel and Aiden alone tonight.

Laurel smiled and acted like she hadn't seen Cassie's expression. "Yes, of course. Cassie, if you want to use the bathroom in the master bedroom, Sean can use the guest bathroom upstairs. I'll put some appetizers together and then shower when you guys are done."

"I'll run home and shower and be back shortly to help," Aiden said as he turned and walked across the yard.

"Great. See you soon." Laurel turned back to Cassie and Sean. "Cassie, there are extra towels in the linen closet in the upstairs hallway. Scream if you need anything else, okay?"

"Thanks, Laurel." Cassie grabbed the clothes they had arrived in and led Sean up the stairs.

Laurel could hear them chatting away the entire time. It made her smile, feeling that perhaps Cassie and Sean were getting closer by the day.

Laurel busied herself in the kitchen. She placed the au gratin potatoes in the oven on low so they could warm through. She pulled the Tuscan Lemon chicken she had been marinating since yesterday from the refrigerator. Then appetizers went on a couple of chalkboard slates. Laurel and her mom had found them in a shop, and she couldn't resist buying them. They had never been used, as Graham wasn't one for entertaining—well, unless it was beer and chips. Laurel immediately pushed that thought from her mind and carried on setting things up for her friends.

Aiden arrived at the French doors carrying a couple of bottles of wine. At his side was Sophie, who, after greeting Laurel, wandered into the living room to find Socks.

"You didn't need to bring anything, Aiden. But thank you," Laurel said.

"Hey, you've done enough. It's the least I could do. What can I help with?" Aiden asked, just as they were joined by Sean and Cassie.

"Well, you can all help yourselves while I go up and shower and change." Laurel smiled at her friends.

"I'll open some wine. Would you like to take a glass with you?" Aiden asked.

"Ah, that sounds perfect. Thank you," Laurel said. "I won't be long. Please make yourselves at home."

Aiden handed her a glass of wine, and she disappeared upstairs.

Laurel rinsed out her swimsuit and hung it on the drying rack. She turned on the shower, took a sip of wine, and stepped under the water. As she washed her hair, she smiled, thinking about how much fun she had had today. She washed off the remnants of sunscreen and lake water and turned off the tap.

Wrapping a towel around her, she stepped out of the shower and looked in the mirror. There was something different about her. She not only saw it, but more importantly, she felt it. She was happy—happy with her life, happy with her work, happy with her friends. Happy with herself.

She dried off and applied lotion while humming to herself. After towel-drying her hair, she combed it and decided to let it dry naturally. Laurel didn't want to waste time while her friends were waiting downstairs. She quickly applied a little mascara and lip gloss. She carried her glass of wine into the bedroom and opened the closet door. She chose a pair of jeans and a soft blue T-shirt. Slipping on a pair of flat sandals, Laurel stopped in front of her jewelry box. A pair of hoop earrings and one of her favorite necklaces, which said "scatter joy," completed her outfit.

Laurel returned downstairs to find everyone sitting on the deck, the conversation entertaining and animated. Aiden stood as she walked outside.

"We've only started on the wine," Sean said from where he was seated—close to Cassie, Laurel noted.

"What? Why haven't you eaten anything yet?" Laurel took a seat next to Aiden.

"You haven't been gone that long, Laurel. We've been busy talking," Cassie said. "But, now that you mention it, I am starved." She reached for a piece of cheese and a cracker.

Sean and Aiden followed suit. Laurel reached for a couple of olives and a piece of cheese.

"Those potatoes smell incredible, Laurel," Aiden said. "But I'm not sure there will be enough for anyone else." He smiled, leaning against her shoulder. Laurel laughed in response.

They devoured the appetizers, and Aiden kept their wineglasses topped up. When the cheese and crackers were gone, Laurel and Cassie picked up the slates and carried them inside.

Once out of earshot of the guys, they both started talking at once. Whispering as they put things away, Cassie asked, "So, what's happening between you and Aiden?"

Laurel looked at her and turned her back to the door. "Um, I'm not sure. We're just friends, and you know I'm not looking for anything, but—" She looked over her shoulder to make sure they were still alone. "I swear when we finished the race and fell into the water that, well, he was going to kiss me."

"What? That's great." Cassie grabbed Laurel's hand and squeezed it. "Listen, I know you say you aren't looking for anything, but...Aiden is a great guy!"

"I know, he really is. I just don't want to rush anything. We've become good friends. I don't want to lose that." Laurel gave Cassie's hand a squeeze in return. "Hey, what about you and Sean?"

"Well, you know I don't want anything to start before I finish this branding contract with his company, but I don't know. We're growing closer every day. Today, while we were paddle boarding, he told me how much he enjoyed spending time with me, and we both agreed we want to do more of that." Cassie twirled a lock of hair between her fingers. "So, oh gosh, I don't know."

"Sounds like we're both in the same boat. Guess we just have to calm down and see what happens." Laurel hugged Cassie.

"Hey, is there anything we can help you lovely ladies with?" Aiden poked his head into the kitchen, startling them both.

"Yes, actually, could you light the grill?" Laurel asked.

"Sure thing." Aiden smiled as he turned and walked back out to the deck.

Laurel clapped her hands together. "Okay, let's get things going here. Can you get the salad out of the fridge?"

Cassie pulled out the salad, then opened the cabinet above the counter and pulled out plates and bowls and placed them on a tray.

Sean came inside as she added the cutlery to the tray. "I'll take this outside and set the table," Sean said, as Cassie placed napkins on the tray and smiled.

"Thank you," Cassie said.

Aiden appeared at the open door and announced the grill was warmed up.

Laurel handed him the chicken. "The chicken may cause a flare-up, so we'll have to keep an eye on it."

"Wow, this smells amazing. Lemon, rosemary, and garlic?"

"Yes! It's one of my favorite recipes. I hope you all like it," Laurel said.

"I'm sure we'll all love it," Sean said.

Dinner was indeed loved by everyone; Aiden even shared the au gratin potatoes. After dinner, the guys cleared the table, and Aiden loaded the dishwasher.

"He sure looks like he knows his way around here, Laurel. Is there something you haven't told me?" Cassie teased her.

"Ha, ha. No, I have nothing to tell. He had dinner here before and helped me clean up afterward. That's all."

Cassie giggled. "Okay, if you say so."

When the guys returned from their kitchen duties, they all walked down to the dock and sat in the Adirondack chairs under the stars. The lake was still but for the occasional fish jumping. They spoke in hushed voices, knowing that sound carried across the water. Laurel's dad had taught her that when she was a child and had instilled in her how important it was to respect the neighbors around the lake.

"Aiden, have you always had your own carpentry business?" Sean asked.

"No, this is something new for me. I used to be a financial advisor for one of the largest global investment companies."

"Oh, wow, so this is a big change for you," Cassie said.

"Yes, it is, but it's a good change. I don't miss the pressure of the job," Aiden said. "Truthfully, I don't miss anything about that old life."

"I know a few people in that line of work, and it's pretty intense," Sean said. "If you don't mind me saying—you don't seem the type."

"In hindsight, I agree with you. I was good at what I did, and I fell into all the perks of that lifestyle. When I look back now, it doesn't even seem like me. Well, it wasn't the real me. It's interesting; when I quit and told the people I thought were my friends what my plans were—well, they acted like I had lost my mind." Aiden stared out at the lake. "The friendships turned out to be as superficial as everything else about that life. If only they could see me now."

Sean looked into the darkness of the lake, then at Cassie. "If you ask me, this is how life should be spent."

"I couldn't agree more." Aiden winked at Laurel.

"Isn't it funny how we thought there were things in our lives that we couldn't live without, but now we're on different paths? What I thought I couldn't live without is becoming a distant and no longer welcome memory." Laurel leaned back, gazed up at the stars, and sighed.

Cassie reached over and squeezed Laurel's hand. "I sure am glad you are here."

"Me too."

As if to lift the mood, Sophie chose that exact moment to run over and drop her ball at Laurel's feet.

Aiden laughed. "Looks like it's unanimous!"

They all took turns tossing the ball for Sophie. Socks wandered down and climbed into Aiden's lap. Laurel smiled and reached over to pet Socks as she attempted to stifle a yawn. Of course, Aiden noticed.

Standing with Socks cuddled in his arms, Aiden yawned. The contagious nature of yawns meant that they all started yawning.

"Guess we had better get going," Sean said. "Thank you so much for a wonderful day and an excellent meal."

Cassie chimed in. "Laurel, thanks so much! I've had a great day, especially teaching these two how to paddleboard. Dinner was amazing, as always."

As they walked up to the house, Aiden handed Socks over to Laurel.

"So, I'm guessing we'll see you back again soon for more paddle boarding, Sean?" Laurel asked.

Aiden laughed, as did Sean. "I think Sean and I will borrow the boards to work on our paddleboard racing game."

"Yes, we can't let them think they can beat us again," Sean agreed.

Sean and Cassie drove away, and Aiden and Laurel walked around the house to the deck. She put Socks down on the chair and looked up at Aiden.

"I can't thank you enough for all of your help with the studio."

Aiden chuckled. "I thought we settled this. There's nothing to thank me for. This is what friends do for each other. And you've paid me back with your wonderful dinner. Thank *you*."

Without another word, Laurel stood on her tiptoes and kissed Aiden on the cheek. When she stood back, he reached his hand out and caressed her cheek with his thumb.

Aiden bent down and gently kissed Laurel. It was the briefest of kisses. Aiden caressed her cheek once more before he said, "Sleep well, Laurel. I've enjoyed our day together."

Laurel stood there in a daze as she watched Aiden turn and walk toward his house. At the last moment, before he disappeared around the house, he turned back and smiled. Laurel waved at him, picked up Socks, and walked inside.

Sixteen

Laurel wasn't sure what had just happened. Okay, she knew what had happened. Aiden had kissed her. OMG, Aiden had kissed her. It was the softest, sweetest kiss, and she could still feel his lips on hers. She touched her lips and sighed.

As she locked the house and turned off the lights, she tried to convince herself it was just a friendly kiss. Nothing more. She wasn't looking for anything more, she reminded herself.

Laurel was still trying to convince herself of that as she climbed into bed and turned off the light.

As EXHAUSTED AS LAUREL WAS, SHE SEEMED TO SPEND the night tossing and turning and dreaming. Oh, the dreams. She woke up with a smile on her face and a bundle of energy. Sunday morning was usually a restful time for her, but she couldn't wait to get into the studio. She still had a lot to do for Hettie's order, and she was feeling extremely creative this morning. She fed Socks and herself, and then they both went out to the studio. The windowsills were deep, which gave Socks a perfect place to stretch out and supervise Laurel's work.

She turned on a favorite playlist and had a look at her detailed order for Hettie. With a vision in her head, she sliced some clay and sat down at the wheel. The music seemed to be the perfect rhythm for the speed of the wheel and the feel of the clay as she effortlessly created several pieces. Once Laurel finished the pieces and placed them on the drying rack, she sliced more clay and continued working like this for several hours.

The time seemed to fly, and she was able to finish all the pieces for Hettie's order. The drying rack was full once again. While waiting for the pieces to dry before she fired them, she would work on painting and glazing some of her stock pieces. Thankfully, Hettie wanted some simple items that Laurel had already created.

After lunch, Laurel was back in the studio adding the perfect little painted touches to the tall vases and the place settings. She worked well into the afternoon, and as she stood from her workbench, Laurel looked around and felt very accomplished. Hettie's order was important, and Laurel was impatient in wanting to deliver it. She knew it would be a few weeks before it would all be fired and painted or glazed. Patience was a virtue, she told herself as she cleaned up.

Locking up the studio, Laurel looked toward Aiden's house. She hadn't seen him all day, though she had heard Sophie barking earlier. Deciding to play it cool and not push things, Laurel went inside and changed into a swimsuit. A little time on the paddleboard would loosen her tight muscles—and, if she was lucky, keep her mind off the kiss and the man.

For the next hour, she glided slowly around the lake. The tension in her neck and shoulders eased, and her mind even wandered away from Aiden—well, for a short time. The birds chattered away in the trees as she paddled by. She waved to neighbors enjoying time on their boats or docks.

Making her way back to her dock, she saw someone sitting in

one of the Adirondack chairs. Laurel could tell immediately that it was Aiden. Sophie was running around and dropping the ball at his feet, where he would toss it over his shoulder for her.

She wished the butterflies in her stomach would calm down, or at the very least, all fly in formation. One of her hands slipped on the paddle, and she tried to wipe the sweat from her palm on her swimsuit. Why were her hands suddenly clammy? *It's Aiden. Calm down.*

"Hey you, how is it out there?" Aiden asked.

"Peaceful. I've been in the studio all day and needed a change of scenery and to work out some knots in my shoulders."

"Did it help?" He looked at her inquisitively.

"Yes, it did. It was exactly what I needed. I realize how much I love being on the water," Laurel said. "What have you been up to today?"

"Well, I finished the kitchen. I woke up full of energy and decided to just work until it was finished. And about thirty minutes ago, I finished it."

Laurel stopped wiping down the paddleboard. "Aiden, that's great! What an accomplishment. Can I see it?"

"Of course," he said. "I'm ready when you are."

Laurel stored the paddleboard in the shed and pulled on shorts she had left there. With Sophie leading the way, they walked over to Aiden's house.

Laurel walked into the kitchen as Aiden closed the sliding screen door behind them.

"Oh, Aiden." Laurel spun around, taking it all in. "This is absolutely gorgeous. It's like a completely different space. It's so open, and the light is amazing."

Aiden smiled as he looked around. "Thanks. I'm happy with how it turned out."

Aiden had removed all the over-the-counter cabinets and added a large window. The dining room access had been through a door with paneled walls on either side of the door, but he had removed one wall completely to make the kitchen and dining area one space. So as to not lose the cabinet space, he had converted the other wall to all cabinets and cupboards.

Laurel walked around, opening drawers and cabinets, commenting on little details. The tiniest detail didn't escape her.

"Aiden, this is gorgeous. You are so talented." Laurel leaned against the counter.

"Thank you." He beamed. "Kitchens are always the worst room to remodel, but now it's done. Finishing the rest of the house should be easy."

Laurel walked across the kitchen to the other side of the dining room table. "So, what else are you going to do?"

"Let me show you." Aiden led the way through the dining area. "I'm taking out this wall between here and the living room."

In unison, they both said, "That way, it isn't so boxed in."

Laughing, Aiden said, "We certainly think the same, don't we?"

"Yes, we do." Laurel giggled.

Aiden turned toward Laurel and took a step, closing the space between them. "Do you want to know what I've been thinking about all day?" Aiden asked.

Laurel nodded, because suddenly her words wouldn't form.

"I've been thinking about kissing you again."

"Me too," she managed to say.

Aiden cupped her face as he leaned down and kissed her. The kiss started soft and gentle. Laurel leaned into the kiss and wrapped her arms around his neck. As Aiden held her closer, the kiss intensified. Aiden's tongue explored her mouth, causing a soft moan to escape. Just when she leaned in to deepen the kiss, Aiden slowly pulled back.

Her eyes fluttered open.

"Wow," they said in unison.

Aiden brushed a strand of hair away from Laurel's face. "I have wanted to kiss you since the day we met."

She caught her breath as she stood locked in his embrace. "What stopped you?"

"Well, you were going through a lot of changes, and I wanted to give you the space to work through things first."

Laurel kissed him briefly. "Thank you."

"You're welcome," he said, then continued kissing her.

Laurel couldn't believe this was happening. It felt as if she were floating. She wanted Aiden, but was she rushing into another relationship? *No*, she told herself, kissing Aiden more intensely.

She pulled back and opened her eyes, gazing at him as his thumb caressed her cheek.

"Are you okay?" Aiden asked.

"Yes, very okay." Her heart seemed to be beating double-time, and her knees felt a bit wobbly. *Can a kiss really make you weak in the knees?*

"Listen, why don't you come over for dinner tonight? I've been in the studio all day and then in the lake. I'll shower and make us some dinner." Laurel smiled up at him. "Sound good?"

"Okay...but I really don't want to let you go." He leaned in for another kiss, but Laurel took his hand and guided him to the door.

"See you in, say, an hour?" She kissed away his disappointed frown.

"I look forward to it." Aiden reluctantly let go of her hand. She could feel his gaze as she walked the short distance to her house. She stopped and looked over her shoulder before disappearing around the corner.

LAUREL WALKED INSIDE AND WANDERED UP THE STAIRS in a daze. She took a shower and slipped on a sundress. She couldn't wipe the smile off her face—not that she tried. Although Laurel was excited, she wasn't nervous. She felt so at ease around Aiden. She didn't feel the need to be anything or anyone but herself. Had she ever felt that way before? No, not if she was being honest.

In the kitchen, she fed Socks and started dinner. She hadn't gotten far when Aiden and Sophie arrived at the French doors.

Aiden tapped on and opened the door. "Hi."

"Hi, c'mon in. I am just starting dinner."

"Can I help with something?" Aiden walked up behind Laurel and kissed the back of her neck.

Laurel let herself lean into his arms briefly. Bringing her focus back to making dinner, she said a bit breathlessly, "Well, I think maybe we should refrain from any more of that so I can focus on feeding us."

Aiden smiled. "Okay, good point. I'll open some wine and set the table. Do you want to eat outside?"

"Yes, thanks."

Laurel looked up at him as he reached into the cupboard and pulled out the bowls. He popped them into the microwave to warm them. When he reached around her to get the corkscrew and brushed against her, he paused to look at her and winked.

She put the water on to boil and then cut up some tomatoes. She pulled out a pan for the sauce and added a little olive oil. Turning, she found Aiden right behind her.

"For you." Aiden handed her a glass of wine.

"Thank you." She winked at him as she took a sip of wine, then returned to making dinner.

Aiden busied himself with setting the table. Every time he was in the kitchen, he seemed to brush up against her.

Finally, Laurel couldn't stop herself from giggling. She stopped what she was doing and turned to Aiden. "It's really amazing," she started.

"What's that?"

"I never realized how small this kitchen was until now. I mean, isn't it crazy how we can't seem to both be in the kitchen without brushing up against each other? I never noticed that when you've been over here before."

"Small?" Aiden placed his hands on her hips and pulled her closer. "I think it's the perfect size."

"Hmmm...maybe you're right." Laurel leaned forward and kissed him.

He deepened the kiss as she wrapped her arms around his neck. Just as they were starting to get lost in each other, the timer startled them back to reality. Still in his embrace, she reached over and turned the timer off. Laurel smiled. "To be continued."

"Yes, to be continued." Aiden's voice sounded a bit husky— and very sexy.

"Do you know what else I discovered about this kitchen?" Laurel drained the pasta and tossed it with the sauce.

"No, please tell me." Aiden handed her the bowls and their hands touched.

"It seems to be hotter in here all of a sudden," Laurel said. "Have you noticed?"

Aiden leaned in close and whispered in her ear, "Yes, it is definitely hotter in here."

"Stop that now!" Laurel laughed as she gently pushed him away.

"Okay, but technically, you started it. You kissed me." Aiden picked up their wineglasses and carried them out to the deck, throwing a grin over his shoulder.

Laurel giggled as she carried the bowls outside. Sitting down, she said, "Yes, I did. I couldn't help myself."

"I think you actually did 'help' yourself." Aiden winked as he raised his wineglass to toast.

Laurel raised her glass and clinked it to Aiden's. "Touché."

"Oh, and please feel free to help yourself anytime you want." Aiden took a bite of pasta.

"I'll keep that in mind."

"Wow, this pasta is delicious. You know what they say, 'the way to a man's heart...'"

"Is that so? Well, you've had a few meals here, so perhaps that was my ploy all along."

Aiden reached over, taking Laurel's hand and lifting it to his mouth to place soft kisses on it. "Then your ploy worked."

They were both quiet for a few minutes while they ate their dinner. Laurel lifted a fork full of pasta and brought it to Aiden's mouth. His lips parted, and he took the bite of food, watching Laurel as she lowered her fork to her bowl.

Aiden followed suit by feeding Laurel a bite of his pasta. Laurel took a sip of wine while she looked into Aiden's eyes. His eyes held hers as his smile seemed to convey words he hadn't spoken aloud.

They carried their dishes into the kitchen and Laurel loaded the dishwasher while Aiden took Sophie outside for a break. Laurel refilled their wineglasses.

When Aiden and Sophie walked back in the door, Laurel locked the door behind them. She turned off the lights and turned to Aiden. Without saying a word, she picked up her glass and handed Aiden his glass. Then she reached out, took his hand, and led him upstairs.

LAUREL AWOKE HOURS LATER, NESTLED IN AIDEN'S arms. As she opened her eyes, she found him smiling as he looked at her.

"Hi," she whispered.

"Hello, beautiful." He caressed her arm.

"How are you?" Her fingers trailed across his chest.

"Wonderful. How about you?"

"Well, that was an amazing night. You were amazing."

"Look who's talking. You are an incredible woman."

Laurel reached up and kissed Aiden. He pulled her closer. To Laurel, being in his arms felt like a little haven. Snuggled together, they alternated between talking and kissing. Both drifted off to sleep until the sunlight peeked through the window.

They woke in each other's arms, and Laurel couldn't believe

how this all felt so perfect, so comfortable—but in a *this is where we belong* sort of way.

Laurel took a shower while Aiden went downstairs, made coffee, and let Sophie outside. It seemed like the most natural thing to walk into the kitchen and have Aiden hand her a cup of coffee. They worked together in the kitchen, cutting up fruit to have with the homemade blueberry muffins.

Eating breakfast, they talked about the day ahead and what each of them had going on. Laurel would be spending the day in the studio, working on Hettie's order. Aiden had a remodel job in Willow. They lingered at the door saying goodbye, not able or wanting to stop kissing each other. Then Aiden and Sophie walked across the yard and disappeared around the corner of the house.

Laurel sighed as images of their night together filled her mind. *Wow, I'm falling hard for him.* As she prepared for her day, she couldn't help wondering where this was all heading with Aiden. *Is this what true love feels like?*

Seventeen

L aurel spent the day in the studio, her playlist blasting away with her singing along. A smile was planted on her face. Her thoughts kept wandering back to last night. Memories of making love with Aiden were fresh in her mind. Why did it feel so easy with him? It had always been easy with Aiden. Ever since they met, their friendship just flowed. She had never felt this way before—just completely comfortable with herself, not trying to be someone else to impress or attract Aiden.

She wasn't—well, hadn't been—looking for another relationship. The past couple of months getting to know Aiden had built a strong friendship. He had been there when she needed him. They made each other laugh. Maybe that was what was different. She, for once, was staying true to herself. And Aiden liked her just the way she was.

He sent her a quick text while he was having lunch to ask her out for dinner.

> Of course, looking forward to it.

Aiden arrived at Laurel's front door with a bouquet of flowers.

"Wow, thank you. They're beautiful."

"Not as beautiful as you." Aiden captured Laurel in his arms and kissed her with a gentle longing. "I missed you."

"That was some kiss. I missed you too."

"Shall we go? I made a reservation at Flaherty's."

"I've heard great things about that place. I'm ready when you are."

Flaherty's was a family-owned restaurant that had been a local favorite for as long as Laurel could remember. Strangely enough, she had never been there.

Aiden held the door for her, and the hostess led them to a lovely table tucked in the corner. The lighting was soft and accompanied by candlelight at each table. The crisp, white table-cloth was topped with a slender vase holding wildflowers. The table setting was elegant, but not pretentious.

Once the waiter took their orders, Aiden reached over and took Laurel's hand in his. He gently rubbed his thumb along her hand, and she lifted her eyes to his.

"This is nice. Thank you," Laurel said.

"You deserve it."

"I do? Why is that?"

"Well, I've heard that you have this very needy neighbor who keeps mooching meals off you. Seems to eat more at your house than he does at his."

"Ah, yes, him. Well, he's not all bad."

"He isn't, huh?"

"No, but he certainly has an appetite." Her eyes sparkled with mischief.

"Oh, you haven't seen anything yet." He took her hand to his mouth and placed several kisses on it. He would have continued if the waiter hadn't brought their starters.

Laurel giggled as she moved her hand back. "Is that a promise?"

"Yes, it is."

"I look forward to it."

They talked about anything and everything over dinner, just like they did at her house. Dinner was wonderful, and they shared a crème brûlée for dessert, along with coffee. When they weren't holding a coffee cup or a spoon, they were holding hands.

As they walked outside, Aiden stopped and pulled Laurel into his arms, gently kissing her. His lips tasted sweet, like the crème brûlée. "I've waited long enough to kiss you. That seemed like the longest dinner ever."

Laurel laughed and kissed him again. "What did I say about that appetite of yours?"

Pulling her closer, he lifted her chin with his finger and looked longingly into her eyes. "Hmm, it seems to me you have the same appetite."

"I think you'll have to wait to find out." She took his hand and walked to the truck.

THE NEXT DAY, LAUREL VIDEO CALLED MAGGIE TO TELL her the news.

"So, y'know how I said I was swearing off men?"

"Yes, I believe you said that several times. So, who is it? Tell me everything." Maggie settled in a chair for the chat.

"Well, I've told you about Aiden, who bought the place next door. He rebuilt the studio for me."

"Yessssssssssssss," Maggie urged her on.

"We've spent a lot of time together and, well, y'know one thing led to another and dot, dot, dot..."

"Dot, dot, dot. That's all you're going to tell me?!"

Laughing at Maggie's question, Laurel replied, "It just started a couple of days ago, but I have to admit it feels so right. We've been friends for a couple of months, and he's seen me at some of my worst moments, but that didn't scare him off. I wasn't looking for anything, so I, for maybe the first time, wasn't trying to be what I thought the guy wanted. You know what I mean? I was just me, and that's who he likes."

"Aw, Laurel, what's not to like? You're such an amazing person. I am so thrilled for you."

"Thank you. You know, what I've really noticed is how much he makes me laugh. I feel like I haven't laughed this much in ages."

"That's wonderful. You deserve all the happiness the world has to offer. Remember that."

"Thanks. I can't wait for you to meet him."

"Me either. I'll have to see what my schedule looks like."

LAUREL AND AIDEN FELL INTO AN EASY ROUTINE, working during the day and spending most evenings together. Laurel was busy with finishing Hettie's order. So, many nights she took a break to have dinner with Aiden, but then went back to the studio for a few more hours.

Her hard work paid off, and she finished the order two days before her promised delivery date. She carefully packed up the pieces and loaded her SUV. Driving to Hettie's, she couldn't help but feel proud of what she had just accomplished. *Look, Mom and Dad, I did it. I'm doing it. Finally. Wish you were here to celebrate with me.*

Hettie greeted her with a hug and was just as excited about seeing the pieces as Laurel was about to show her. They unloaded the boxes from the car and placed them on the large kitchen island and table.

Hettie stood back and looked at Laurel. "Well, which one should we open first?"

Laurel pointed to the largest box on the island.

Hettie was like a child at Christmas—well, except that she knew there was something fragile in the box, so she took great care in opening it. She hadn't even lifted the centerpiece bowl out of the box before she gasped, and a tear escaped her eye.

Lifting it out carefully with Laurel's help, Hettie said, "Oh Laurel, this is absolutely beautiful. You are so talented. I love it."

She carefully carried it into the dining room and placed it on the long sideboard. Standing back, she smiled and gave Laurel a big hug. "It's perfect."

"I'm so glad you like it. It looks perfect there," Laurel said. "Now, let's go open the other boxes."

Hettie loved all the pieces. She and Laurel unpacked everything and then spent an hour or so distributing the pottery throughout the bed-and-breakfast. Laurel helped Hettie install the new wall plates in the guest bedrooms. They both agreed that they gave a perfect touch to each room.

"How about some lemonade in the garden while I cut some fresh flowers for the new vases?" Hettie asked as they headed downstairs.

"That would be lovely. Thank you. I would like to take some photos of the vases with flowers to add to the other photos that I've taken. Hopefully adding those to my website and social media will bring more customers."

Hettie brought the lemonade outside and set about cutting some flowers.

"Hettie, you've truly transformed this place. I can't believe the change since I was here last. Have you started taking bookings yet?"

"Thank you. It's amazing what a bit of paint and new decor will do. Yes, I have bookings starting this weekend, and I'm having a little gathering this Thursday evening before the craziness starts. I hope you can attend. There will be friends and family, but also many people from the business community. I even have the local newspaper, *Lake Life*, coming out."

"Oh, that's sounds amazing. Of course, I would love to attend. Thank you."

"Feel free to bring someone, if you'd like."

"Thank you. I just might do that."

Hettie filled the vases, and Laurel took plenty of photos. Everything looked perfect. Laurel was proud of her first order.

"Well, I had better get going," Laurel said.

"Yes, of course. Thank you so much for everything, dear. I am thrilled with the pieces," Hettie said as they walked to the front door. "Just a moment."

Hettie walked into the office and quickly returned with a check for Laurel's work. She handed it to Laurel. "You are very talented. I think this is the beginning of your success. Thank you again."

Laurel did her best to act professionally as she took the check from Hettie and slipped it into her bag. She really wanted to jump up and down, but that would have to wait.

"Thank you so much. I'll see you Thursday."

"Great. See you then. Bye," Hettie said, as Laurel walked to her car and drove away.

Laurel drove down the street, and when she was sure she was out of sight, she pulled over and put the car in park. First, she sent a text to Maggie because she was her loudest cheerleader. She would have called, but she knew Maggie was at a function and wouldn't be able to take the call.

Then she called Aiden and told him the news.

"Oh baby, congratulations! Of course, Hettie loved them. Your pieces were beautiful. I'm so proud of you."

Laurel's cheeks hurt from smiling so much. "Thank you! I feel on top of the world right now."

"Listen, how about we celebrate tonight? I can grill some steaks, and we can open a very nice bottle of wine."

"Sounds perfect. See you later."

When Aiden arrived that evening, he greeted Laurel by wrapping her in his arms and swinging her around. This started both of them laughing.

"Congratulations! I really am so proud of you, Laurel," he

said as he stopped spinning her. "I know you've had some hurtles to cross, but you did just that."

"Thank you. It's a bit surreal, thinking back over the past eight months. A year ago, I had no idea how much my life was going to change. Losing my mom. Leaving my old life behind and pursuing this long-lost dream of mine. So much happened to lead up to this point."

Aiden leaned down and kissed her. "I bet you wish your mom and dad were here to cheer you on."

"Yes, I do. I miss them so much." Laurel's eyes got misty for a moment, but she managed to blink away the tears. "I do know that they're here in spirit every day, which helps."

"You persevered through all that life has thrown at you this past year. Look at where you are now. You are an amazing woman."

"I'm thinking you might be a bit biased, now. Thank you for being here to help me celebrate."

"I can't think of anywhere else I would rather be."

Laurel kissed Aiden and whispered, "Me either. Thank you for being so supportive. I'll be honest. I'm not used to that in a relationship."

Aiden pulled her closer and whispered in her ear, "Baby, I am not Graham or anyone else from your past."

"I know. You're so different from anyone I've dated before. It's still so new for me. I'm sorry."

"Hey, there's nothing to be sorry for. You are completely different from any woman I've dated. We both deserve better, and I think we've found it."

"Me too. So, let's get this celebration going. I bought some Spanish cava on the way home. Maggie—oh, I can't wait for you to meet her—anyway, she and her husband love Spain, and she's always turning me on to their wines and cava."

"Sounds great." Aiden opened the cupboard for glasses. "I've been to Spain a couple of times. I know why they love it."

"You have? Oh wow. It's on my bucket list. Someday."

"Well, I say we make that happen. Tell me what else is on your bucket list. I want to make all your dreams come true." Aiden poured the cava and handed her a glass.

Laurel couldn't help herself from blushing. "Oh, believe me. You have already."

Aiden threw his head back, laughing. "Dreams or fantasies?"

"Oh, yes, sorry. I was thinking of something else."

Laurel leaned against the counter, lifting the cava to her lips. She looked up at Aiden, who smiled and sipped his cava.

"What is it?" he asked.

"This all just seems so right. Us."

"It is right. I think we were supposed to meet and fall in love. This is meant to be." He kissed her gently and stood back.

"These feelings are so strong. I'm a little scared of how good it is. I don't want it to change between us."

Aiden took her cava glass and placed it along with his on the counter. He pulled Laurel into his arms and lifted her chin with his finger. "Laurel, I love you."

Laurel's mouth fell open in surprise.

Aiden continued, "I have never felt this way about anyone before. We were meant to be. I believe that with my whole heart."

Laurel smiled as a single tear found its way down her cheek. "I love you too. It's as if you were put in my life right when I needed you, although I didn't know it at the time. I sure am glad you're here."

"Me too," he said, sealing it with a kiss full of promise.

They clinked their cava glasses together. "To us," they said in unison, which made them both smile.

The moment was interrupted by the sound of a stomach grumbling. Laurel burst into giggles as Aiden looked at her.

"What? I can't help it. I'm hungry. Someone promised a grilled steak."

Aiden laughed. "Laurel, did you eat lunch today?"

"Um, well, come to think of it...no, I didn't."

"Why not?" Aiden opened the fridge and pulled out some

cheese and grapes. He sliced a couple of pieces of cheese and placed them on a plate, along with a few crackers and the grapes, while she answered his question.

"Well, I meant to. I just didn't get around to it. I guess the day just got away from me with delivering Hettie's order. Then I was too excited when I got home to even think about food." She stuffed a piece of cheese and cracker into her mouth. "Oh, that tastes good."

Aiden shook his head at her and laughed. "What am I going to do with you?"

"I'll tell you later." Laurel winked. "Now, let me get a salad made. Do you want to throw a couple potatoes on the barbecue?"

Aiden was one step ahead of her. He had washed and pricked two potatoes with a fork and was wrapping them in foil by the time Laurel finished her question.

"Wow, you're pretty handy in the kitchen," Laurel said when she noticed what he had been doing while she was pulling veggies out for a salad. "I think I might keep you."

"That seems only fair. I'm keeping you because of your au gratin potatoes."

In unison, they said, "The way to a man's heart..."

Laughter filled the kitchen as they prepared dinner and talked about their days. Laurel loved this feeling of having a partner who was interested in what she thought and how her day affected her.

Over dinner, they toasted to her, delivering her order to Hettie. Laurel showed Aiden the photos she had taken, and they picked out a few for her website and social media.

"Oh, by the way, Hettie said I could bring someone to her party on Thursday. Would you like to go?"

"Sweetheart, I wouldn't miss it for anything. I want to see all your pieces on display."

"Do I really deserve you?" Laurel squeezed his hand and looked into his deep blue eyes.

"Baby, I'm just me. You deserve all the happiness in the world. I just hope I'm the one to help make that happen."

Fighting back tears, Laurel said, "Thank you. I hope that I'm the one to bring you all the happiness as well."

THE CELEBRATION WAS IN FULL SWING WHEN LAUREL and Aiden arrived. There were a lot of familiar faces, and Hettie introduced Laurel to everyone. Hettie sang Laurel's praises to the point that Laurel was blushing.

The reporter from *Lake Life* newspaper even asked for Laurel's contact information for the article. It seemed that when he interviewed Hettie and she gave him a tour, she had been intentional to highlight Laurel's pottery. Since the newspaper was about all things local, the reporter wanted to be sure he had Laurel's information.

Cassie was the first of the ladies to see Laurel and Aiden officially together. By the smile on her face when she greeted them both, she approved of their relationship.

"Laurel, your pieces are gorgeous! They look amazing." Cassie gave her friend a hug.

"Thank you."

"Hi Aiden, how are you?" she asked as he gave her a hug.

Aiden lifted Laurel's hand to his mouth and kissed it. "Cassie, I'm great. Thanks to this beautiful lady. How are you?"

"Is Sean with you?" Laurel chimed in.

"Wow. You two look perfect together." Cassie smiled. "I'm great. Busy with Brady Tech and, well, life is good. Sean should be here shortly. He had an overseas call that was running late."

Laurel winked at her friend. "Good. We were hoping you would both be here."

Lena and Hank were the next to arrive. Lena and Cassie smiled at each other and nodded.

Laurel caught the look they exchanged and laughed. "Okay, you two. Enough with the knowing looks."

"Aw Laurel, we're happy for you. And Aiden."

"The amazing Aiden." Lena smiled.

"I don't know about that. I just go by Aiden." He laughed.

"Well, the way you've helped Laurel with rebuilding her studio..." Lena clapped Aiden on the arm. "I think you are amazing. And thank you."

"No thanks is necessary. To be honest, I would do anything for Laurel." He wrapped his arm around Laurel's lower back.

"I see." Lena winked at Laurel. "By the look of her smile and the way she keeps looking at you, Aiden, I think that feeling is mutual." Lena reached over and hugged Laurel. "I'm very happy for you guys."

Beaming, Laurel said, "Thank you."

Brad, Bailey, Holly, and Joy crossed the room to join them.

"Great to see you guys." Bailey winked at Laurel, who was still wrapped in Aiden's embrace.

"Aiden seems like you're the center of attention. Would you lovely ladies mind if I tear him away to talk about a renovation project?" Hank asked.

Laughing, Laurel said, "I guess that would be okay."

Hank, Aiden, and Brad became engrossed in a discussion about some reno project Lena and Hank wanted to do at the winery. This gave Laurel's friends time to grill her for information.

"So, tell us everything. Okay, not everything. This looks like something pretty special." Bailey sipped her wine.

"By the looks of things, he's helped you with more than rebuilding your studio." Lena winked.

Cassie interjected, "I think what we're trying to say is that we're all super happy for you and Aiden. That smile looks good on you."

"Yes, we're all happy for you, Laurel." Joy smiled as Holly hugged Laurel.

"Aw, thanks ladies. I can't describe how *right* this feels. It was so unexpected. I mean, I wasn't looking for another relationship

—especially this soon—but, well, one thing led to another." Laurel glanced over at Aiden.

"It's better when you aren't looking for it. When it happens naturally. You've got to know each other and build a friendship before starting a relationship. I always think that's a good basis for a great relationship." Lena rolled her eyes. "'Cause I am the relationship queen...which is why I am single."

Bailey bumped her shoulder against Lena's, "Well, looking at the way you and Hank carry on together, you might not be single for long."

"What are you talking about? No, not Hank and me. We work together. We're not relationship material."

"Methinks she doth protest too much." Cassie smirked at Lena.

"Enough, let's talk about something else. Like how amazing Laurel's pottery looks here." Lena diverted the conversation elsewhere.

The diversion worked, and suddenly they were all wandering from room to room, checking out the changes Hettie had made and, of course, Laurel's beautiful pottery. When they returned to the living room where they had left the guys, one look at Cassie's smile said that Sean had arrived. They had yet to take the next step towards becoming a couple, as Cassie was adamant about not mixing work with pleasure, but it seemed obvious to Laurel that it was destined to happen soon.

By the looks of the crowd at the B-and-B, Hettie had a lot of local support and reopening the doors would be welcomed. The party was a big success, and Laurel was thrilled her pottery was going to be part of such a beautiful place. Hettie had insisted that Laurel leave some business cards so Hettie could share them with her patrons.

As the party wound down, Laurel made her way to Hettie to say goodnight. Hettie wrapped her in a tight hug and thanked her for what seemed like the millionth time.

"Hettie, I'm the one who should be thanking you," Laurel

protested. "Your confidence in me has come at a crucial time, and I wish I could tell you how much that's meant to me."

"Don't doubt yourself, and don't doubt your talent, my dear," Hettie replied. "You have a bright future ahead of you. Oh, and I will be ordering more from you. Now, go enjoy the rest of your evening. We'll chat soon."

Laurel fought back the tears as she hugged Hettie again and said goodnight.

LAUREL UPDATED HER WEBSITE AND SOCIAL MEDIA with all the new pieces she had made for Hettie. The newspaper article had brought new followers to her sites, and she was hoping that might turn into more orders. A couple of weeks after the party, Joy told her that her display at the bookshop was getting more attention, too, and she would need replacement pieces. Joy also suggested that they add a bit more display space for her. Of course, Laurel jumped at the chance, and she worked on a few new items she thought would sell well in that location.

With the increase in traffic to her online store, Laurel was pleased when she started getting a few orders. She knew that she had a long way to go, but at least things were moving in the right direction.

Aiden was busy with his projects and gearing up to start the big renovation at the winery. Everything was going well for them both—especially their time spent together. As she sliced another finished piece from the wheel and placed it on the drying board, Laurel thought about how her horrible year had turned around. Of course, she was still grieving her mom, but she was finding her own strength and making a new life for herself.

Her phone rang just as she finished washing her hands.

"Hello? Laurel Hardiston."

"Well, hello beautiful! Sorry it's been so long," Tim's familiar, deep voice said.

"Oh my gosh! How are you? Where are you?"

"On the road, but I have to stop in Jackson. I wondered if you want to meet me for lunch."

Laurel looked at her watch and then down at what she was currently wearing. "Of course, I just need to change clothes. Where do you want to meet?"

His deep voice chuckled at the excitement in her voice. "How about Delaney's? They still have that nice outdoor dining, don't they?"

"Yes, they do. That's perfect. I'll be there in forty-five minutes, okay?"

"That's great. Looking forward to it."

"Me too. You're the last person I thought I would hear from today. See you soon."

She rushed inside and changed her clothes, thankful she had put makeup on earlier. Checking her face for any smears of clay, she brushed her hair and smiled in the mirror. "I can't wait to see him," she said aloud as she backed her car out of the garage.

AIDEN SHOOK HIS HEAD, CURSING AS THE HACKSAW blade snapped. He didn't have a spare with him, and he didn't have time for this. He needed to get to the hardware store and back quickly if he was going to finish this job today. Reluctantly, he hopped in his truck and pulled onto the road. Then, to add to his frustration, he missed the turn from his client's office to the hardware store, so he was stuck driving through the busy downtown area.

The car in front of him stopped abruptly, and Aiden slammed on the brakes. *What now?* It was one of those days where everything was taking longer than it should—the blade breaking, and now the lunchtime traffic. It was all trying his patience. He wasn't normally like this, but this job was important, and he wanted to finish it today, as he promised.

Waiting for the passengers to get out of the car stopped in front of him, Aiden saw someone out of the corner of his eye. It was Laurel. She had just crossed the street and was throwing herself into the arms of—some guy. The guy picked Laurel off her feet and swung her around as he hugged her close. Laurel was laughing and holding on for dear life. Finally, the guy put her down. It was obvious from the way they were looking at each other and laughing that they knew each other very well.

Aiden sat there, staring. Dumbfounded. *What the hell? Who is that? Was that Graham?* No, couldn't be. Laurel swore it was over between them. If not Graham, then who? He watched as they sat at a table—next to each other. Leaning into each other. Laughing. Laurel was glowing.

The car behind him honked its horn several times before Aiden realized he had stopped traffic. He slowly pulled away from the scene that was breaking his heart. *I can't believe this. Who is this guy? I thought what Laurel and I had—I mean, have—was solid.*

He didn't have a choice but to finish the run to the hardware store and return to the job site. What could he do? Go and confront Laurel at the restaurant in front of everyone? He couldn't do that.

Late that afternoon, Aiden shook his head in frustration knowing he wasn't going to get the job done that day. Since he had seen Laurel with that guy, he had struggled to keep his focus on the job and made several measuring mistakes. That just frustrated him, causing him to make more errors that delayed finishing even further. The client was very understanding, but Aiden was disappointed in himself. As he drove home in rush hour traffic, his mind was still on Laurel and the guy she had been with. Aiden's mind had run through all sorts of scenarios. Most of them assumed the worst. By the time he turned into his driveway, he was sure it was over between them. That's when he saw the extra car in Laurel's driveway.

Sophie greeted him like he had been gone for years instead of hours. She danced around his feet and ran to the back door. "Okay, girl. Hold on. I'm coming."

He opened the sliding door, and Sophie bolted out to do her business. Aiden set the mail on the table and went out to see what Sophie was up to.

What he saw was Laurel and the guy from earlier sitting on her dock. Her head was on his shoulder and his arm was wrapped protectively around her. Sophie ran to Laurel and Aiden cursed as he ran after her, not wanting to have to face what was happening.

"Sophie, come here, girl. Sophie. Stop."

Laurel turned at the sound of his voice.

Fumbling over his words, Aiden tried to apologize. "I'm sorry to interrupt. I didn't mean to—it's just that Sophie...I'll just grab Sophie and leave you two alone. Sorry."

Laurel stood and gave Sophie a quick pat on the head. "Hi. How was your day?" She walked to Aiden and reached for him, but he stood there, not making any move for her.

"You have company. I'll see you later."

"Aiden, what's wrong? Why are you acting this way?" Laurel grabbed his hand to stop him from leaving. "I want you to meet someone."

Aiden clenched his jaw, dreading what was to come. This was just getting worse.

Suddenly, the guy was in front of Aiden, holding out his hand. "Hi, I'm Tim. You must be Aiden. Laurel's told me so much about you."

Not wanting to appear rude, he shook Tim's hand. "Well, you have the advantage, then."

"Aiden, this is Tim. Maggie's brother."

All at once, it dawned on him. *How could I have been so stupid and non-trusting?* "Ah, Tim. Maggie's brother. Pleasure to meet you."

Tim's phone rang. "Sorry, I have to take this." At that, he walked up to the deck and sat there while chatting on the phone.

"Aiden, are you okay?" Laurel's eyes searched his. "You're acting a bit strange."

He swept Laurel into a kiss that took even his breath away. "I've been an idiot. Ever since I saw the two of you in Jackson, earlier today..." Aiden recounted the story to Laurel and all the stupid thoughts he'd had all afternoon. He'd known it couldn't have been true, but somehow his mind had gotten the better of him.

Laurel listened intently without saying a word.

"Laurel, can you please forgive me?" His eyes were shiny with tears. "I'm so sorry."

She looked down at the ground and then back into his eyes. Slowly, a smile started to show. "You have a vivid imagination; do you know that? Me and Tim? That's laughable."

"But if you saw the hug that I saw. He lifted you off your feet and swung you around. Looked pretty intense."

Laurel rolled her eyes. "Aiden, that's the way Tim has hugged me since we were kids. A big bear hug while swinging me around. I call him my dorky big brother, and he calls me his extra kid sister. We're family more than friends. Nothing else, okay?"

Aiden swept her up in his arms and kissed her again. "I love you, Laurel."

In between kissing him back, she said, "I love you too, Aiden. Are we okay, now?"

"Yes. Forever."

Tim stood watching them from the deck, having finished his call. "Hey, is it safe to come back down there?"

Aiden took Laurel's hand as they walked to the deck. "Hey man, sorry about that. Really, it's a pleasure to meet you."

"He saw our hug when we met in Jackson. Having no idea who you were, well, you can imagine." Laurel squeezed Aiden's hand.

Tim shook his head, looking down. When he looked up, he had a huge smile on his face. "Yeah, I can just imagine how that must have looked." He extended his hand to Aiden in apology.

"Sorry about that. Believe me, she's just a kid sister to me. You can have her!" He winked at Laurel.

"Thanks," Aiden replied, feeling sheepish yet relieved. "I'll keep her, if she'll have me."

"Well, now that everything is cleared up, how about we open a bottle of wine and order some takeaway?" Laurel asked as she headed to the kitchen.

They spent the evening telling stories about their childhood to Aiden. Aiden and Tim bonded over books they'd read, the places they'd traveled to, and most importantly how much they both loved Laurel.

"Where are you off to next?" Laurel asked.

"South of France for a couple of weeks. After that, it's Spain and Switzerland. Then back here."

"Wow, sounds great. Maggie and Martin are off to Spain again in a couple of months. One of these days I'll get there."

Aiden put his hand on her thigh. "I told you, we need to make that happen. We should start planning it."

"You really should, Laurel. Travel changes your perspective. You should go to Spain while Maggie and Martin are there. They can show you around." Tim looked at Aiden. "I think it's crazy that I met you before my sister did."

"I know. Really looking forward to meeting them."

Tim reached for his phone. "Let's take a photo and send it to her to make her jealous!"

They took a few photos and sent them to Maggie, who predictably texted back,

JEALOUS!

"Exactly the reaction I wanted from my sister." Tim laughed. "She doesn't know that I'm surprising her tomorrow. Martin and I have it all arranged."

"That's awesome, Tim." Laurel smiled at her dorky big brother. "It's so good to see you. Next time, you need to stay longer. You had talked about having some time on the lake, so you need to come back and do that."

He hugged her as they said goodnight at the door of the guest bedroom. "I will. I promise to block out time for a longer visit." He tilted his head to the master bedroom, where Aiden was waiting for Laurel. "You did good, kid. Aiden's a great guy. I'm happy for you."

"Thank you. He is great." She hugged him again. "Sleep well. See you in the morning. Love you."

"Love you too."

As Aiden held Laurel in his arms, they started making plans for that trip overseas. He wanted to show her the world, and he planned to do just that. After Laurel fell asleep, he laid there mulling over the one thing he still needed to tell her—the one thing that stood in the way of him being happy.

Eighteen

Aiden had been struggling with not telling his parents the truth. When he left his job and bought the house, he told them he was making some changes in his life. They were worried about him since he had changed so much with his finance job. He didn't tell them he was remodeling the house himself or that he was pursuing carpentry work. Aiden knew he had disappointed them with his old lifestyle, and even though he wanted to tell them he had changed, he wanted to prove to himself that he could do what his dad had taught him.

So, their relationship was still a bit strained. Their phone calls were short and cordial, but Aiden knew he was hurting them. The saving grace was that they had been on an extended trip, so he had had a bit of time. They had just returned home, and Aiden was thinking it was time to invite them to see his new home. Now that he had had a few paying jobs, and he had just signed a contract to remodel the tasting room and store of the winery, he felt more confident in telling them the truth.

Aiden smiled as he parked in his driveway. Of course, then there was Laurel. He wanted to introduce her to his parents. He was sure they would love her. Now all he had to do was talk to Laurel about it and see if she was ready to take that step with him.

They had a date to go swimming, and his plan was to talk to her about it when they finished.

That was the plan.

"Are you going to tell me what's bothering you?" Laurel asked after they had only been in the lake for ten minutes.

Treading water, Aiden tried to sound nonchalant. "What are you talking about? We're just having a swim. What could be bothering me?"

Laurel swam up to Aiden and placed her hands on his shoulders. "Aiden, come on. What is it? You're worrying me."

"Oh, I didn't mean to worry you. I just wanted to wait until after our swim to talk about it."

Laurel swam the short distance to the dock and climbed up the ladder. "I'm done swimming until you tell me what's wrong."

Aiden reached out to her as he climbed to the top of the ladder. "Hey, nothing is wrong. I just wanted to talk to you about something."

Laurel crossed her arms. "So, start talking."

Aiden grabbed their towels and wrapped one around Laurel's shoulders. "Well, I've been thinking of inviting my parents to town."

"And?"

"Well..." Aiden hesitated while messing with his towel. "I haven't told them what I'm doing here."

"What do you mean, you haven't told them what you are doing here?"

He led her to the Adirondack chairs. "Let's sit."

Once they were both sitting, he took her hand and began. "My relationship with my parents has not been good for many years. They were and still are very disappointed in me and the career path I took."

Laurel squeezed his hand. "I don't understand why. You said you were good at your job. Why would they be disappointed in you?"

"My dad was disappointed I didn't become a carpenter like him. Like he had taught me."

"That seems a bit harsh."

"Well, that's where it started, but once I became successful, I got sucked up in the lifestyle."

"Yes, you've mentioned a little about that. I can't imagine you being—well, not being who you are."

"I'm glad you can't imagine that person. Listen, I wasn't evil or anything like that. But my life and relationships were very superficial." Aiden lowered his head into his hands. "I was so caught up in the glamorous life, the vacations, the dinners at the finest restaurants, cocktails at the latest club. Doors being opened because of who I was and what I did. It was all so fake."

Laurel reached over and caressed his arm. "Okay, well, we all do things we aren't proud of in hindsight. Surely your parents now see that you've changed your life and are heading down a better path."

Aiden's reply was barely audible. "I haven't quite told them."

Laurel leaned in, as if she wasn't sure she heard him correctly. "What do you mean you haven't quite told them? What haven't you told them, Aiden?"

"I haven't told them about the carpentry. I just told them I was reevaluating my life and working out what job I wanted to pursue next."

"Why haven't you told them?"

Aiden looked out across the lake and took a deep breath. "Well, I wanted to prove to myself that I could make a living doing carpentry. I wanted to know I could do this before getting their hopes up. They were so disappointed in the person I'd become that I needed to show myself that I have indeed changed."

Laurel reached over and squeezed his hand. "Oh Aiden, I can't believe your parents wouldn't be proud of you. I don't know the person you were before, but I can certainly attest to the wonderful man you are now."

Aiden leaned over and kissed her. "Thank you. They've just

returned home from their trip, and I was thinking it was time to invite them for a visit."

"Oh, Aiden, I think that's great. I would love to meet them! Call them now." When Aiden made no move to grab his phone, she elbowed him. "Go on. No time like the present."

"You are very persistent; do you know that? Are you sure you're ready to meet the parents?"

"Thank you. Persistence pays off." Laurel winked at him. "Aiden, I want to meet your parents. Please, call them."

Aiden reached for his phone on the table, looking at Laurel smiling back at him, and dialed his mom's cell.

His mother answered on the second ring. "Aiden, hi dear. We were just talking about you. Is everything okay?"

"Hi Mom. Yes, everything is great. How are you and Dad?"

"Good, good. We had a great trip, but it's nice to be home. Now that we're home, we—"

"Mom, listen, I would like you and Dad to come visit and see the new house. I have a lot to tell you."

"You want us to visit? Lots to tell us? Are you sure everything is okay?" his mother asked, then seemed to pull the phone away from her mouth to call her husband. "Ed, it's Aiden. He has something to tell us, and he wants us to visit." His father's response was barely audible, but his mom said, "Aiden, honey, your father and I can be there the day after tomorrow. Will that be soon enough?"

Aiden gave a thumbs up to Laurel and smiled. "Yes, Mom, that's great. It's nothing urgent. Okay, I'll text you the address."

"Oh honey, I am so excited to see you. It's been too long. Yes, send the address. Should we book a hotel?"

"I'll book a room at the B-and-B in town. My guest room isn't quite ready. The B-and-B is wonderful; you'll love it."

They talked a bit longer before disconnecting. Aiden texted his address to his mom's cell before putting his phone down on the table.

"Well, that's done," Aiden said as he looked over at Laurel.

"They will be here the day after tomorrow. I need to call Hettie and book a room."

"Let's call her now. Make sure she has a room available," Laurel said.

Aiden called Hettie. She did have a room available, and she promised to make his parents very comfortable.

"Okay, I guess this is happening." Aiden smiled.

Laurel reached out and squeezed his hand. "I think they're going to love all your news. Your beautiful home after all the work you've done, your new contract at the winery—but more importantly, how you decided that the life you were living wasn't right for you and made the changes needed to turn that around."

"Well, when you put it like that, it sounds good. It is good." Aiden sighed and rubbed the back of his neck. "I really miss having my parents in my life. Hopefully this will put us back on track."

Laurel looked out across the lake and took a deep breath. "I completely understand that feeling. I'm sure this will change things with you and your parents."

Aiden caressed her arm as he leaned over and kissed her. "Baby, I'm so sorry. All this talk about my parents. This must be hard on you."

She shook her head. "No, believe me, it isn't talking about your parents that makes me miss mine. I do that every minute of every day. Some days or moments are harder than others, but I know my parents wouldn't want me to wallow in my grief and forget to live. So, to honor them, that's what I am trying to do."

Aiden kissed her again. "You are the most remarkable woman I have ever met. I'm so lucky to have you in my life."

"I'm pretty sure I'm the lucky one." Laurel closed her hand over his. "Now, your parents will be here the day after tomorrow. What do we need to do to get ready for their visit? Are there things you would like to do at the house, or any food we should prepare?"

Aiden paled as the short timeline dawned on him. "Oh jeez, I didn't think they would arrive so quickly. I guess I'd better make a list and a plan."

"Well, let's do that now." Laurel stood. "I'm going to go get out of this wet suit."

Aiden stood and gathered her in his arms. "Well, that gives me some ideas about how to spend this time."

He seemed to take her all in, in one seductive glance, but Laurel lifted his chin with her fingers to bring his focus to her eyes. "As much as I like the sound of that—and believe me, I do—I think we have other things we need to do first."

Aiden pulled her closer and whispered in her ear and made her blush. Gently kissing her on the mouth, he stepped back.

"Okay, well, I guess we'd better get started on this list."

Laurel, clearly flustered, said. "Um, yes. That's what we should do. I'll go get changed and meet you at your place, okay?"

Amused at the effect his words had on her, he looked at her seductively. "Have it your way. See you shortly."

With that, he gathered up the towels and took her hand as they walked across the yard and went to their separate homes.

THEY MADE A LIST OF WHAT NEEDED TO BE DONE AND mapped out a plan of attack. Aiden straightened up his tools and swept up the rooms where he was still remodeling while Laurel worked on making the house look homey. She darted back to her place and chose a few of her pottery pieces to add to the home, then returned to grab one of her tall vases and wander around her yard, cutting fresh flowers to add to it.

Aiden had finished the remodel of the kitchen, dining room, and living room. Only the bedrooms and bathrooms were still in disarray. Aiden had purchased a few pieces of furniture, too, so at least the living area was ready to welcome his parents.

After Laurel's touch, it looked like a welcoming home. She

placed the vase of fresh-cut flowers on the dining room table and stood back to survey the room.

Aiden walked up behind her and wrapped his arms around her waist. "Wow, Laurel, this all looks beautiful. Thank you."

"You're welcome. I just want it to look nice for your parents."

"You know they're going to take one look at this place now and know I have a wonderful woman in my life before I even get a chance to tell them, don't you?"

Laurel turned in his arms to face him. "So, have you thought about what you will say to them?"

"You mean the conversation that I've been rehearsing for weeks?" Aiden caressed her cheek with his thumb. "You know what I've been trying to tell myself all afternoon?"

"What?"

"These are my parents. We love each other, and what I'm going to tell them is all positive news. So, there is nothing to worry about. I just want our old relationship back, and I hope this heals us."

Laurel leaned in and kissed him. "I think it will. This is going to work out fine."

"Are you nervous about meeting them?"

"A little. I don't know why...what's not to love about me, right?" she asked, laughing.

"I love everything about you. I'm sure they will too."

"I love you too, Aiden. I hope you're right."

AIDEN'S PARENTS ARRIVED AT HIS HOUSE LATE IN THE morning. When he heard the car in the driveway, he took a deep breath. *Okay, let's do this.*

Both of his parents greeted him with hugs, and all three of them tried to talk at once as he led them inside. His parents poked around the house while Aiden got them some iced tea. His father was running his fingers across the wood, inspecting the workmanship as Aiden knew he would.

"This work is top-notch, Aiden. You hired the right guys," his dad said as he took a sip of the iced tea.

"Aiden, this kitchen is gorgeous," his mom praised. "I love this large window looking out with a view of the lake."

"Thank you both. Listen, let's sit down for a minute."

His mother touched his arm as she walked past to take a seat at the dining room table. "You're scaring me, Aiden. Are you okay?"

"Yes, Mom. For the first time in a very long time, I am."

"Please, son, tell us what's going on. We've both been worried about you since you told us you were reevaluating your life," his dad said.

"I resigned from my job a few months ago," he began.

"Oh, do you need money? I'm sure we can help you out." The look of concern deepening on his mom's face.

"No, Mom, thank you. I don't need any money. If that job was good for one thing, it was for me to earn and save a chunk of money. Listen, I know you both have been disappointed in me since I took that job."

"Son, we weren't disappointed that you took the job," his dad started as he looked over at his wife. "We were proud of you for everything you accomplished. But to be honest, it was the person you became that we were disappointed in."

Aiden looked down at his hands and then at each of his parents. "I'm disappointed in myself, too. I got sucked into that lifestyle and all the perks it offered and the doors it opened. I became a person that I despised. For that, I am truly sorry. I'm so sorry that I disappointed you."

"Honey, why don't you tell us what else is happening?" his mom suggested. "You left your job, bought a house, and now what?"

Aiden smiled. "The rest is all good news, so please relax. Dad, do you remember that comment you made about me hiring the right guy to do the remodel?"

"Yes." His dad looked around the room. "Why?"

"Well, that guy is me."

"What? You're remodeling your own home?" his mom chimed in.

"That and more. I've opened my own carpentry business. I am finally doing what you taught me all those years ago, Dad."

"What? Really?" His dad's voice caught. "Aiden, that's the best news. I mean, if this is truly what you want to do."

"It is, Dad. I always loved it when we worked together on projects. I love creating something and watching it go from concept to the finished product."

His mom stood and came around the table to hug him. "I love this idea, sweetheart."

"I do too." His dad also stood to hug Aiden.

Aiden opened his arms wide as his parents wrapped their arms around him. "Thank you, guys. I'm sorry things have been strained between us. I'm not proud of the person I was. I hope we can mend the fence between us."

"I think we all just did that, son."

"Sweetheart, we love you. Remember that." His mom gave him another hug.

"So, you've set up your own business and you've certainly been busy remodeling this place. What else have we missed while we've been away?"

"Dad, I've actually had a few small projects already, and more news...I just got a big reno job at the local winery."

His dad slapped him on the back. "That's my boy! So proud of you, son!"

"Thanks, Dad! This project is going to be amazing. I'm redoing the tasting area and the gift shop. I'll show you the plans later."

His mom stood at the side of the table, watching them interact. "I can't tell you two how much I love this. Family again."

Aiden gave his mom a big hug. "Me too, Mom. Me too."

"Now, I have some more news for you."

"More good news, we hope," his dad said.

"Yes, I think it's actually the best news," Aiden started. "I've met someone. Someone who has become an important part of my life."

His mom couldn't contain herself and she bombarded him with questions.

"Let the boy talk," said Dad, laughing.

"Well, her name is Laurel. She lives next door. We met shortly after I moved in here. Things have started getting serious between us."

Fidgeting, his mom asked, "We're going to meet her, aren't we?"

Laughing, Aiden said, "Yes, Mom. We're having dinner at her place tonight."

"How lovely. Now tell us more."

Aiden answered all his parents' questions. He told them so much that he couldn't believe they would have anything to ask her when they met Laurel. His mom loved her pottery in the house and couldn't wait to see more.

Aiden drove them into town for lunch at Lyman's Café. Holly and Joy both stopped by to say hello. "Aiden, isn't Laurel with you?" Joy asked.

"No, she's in Addington today," he answered. "She had a meeting with her lawyer and the real estate agent about her parents' house. We're having dinner with her tonight."

"We can't wait to meet her," his mom said.

Holly smiled at her. "You will love Laurel. She is such a sweetheart. She has been through so much recently, but she always has a smile for everyone."

Aiden sat back and looked at his parents as they waited for their lunch to arrive. He was feeling so much better about their relationship already.

When they had finished their lunch, Aiden drove them to the

B-and-B to check in. Aiden proudly pointed out Laurel's pottery, and of course Hettie chimed in.

"Oh, Laurel's pottery is just so beautiful. She's so talented," Hettie said as she showed them to their room. "These light switch wall plates were her idea. Each room has one that matches its decor. Isn't it beautiful?"

His mom ran her fingers over the wall plate. "Oh, honey, I think we need these in our house. Look how beautiful this is."

"Mom, I'm sure Laurel would make you some. We'll talk to her about it over dinner."

"Yes, dear, I think they would be great in our home. We'll talk to her tonight," his dad said.

Hettie showed them around the room and explained about the house and gardens. She told them breakfast was served in the sunroom overlooking the garden from seven to ten in the morning. She handed them their key and left them alone in the room, saying, "You let me know if there is anything you need."

"Thank you, we will."

Aiden sat in the overstuffed chair as his parents unpacked. They chatted about the B-and-B and how it was the big break Laurel needed. Aiden then told them about the tree falling on her studio when she had the pieces on the drying rack.

"Oh, how awful. What a story," his mom said.

"It was very scary. I heard the tree crash onto the studio and Laurel scream. I went running across the yard, thinking she was working in the studio. Thankfully, she had already stopped for the day. When I arrived, I found her standing on her deck. I was so relieved she wasn't inside."

His dad clapped a hand on Aiden's shoulder. "And let me guess, you repaired the studio for her."

"Yes, Dad, I did. The next day I picked up the lumber and by the end of the day it was finished. I was glad I could help."

"Aw, what a story, honey. Is that when this all started between you two?" his mom asked.

"No, it was awhile after that. Although, ever since we met,

there has been something between us. She is so down-to-earth and funny and an amazing cook, and as you've seen with her pottery, she's very talented."

His dad nudged his mom's shoulder. "Honey, our boy has it bad for this girl."

"It certainly sounds like it."

Aiden laughed. "You two are hilarious. Yes, I have it bad. I will admit that. Now, bring your swimsuits and whatever else you need, and let's go hang out by the lake until Laurel is back, okay?"

His parents gathered their things, and they all headed back to Aiden's house.

LAUREL ARRIVED HOME FROM HER MEETING WITH Frank, their family lawyer. She was grateful her mom had placed him in charge of her estate. Since he had been with them for years, he felt more like a family friend. He understood the emotional rollercoaster of grief and was sensitive to that.

She had mixed feelings about meeting Aiden's parents today. Talking with Frank brought all her raw emotions to the surface. She would much rather soak in a hot bath and curl up in bed with a good book, but the other part of her was excited about meeting Aiden's parents. She figured she had time for a quick swim before getting dinner prepped. She changed into her swimsuit, grabbed a towel, and headed down to the dock. She draped her towel over the Adirondack chair and climbed down the ladder into the water.

She floated on her back and looked up at the sky—a position that always made her feel small compared to the universe around her. Tears of grief leaked from the corners of her eyes. She took a few deep breaths before she turned over and swam some laps. Her cupped hands dug into the water as she focused on her strokes, and the tension in her shoulders eased as she swam.

After drying off, she walked up to the house and climbed the stairs to the bathroom. She took a hot shower and afterward felt like she could take on the world. Well, at least she felt up to meeting Aiden's parents. She slipped on a summer dress of cobalt blue. The dress was flattering, and the color complimented her eyes and her tan. She added a lapis heart necklace and earrings to complete the look. One last glance in the mirror and a deep breath, and she was ready.

She was in the kitchen when she received Aiden's message that they were back. They were going to have a swim and then join her.

> Of course, you are welcome to join us, but if I could guess, I would say you have been home, had a swim, a shower, and are now in the kitchen.

Aiden added a kissing emoji.

Laurel laughed as she read it. He knew her so well—and in such a short time. She typed,

> How do you know me so well? Yes, I had a swim, a shower, and am now in the kitchen, just like you said. I'll get things prepped and bring drinks down to the dock in a few.

> Have I told you lately that I love you? If not, I love you, Laurel. See you soon.

> I love you too.

LAUREL PUT THE DRINKS AND APPETIZERS ON THE TRAY. She took a quick look in the mirror in the bathroom to make sure she didn't have any food smudged on her face from prepping dinner. She straightened her shoulders and said aloud, "Let's go meet the parents."

Laurel walked down to the dock and set the tray on the table.

Aiden and his parents were all floating on their backs, chatting away. None of them had seen her arrive.

"Well, hello everyone!" Laurel said, which caused quite a commotion of splashing as they all tried to turn over and face her. This sent Laurel into a fit of giggles.

"Mom, Dad, this is Laurel." Aiden made his way over to the swim ladder. "Laurel, these are my parents, Jean and Ed." Aiden leaned in and kissed Laurel as she handed him a towel.

"Hi, it's so wonderful to meet you both," she said as they climbed the ladder, and she handed them each a towel.

"Laurel, it's such a pleasure to meet you. Aiden has told us so much about you," Jean said.

Ed thanked her for the towel. "Laurel, great to meet you."

"I didn't mean to interrupt your swimming. I did bring some drinks and appetizers, if you're ready."

"That is so sweet of you. Thank you," Jean said. "This has been such a wonderful day, hasn't it, Ed?"

Ed made his way to the tray of drinks and grabbed a beer, taking a sip before raising the bottle in a toast. "Yes, it has. Aiden, it's so wonderful to have the real you back again, son. We've missed you."

"Yes, we have, dear," Jean said.

"Thanks, Mom and Dad. I've missed you guys too. Sorry I messed things up."

"I'm so glad you've patched things up. Aiden has been quite stressed about it," Laurel said.

"Well, it's all behind us now." Ed continued, "Now, Laurel, tell us all about yourself."

"Gosh, Dad, nothing like putting her on the spot," Aiden teased.

Laughing, Laurel started her story with her birth and told of her accomplishments of being able to ride her bike without training wheels by the time she was ten. "Just kidding, I was actually nine, going on ten."

"See, I told you she was amazing, didn't I?" Aiden asked his parents.

They chatted and enjoyed the food and drinks.

"Laurel, I love your pottery," Jean said after a while. "Is it possible to buy a few pieces before we head back home?"

"Oh, thank you. Of course. I have pieces in my studio that are available."

"Great. Why don't we go get cleaned up, Ed, and then we can have a look?"

"I put some towels in the master bath for you guys," Aiden said. "I'll help Laurel take these things back to her house and see you in a few minutes."

"We can take a hint, dear. You want to be alone." His mom squeezed his arm as she walked past him.

When his parents reached the sliding door, Sophie was sitting there. "Honey, can we let her out?"

"Sure, she'll run over here to see her buddy, Socks."

Sure enough, as soon as they opened the door and Aiden whistled for Sophie, she came running over, looking for Socks. Laurel opened the French doors, and the two friends greeted each other.

Aiden and Laurel walked into the kitchen, and she put the tray on the counter.

"Well, it looks like your talk with your parents went well. How do you feel about it?"

"It did go well, and I feel like I wasted time not being honest with them earlier." Aiden sighed. "But it's done now, and the rest of the day has been great. Like old times."

Laurel wrapped her arms around Aiden's waist and kissed him. "I'm so glad everything is better between you guys. They seem really nice. I like them."

"And they like you. Of course, Hettie, Holly, and Joy all sang your praises on the 'we love Laurel' chorus, so my parents probably fell in love with you before they met you."

"Well, that's good to know. Now I don't need to be nervous about making them dinner tonight."

"They will also fall in love with your cooking, just like I have." Aiden kissed her. "Now, tell me about your meeting with Frank. How are you?"

Laurel looked down and then looked up into Aiden's eyes. She took a deep breath before she replied. "Frank is great. He has such patience with me. Everything is good. There is another open house for my parents' house this weekend, so we'll see if we get some good offers. Frank went over what that process will be like for me, so I know what to expect. He was also able to sell my mom's car, so that's another thing done." Laurel sighed. "I'm so glad that my mom thought to set all of this up with Frank, because I have no idea how I would be handling all of this without him."

Aiden tightened his arms around her waist and kissed the top of her head. "I'm so sorry you have to go through all of this. But I agree. I'm glad your mom had the wherewithal to plan things with Frank. He sounds like he's taking good care of you and the estate. If there's anything that I can do to help, I'm here for you, Baby."

"Thank you. Don't worry, when I fall into a crying heap of a mess, your arms are the ones I want to crawl into."

"Anytime. I'm always here for you."

Laurel stood straighter and smiled. "Okay, why don't you go get changed and I'll see you all back here in a little bit. You can leave Sophie here."

"Okay, we won't be long. You had better get a big box ready, because I think my mom is going to buy a lot of your pottery."

Laughing, Laurel said, "That sounds great to me."

A SHORT TIME LATER, THEY WERE ALL IN THE STUDIO, looking at Laurel's pottery. She and Jean talked about the colors in Jean and Ed's home and what would match well. Ed encouraged Jean to buy anything she wanted.

Aiden just stood back and watched their interaction. He smiled as his parents bought a dozen pieces from Laurel.

Laurel was over the moon and felt they were being too kind.

Jean gave Laurel a side hug. "No, I've just become one of your biggest fans, dear."

"Thank you! I really appreciate that. I will get these boxed up in the morning for you." Laurel clapped her hands together, beaming. "Now, is anyone hungry?"

Ed's stomach growled as if on cue.

Aiden laughed. "Well, there's something that hasn't changed. Dad is always hungry."

Jean took Ed's hand as they walked up to the house. "You're right Aiden, he is always hungry."

"Well, we have plenty to eat, so if he's hungry after this meal, then it's his own fault," Laurel teased as she walked into the kitchen. "Aiden, can you take care of—"

Aiden reached around her to pick up the corkscrew. "Already on it." He kissed her before moving to the cabinet with the wineglasses.

"Thank you. I just need to put the water on for the pasta."

Jean asked, "What can we do to help, dear?"

"You two can sit and relax. Everything is prepped, so it won't take too long."

"Red or white?" Aiden asked his parents, then popped his head into the kitchen. "And Laurel, red for you?"

Over dinner, Ed started telling his many "Dad jokes," and to Aiden's surprise, not only did Laurel laugh at all of them, but she told her Dad's "Dad jokes." Ed and Laurel were in fits of laughter throughout the meal.

Aiden leaned over to his mom and whispered, "I can't believe this. No one laughs at Dad's jokes."

"I know! I think you may have found a keeper in Laurel."

"I think I have, Mom." Aiden smiled.

THEY STOOD IN THE DRIVEWAY HOLDING HANDS AND waving until his parents' car was out of sight. The time had passed so quickly, but they promised to return for a visit soon.

"I really like your parents," Laurel said. "Your mom is so sweet, and your dad is hilarious."

Aiden lifted her hand to his mouth and kissed it. "They think the world of you. And my dad is thrilled that you share his warped sense of humor."

"The best part of the visit was that you and your parents talked things out. I'm so happy about that."

"Me too. I've missed having a close relationship with them for so many years. Now that's all in the past," he said as they walked inside and were greeted by Sophie.

Laurel bent down to cuddle Sophie, who acted like she hadn't been smothered with attention for the past several days. "I know, I know. You haven't had any cuddles in so long. I know. You are so abused."

Aiden rolled his eyes. "No, she hasn't had any attention at all. Poor baby."

Laurel stood. "Listen, I had better go get some work done. I have some orders to fill. And your mom, thankfully, bought a lot of my stock, so I need to get to work creating new pieces."

"No problem. I'm going to work on this place for a few hours, and then I have a meeting with Lena this afternoon to go over a few ideas for the winery." Aiden walked her to the sliding door and opened it for Sophie. "Hey, did Maggie and Martin pick a date to come visit yet?"

"I'm not sure, but I'm going to call her today. She'll be wondering how the 'meet the parents' event went. I'll ask her then."

Aiden kissed Laurel and watched as she walked down the stairs and across the yard. She turned around and smiled at him. "Tell Lena I said hi. See you later."

"Will do. Dinner tonight?"

"Of course."

Aiden leaned against the wall and sighed. He was relieved that he and his parents had smoothed things out between them. Though he knew how much it had played on his mind, he was still surprised a weight had been lifted off his shoulders. He was thrilled Laurel and his parents got along so well. He'd thought they would, but it was better than he had hoped.

"Now I'm ready for what the future has to offer." He smiled as he got ready for his day.

Nineteen

"**W**ell, how did the visit with Aiden's parents go?" Maggie asked.

"It actually went great." Laurel tapped the speakerphone function so she could finish a sketch in her notebook. "They are both very sweet, and we really seemed to hit it off. They were only in town a couple of days, but they'll be back. I'm so glad Aiden and his parents have patched things up."

"Aw, that's wonderful. I can't believe you met his parents, and we haven't even met him yet."

"I know! And Tim has already met him. When are you two coming? Have you figured out your schedule yet? Summer is almost over, and you haven't been here once. You always come to the lake in the summer."

"Get that guest room ready. We're coming next weekend. If that works for you guys."

"*Yes!* Of course. I'm so excited. I miss you, and I haven't seen Martin in so long. How long will you be able to stay?"

"We're planning five days. Is that okay with you?"

"Of course. That's great."

"Don't worry, Martin and I will be working remotely, so we won't interfere with your work schedule."

"I'm not worried. I'm my own boss now, so if my friends come to town, then I can adjust my schedule to spend time with them."

Maggie laughed. "You sound good. Confident. Happy."

"Thank you. I'm feeling pretty good." She picked up a photo of her parents from the coffee table. They were sitting on the dock, laughing. Happier times. She smiled. "I still have times where the grief overwhelms me. But I remember that from losing Dad. The tiniest thing can trigger me, and the tears start falling."

"Yes, that's exactly what happens. You just have to go with the feelings when they hit you."

"Yup. One day at a time." Laurel sighed. "On a good note, I just got another big order. Not as big as Hettie's, but multiple pieces for a florist in town. They want to sell my vases in different sizes in their shop. If it goes well, it will be an ongoing order."

"Congrats! That's great! I'm so proud of you. You've really made your dream a reality."

"Thanks. Some days, I still can't believe how far I've come over these past several months. It's been a complete life change."

"It is pretty crazy how much our lives can change in a short period of time."

"I know. I'm so glad I took the leap."

"I am too." Maggie paused. "Listen, I have to run. I have a meeting with my editor. She has the first run-through done on my book. Wish me luck."

"Good luck! Although, I'm sure you don't need it. Can't wait to see you guys."

"Me too. I'll text you later and let you know how brutal the edit was."

"Ha, ha, I'm sure it will be fine. Love you."

"Love you too."

After Laurel disconnected from the call, she put her phone on Do Not Disturb and headed out to the studio. She couldn't wait to see Maggie and Martin, and thoughts of their incoming visit comforted her as she prepped the clay and got to work.

LAUREL AND AIDEN WERE SITTING ON THE DECK watching Sophie and Socks chase each other around the yard when a car drove up.

"Finally! Now you get to meet my oldest and bestest friend," Laurel said as she and Aiden walked around the house to greet them.

Laurel and Maggie squealed with excitement when they saw each other. Martin greeted Aiden while the ladies were hugging.

"Nice to finally meet you," Martin said, shaking Aiden's hand.

"Great to meet you as well. Laurel has told me so much about you two."

"And as you can imagine, she has told Maggie all about you."

Laurel introduced Maggie, who wasn't one to shake hands. She hugged Aiden as she greeted him. "So great to meet the guy who's made my best friend so happy."

Aiden winked at Laurel. "Thank you. Great to meet you as well. Are all the stories Laurel told me about you true?"

"What?" Maggie gave Laurel a side-eye look. "Whatever stories she told you about me, I have stories about her. We need to talk."

Laughing, Aiden said, "Oh, I can't wait to hear those."

"Hey, you two. That's enough." Laurel laughed.

"Martin, let me help you with your bags." Aiden walked around to the back of the car.

They put their things in the guest room and Laurel said, "You guys get settled and we'll get some snacks and meet you on the deck. Make yourselves at home."

"Thanks." Maggie dropped her purse on the armchair. "We'll just unpack and freshen up. See you in a few minutes."

Aiden and Laurel loaded two trays with food and drinks and took them outside to the deck. Aiden opened the large umbrella to give them some shade. Sophie and Socks were curled up together in one of the chairs, having worn each other out by running around.

When Martin and Maggie came outside, Martin pointed towards the studio. "Listen, before we enjoy this feast, I would love to see your studio. I've heard so much about it."

Laurel grabbed Martin's hand and practically dragged him to the studio. Aiden and Maggie followed behind. When Laurel opened the door, there was no denying that Martin was impressed.

"Wow, you really transformed this space. It's amazing." Martin walked around. "So, this is where the magic happens." He turned and looked at Laurel. "I am so proud of you. You've been through a lot, but you have risen above it and made a great new life for yourself."

Laurel wrapped him in a hug. "Thank you, Martin. You and Maggie have been so instrumental in this, and I couldn't have done it without you. I'm glad you finally got here to see it in person."

He hugged her back, and then he and Maggie perused the finished pieces on the shelves. "You know we're going to buy several pieces before we leave," Maggie said to Laurel over her shoulder.

"No buying for you. You can choose anything you want," Laurel said, standing next to Maggie.

"We'll argue about that later," Martin decided aloud, as if to fend off the impending, good-natured conflict.

"Aiden, you did a great job repairing this after the tree crashed into it," Maggie said, looking around.

"Thanks. I'm glad I was able to help." Aiden wrapped his arm around Laurel.

"I am too." Laurel leaned into his embrace.

"Aw, look at you two." Maggie smiled.

"We're really happy for you both," Martin said. "How about we raise a toast to you two?"

"Sounds good to me." Laurel followed them all out of the door and up the path to the deck.

As they sat around and ate, they talked about Aiden's house renovation and his new project at Lena's winery. Martin shared the golf courses he was currently working on. Maggie was excited to share that she was close to finishing the first draft of her next children's book. Laurel told them about the new contract she had with a local florist.

When the food had been devoured, Aiden and Martin took the dishes into the kitchen and washed up. Maggie and Laurel sat outside talking.

"Wow, he really is something special, isn't he?" Maggie squeezed Laurel's hand.

Laurel looked through the window at Aiden and leaned her head on Maggie's shoulder. "He is. I think I hit the jackpot."

Maggie smiled. "So, I shouldn't remind you how many times you told me that you were over men and were done with them?"

Laurel laughed and gently gave Maggie a shove. "You're funny, y'know that? If you do, then I will only have to praise you and your wisdom when you told me there was someone out there for me and to not give up. Such sage advice."

"Well, thank you. I promise to keep sharing my sage advice with you."

"Thanks, and if I can return the favor, I will."

"Oh, don't you discount all the great advice you give me." Maggie wrapped an arm around Laurel and shook her gently. "Love ya."

"I love you too. I'm so glad you're here."

The four of them went paddle boarding for a couple of hours and then relaxed next to the lake. Aiden gave them a tour of his house after they had all gotten cleaned up. Then the guys cooked dinner, which gave Maggie and Laurel more time to talk.

Maggie and Laurel's phones both chimed with an incoming text message from Bailey.

> Hey, just a reminder that Sunday we are having our end-of-summer barbecue. We're making a day of it this year, since we've all been so busy and haven't been able to get together more often. Come over anytime.

Laurel texted back.

> Hi, can't wait to see everyone. We will come over late morning. That way I can make the potato salad before we come. Maggie is making a blackberry tart. Let us know if you need us to bring anything else.

> Sounds great. We shouldn't need anything else. As usual, everyone will bring WAY too much food. Can't wait to see you guys. XX.

THEY ARRIVED AT BAILEY'S ON SUNDAY AND UNPACKED the car. Maggie and Laurel had told Aiden countless stories about the infamous barbecue at Bailey's. Her grandparents had started the tradition ages ago, and Bailey had continued it. Each year, Bailey set out a photo album of past barbecues that everyone perused.

Aiden hadn't been to Bailey's before, but he immediately fell in love with the old lake house. Bailey gave him a tour and a history lesson peppered with stories of her grandparents and parents.

"I think it's great that both you and Laurel are living in these family homes that hold such wonderful memories," Aiden said when the tour came to an end.

Bailey nodded. "I agree. My parents now have a cabin in the mountains, as they love winter sports. They convinced my grandparents to leave the house to me instead of them. I'm glad they did. I love it here."

"I can see why," Aiden said as they joined everyone outside. "Is that a horseshoe pit?"

Bailey laughed. "Yes, haven't seen one in a while?"

"No, I haven't. My dad and I used to play when I was growing up. This makes me want to put one in at my house. Good memories."

"You should. You have the space. It's always been a part of our get-togethers. Guess we'll find out how good you are today."

Laughing, Aiden said, "Yeah, we'll see if I still have it."

Aiden found Laurel sitting in the shade on the deck. Her face lit up when she saw him.

"Hi gorgeous." Aiden sat next to her.

"Look who's talking." She leaned over for a kiss.

"What a gorgeous spot." He looked across the yard to the lake.

"It is, isn't it? And I love that we have all made the effort to be here this year. I haven't been to this party for a few years. *Someone who shall remain nameless* never wanted to come. So...I didn't." Laurel shook her head as if to clear the memory. "Anyway, I love how you fit perfectly with my crazy, wonderful friends."

"I love your crazy, wonderful friends. They're all such interesting and fun people. Not only did I get the girl—" he planted a kiss on her nose, "—but I lucked out and got all of the friends too."

She leaned into his embrace. "I love you, Aiden."

He pulled her closer and kissed the top of her head. "I love you too, Laurel."

Cassie and Sean walked up and started chatting with them when Hank called out.

"Hey, Aiden, ready for some horseshoes?" asked Hank. "We hear you may know how to play."

Aiden laughed as he walked over to Hank. "Well, let's see if I remember how to do this."

EVERYONE SWAM AND NIBBLED ON APPETIZERS AND SAT around and talked. It was one of the best end-of-summer parties that Laurel could remember. Perhaps it was that even though she had been through so much this year, she had reconnected so strongly with this amazing group of friends.

Brad fired up the barbecue, and the rest of the food was brought to the tables on the deck. Lena opened a couple bottles of special wine to celebrate. Holly and Joy made an amazing chili, Cassie and Sean brought corn on the cob and a green salad, and Bailey made her favorite seven-layer dip. They grilled steaks, burgers, and chicken. As always, there was so much food—but that was the way they did these get togethers.

After everyone ate and then cleaned up, they set up the outdoor movie screen. The fire pit was set to light when the time came.

Laurel couldn't remember when she had laughed this much. Her cheeks hurt from smiling and laughing so hard.

Everyone settled around the firepit and watched "The Sandlot". Afterwards, they had coffee and dessert. Exhausted and happy, they packed up the cars and all headed home.

"That was a fantastic day," Aiden said as they drove away from Bailey's.

"It certainly was. It was so great to spend time with everyone," Martin added.

"Is anyone else full from all of that yummy food?" Maggie asked.

Laughing, Laurel said, "Besides being full, my cheeks are aching from laughing so much. What a great day."

AIDEN WAS AT THE WINERY AND LAUREL WAS IN THE studio when Frank's number showed up on her caller ID.

She answered it.

"I wanted to let you know that we have an offer on your parent's house in Addington. Laurel, it is an excellent offer."

"Oh, okay. How much is the offer?" She sat at her desk, trying to stay calm.

Frank told her the amount and added, "I would recommend that we accept it, Laurel."

Laurel paused. "Yes, yes, of course. That is a good offer. Please proceed with the sale."

"Laurel, I realize how difficult this is for you. I'm sorry."

"Thanks, Frank. Yes, it is difficult. Strangely enough, it makes it all very real—even though it's all been real."

"I do understand. I will proceed on this end and will keep you posted. Escrow should close in thirty days. I'll speak to you again soon. I am sorry, Laurel."

"Thanks, thanks, yes, speak soon. Thanks for everything, Frank." Laurel disconnected the call. She leaned back in the chair. Then she leaned forward and put her head in her hands. The sobs came fast and hard. Laurel struggled to catch her breath between sobs.

Aiden found her there thirty minutes later, rocking back and forth in the chair. The pile of crumpled tissues on the desk and her red, blotchy face told him everything.

"Baby, baby, tell me what's wrong. What happened? What's wrong?" Aiden kneeled and pulled her to him. He held her tight and caressed her hair. "Shhh, I'm here."

The sobs finally slowed, and Laurel took a deep breath. "Frank called. We've had an offer on the house. It is a good offer." She took another deep breath. "I told him to accept it and proceed with the sale."

Aiden hugged her tighter. "Oh, baby. This makes losing your parents so real. Not that it hasn't been, but I'm guessing that reality is hitting you hard right now."

Laurel pulled back and looked at him. "How do you know that? How do you know exactly what I am feeling?"

"I don't know. Maybe my heart is locked with yours. I'm so sorry you are hurting, baby." He kissed her gently.

Laurel took a deep breath and managed to smile. "Thank you. Thank you for being so understanding. I'm sorry I'm such a mess."

"You have nothing to be sorry for. And if I remember correctly, you did tell me, 'Don't worry, when I fall into a crying heap of a mess, your arms are the ones I want to crawl into.' Well, here I am. I will always be here for you."

"How did I get so lucky?" Laurel sniffed and managed a bigger smile.

Aiden smiled back. "I'm the lucky one." He kissed her again. "Let's go inside and get a cool cloth for your face."

"I must look beautiful."

"Always."

A short time later, Laurel and Aiden were sitting on the deck when Maggie and Martin returned from running errands.

"Hi, you two." Laurel smiled weakly at them.

Maggie immediately sat in the chair next to Laurel and reached for her hand. "What's wrong?"

"You always know when I need you, don't you?" Laurel asked. "We got an offer on mom and dad's house. I've told Frank to accept the offer."

"Oh, honey, I'm sorry. I know how hard this is for you."

Laurel leaned her head on Maggie's shoulder. "Yes, you do know how hard this is. You and Tim went through the same thing. I remember how much that tore you both up."

Maggie laid her head atop Laurel's. "It's tough to deal with the emotions. I remember trying to balance knowing it was just a building, but that it was our home and held all of our memories growing up."

Laurel sighed. "I keep telling myself that this is what my mom wanted. It just seems like the final step of saying goodbye to her."

"Honey, you'll never say goodbye to her. She and your dad are always right here with you. Always in your heart. And you are living *here* where you have a lifetime of happy memories."

"I know, and I am so grateful for that. I walk around this cabin with a silly smile on my face most of the time, the memories surrounding me."

Martin leaned over and touched Laurel's shoulder. "That's what you need to hold on to—all of those precious memories."

Laurel looked up at Martin and Aiden, their faces full of concern and love. "Thank you all for being here for me. I couldn't do this without you."

Maggie smiled, "We love you so much."

Aiden and Martin said in unison, "Yes, we do."

Laurel's face brightened into a smile. "I love you all, too. Okay, enough of this crying stuff. Anybody feel like a swim before dinner?"

THEY ALL ENJOYED THE NEXT COUPLE OF DAYS together. Aiden told them that he wanted to take Laurel to Spain someday soon. Of course, they completely agreed with that idea, and the three of them seemed to make it a mission to get something planned. As Maggie and Martin were due to leave on their annual vacation in three weeks, they all decided to plan for the following September. That would give them time to plan and time for Laurel to get her business more established.

Laurel hugged Maggie as they said goodbye. "Thank you so much for being my best friend. I love you so much."

Maggie returned the hug even tighter. "I'm so glad you're my person. Take care of yourself. I love you."

Martin looked at Aiden and shrugged. "Their farewells always seem like they won't be texting in the next two hours."

Aiden laughed. "I see that. Pretty great friendship."

Laurel and Maggie, who had split for just a second, hugged once more. "Thanks for coming. Have a great trip."

Martin laughed. "See what I mean, Aiden."

Aiden nodded, amusement curling his lips. "Yup."

"Okay, okay. Love you, Laurel. Thanks for everything. See you soon." Maggie got into the car.

Laurel and Aiden waved as the car disappeared down the road.

Twenty

Laurel looked around her studio and smiled. Her business was doing well. Hettie had asked her to let her stock a few pieces to sell to guests. Forget-Me-Not Florist in town loved the vases that she had created for them. They had just signed an agreement with Laurel to supply them with vases and pots. Lyman's Bookshop and Café had increased her display area and were selling pieces consistently, so she was always restocking.

Her social media presence was gaining traction, and she was finally getting some sales directly from those sites. Nothing crazy yet, but that was okay with her.

Laurel was able to handle the workload without working all day, every day. There were days and weeks when she had a large order to fill, and those times she worked longer hours. However, she had filled her shelves with stock now, so she was able to stay ahead of restocking her three major clients and fulfilling online orders.

Her confidence had returned, and she couldn't help but feel proud of how far she had come this year. Next month, she was starting something else new. Thanks to Jenny, Lena's assistant, Laurel was going to give classes in pottery making. Jenny and her friend would be Laurel's first students. She had bought a couple of portable wheels, and she and Aiden were rearranging her studio to make it all work. Exciting times were ahead.

A life can change in an instant. For Laurel, it was seventy-two hours. Seventy-two, and her life was forever changed. Laurel had pondered that many times in the past several months—how her seemingly dull, comfortable life became completely unraveled.

A normal Friday night doing laundry led to the discovery of infidelity. The man she had lived with for years was having an affair. Not thirty minutes before discovering the hidden note, Laurel had asked herself the hard question. Would she marry him if he asked her? No. The answer had come quickly. In that moment, she knew she had to leave. She no longer loved him. She no longer saw a future with him. That revelation sparked an energy in her to start packing and making plans to leave.

That Saturday and Sunday, she had spent with her mom. Talk of her new plans, the height of their conversations. They enjoyed time together, visiting their favorite shops, eating in one of their favorite restaurants, and talking late into the night.

By Monday night, her mother was dead. Her poor health took its final toll.

It felt like her life had been split in two—her life before that moment and her life after.

Her life now was not dull. It was comfortable, but not because she settled. She loved how far she had come and how she had created the life that she wanted.

Little did she know the boy next door would become the love of her life.

As if he heard her innermost thoughts, Aiden arrived at the studio door. "Hey babe." He walked over and wrapped his arms around Laurel's waist.

She brushed her thumb along his cheek and kissed him. "I missed you today. How did everything go with the inspection?"

"Passed with flying colors! Lena and Hank are ecstatic. I have a very happy client." Aiden lifted Laurel and twirled her around.

"Congratulations. Of course, they're ecstatic! You did an amazing job on that reno."

"How about we celebrate? They gave me a very nice bottle of sparkling wine."

"That sounds wonderful. I've just finished in here." Laurel took his hand and led him to the door. Shutting off the lights, she closed and locked the studio.

As they walked up to the deck, Sophie came over and greeted them and walked to the door to be let inside. Aiden opened the door and stopped. The enticing smell of Laurel's au gratin potatoes welcomed him inside.

"You made me potatoes." He leaned down and softly kissed her.

"Well, I was hoping you might share some with me." Laurel winked.

"I love you so much that I will even share the au gratin potatoes you made *for me* with you."

"I love you too," Laurel said. "Shall we open that bottle? Dinner will be a few more minutes."

Aiden popped the cork and poured them each a glass. They clinked their glasses together and toasted to his successful renovation at the winery.

He leaned back in his chair and raised his glass again. "I've been thinking about your studio and how we can change things to maximize that space for you."

"I'm all ears. What are you thinking?" Laurel took a sip of her sparkling wine.

"Well, you have a lot of stock now, and as the business continues to grow, you'll need more space. Also, with your classes starting, I thought maybe I could enlarge the studio for you."

Laurel wasn't sure she heard him right. "Enlarge the studio? How?"

Aiden pulled a notebook and pencil from his pocket. "At first, I thought we could move your shelves of stock into the garage, in the second bay. But then I thought..." He paused as he sketched a drawing of the studio and the garage and shaded in the piece between them. "Well, I thought that might be inconvenient to have to carry your pieces into the garage."

Laurel studied the sketch. "Yes, but I already do that when using the kiln."

Aiden started sketching again. "What if we extended the studio from here to the garage? Currently, that area just has pots of flowers in it. We could relocate those. We could open this side of the studio and attach it to the garage and make a larger doorway here." He showed her on the drawing.

Laurel studied it, then walked to the French doors and looked out at the studio.

Aiden joined her and opened the door. "Let's have a look." He led the way down the steps. "So, we remove this wall of the studio, and we build the extension here, and we open up the back of the garage. This way you can easily get to the kiln no matter the weather. It'll give you more space for your stock, and we could add an additional drying rack, if that would help."

Laurel stood looking at the studio and then at the garage. "Wow, that would give me a lot more space. How much do you think it will cost? Not that it matters, really, because I have money to do it now. Oh, Aiden, this is exciting!"

Aiden beamed. "I'm glad you think so. How about after dinner we sketch out exactly what you want? Window, skylights, shelves, how you want it to flow. That way, we can work it into the design and make it perfect for you."

Laurel wrapped her arms around Aiden's neck, reached up, and kissed him. "Thank you. Thank you for thinking of this. I love you."

Aiden returned the kiss and pulled her closer. "No need to thank me. I would do anything for you. Your business is doing so well, and if we can make it work better for you, then let's do it."

Laurel took Aiden's hand and led him inside. "Can you refill our glasses while I serve dinner?"

"Of course." He leaned in for one more kiss.

After dinner, Laurel cleaned up the kitchen, and Aiden ran next door and got some large paper and his drawing instruments. They spent the next couple of hours talking, planning, drawing, erasing, redrawing, and looking online at photos of studios and studio layouts.

"Tomorrow morning, when it's light, we can take the measurements," said Aiden. "Then I can put together a materials list."

"Oh my gosh, I'm so excited. This just takes my business to the next level. I never dreamed..." Laurel paused as her emotions caught in her throat. "It's just that I was so close to giving up on this dream all together. When I look at what I've accomplished and what the future holds, I just can't believe it."

Aiden caught her face in his hands with the gentlest touch she'd ever felt. "Sweetheart, you are an amazing woman. I love watching how you've taken your dream and created this incredible business. You've met some bumps in the road, but you have persevered and come out stronger. I love you."

Laurel couldn't help herself. Aiden's words brought tears to her eyes, and they rolled down her cheeks.

"I love you too, Aiden. With you by my side, I feel like I could do anything."

"You can do anything you put your mind to, Laurel. You've shown that time and time again. I'm just lucky enough to be a part of your journey."

Laurel kissed Aiden and smiled. "What a year of change this has been for both of us. I'd say we're both very lucky."

Are you curious to follow what adventures await the friends from the small town of Lake Benton?

Find out by signing up for my monthly newsletter at www.alexandriavarian.com and you'll receive a free story about their special friendship. I'll also keep you up to date on new releases, share recipes from my books, and give you a glimpse into my life in a vineyard.

Acknowledgments

A huge thank you to Jennifer Crosswhite of Tandem Services Ink for your incredible coaching over the years. Your guidance and encouragement are invaluable.

To my Tandem Services C4 writing group, you guys are the absolute BEST! We continue to learn from and support each other and I can't wait to meet you in person!

And to my sisters, Vicky and Sandy, I love you!

Bob, I'm so glad we made the move to this little hilltop vineyard in Spain. Thank you for helping make my dream of writing a reality. All my love.

And in loving memory of my parents, Richard and Shirley Varian. I hope I'm making you proud.

Author's Note

The inspiration for this story came from a short story I wrote a few years ago.

Although the town of Lake Benton is a fictious place, it is a blending of places I have visited of which I have special memories.

Thank you for taking the time to read my book. I hope you enjoyed reading it as much as I enjoyed writing it. I would appreciate it if you would consider leaving a review. Reviews not only help others find great books to read, but they also help the author build their audience. Reviews can be as easy as you want to make them. One line telling people why you loved the book is all it takes. Don't worry, it's nothing like writing a dreaded book report.

Thank you in advance!

Keep reading for a sneak peak of the next book in the series, *Dream Vintage.*

About the Author

Photo credit: Kim Bordons

Alexandria "Xan" Varian

Born in Connecticut, I have lived in 10 different U.S. states. After meeting my now husband in California, I followed him to Australia. We were married on the start line of the Adelaide Formula 1 racetrack, the first track that my husband, Bob Barnard, designed and built.

After living back in the U.S. for twenty years, in 2017, we moved to a hilltop vineyard in Spain. The change of lifestyle gave me the opportunity to pursue my dream of being an author.

Follow me on social media to see my life in the vineyard and what new adventures inspire my writing.

www.alexandriavarian.com

Facebook: Author Alexandria Varian

Instagram: alexandriavarian_author

Pinterest: alexandriavarian_author

Sneak peek of Lake Benton: Book Two

CHAPTER ONE

Maggie reached over to put her hand on Martin's thigh. Giving it a slight squeeze, he glanced over and smiled.

"How are you doing, babe? Excited to share our news?" he asked.

"Yes. I hope they're as thrilled about the news as we are."

Martin changed lanes to pass a slower car. "I think they will be. Although they may be a little shocked about how quickly our lives are about to change."

Maggie laughed. "Seriously, we're still shocked by how quickly this is all happening."

"True. No second thoughts?"

"Absolutely not. I know it's going to be a big change, but it's an opportunity we couldn't pass up. You don't have any second thoughts, do you?"

"Not one. Like you, I'm still pinching myself that we get to do this." Martin squeezed her hand before gripping the steering wheel again.

"I hope Laurel isn't upset that I didn't tell her first."

"Maggie, she will be fine. Don't worry. We'll be there shortly."

Maggie sighed as she flipped down the visor to check her makeup in the mirror.

Giving her a sideways glance, Martin said, "You look beautiful, as always."

"Ha, thank you. I'm glad I don't look as tired as I feel. But I guess I might be feeling tired for a while."

"Somehow we'll make time to rest, I promise."

Maggie laughed at that. "I'm going to hold you to that promise."

She looked out the window as they took the turn off for Lake Benton. Martin slowed as they drove through the familiar town. They were quiet as they both looked at the town with different eyes.

"It feels weird." Maggie almost whispered.

"It does. It'll be okay though." He reassured her.

"I know."

"I have no idea," Laurel said, for what felt like the hundredth time. "They just said that they needed to talk to all of us at once."

Everyone seemed to speak at once as they greeted each other and started to make their way out to the deck.

"No, they assured me that it isn't health related. They are both fine."

Aiden spoke up. "Listen, everyone, they should be here any minute."

Aiden walked over to Laurel and wrapped her in his arms. Laurel took a deep breath and exhaled. "Babe, they'll be here soon. I know you are just as concerned as everyone else. It'll be okay." He kissed her forehead.

"Thanks. I'm just wondering what the news is, and my mind is all over the place trying to guess at what's going on."

"I know. Just a few more minutes." Aiden kissed her softly on the lips, brushing his thumb along her cheek.

The sound of the doorbell stopped everyone talking, as if they were now all holding their breath. Maggie opened the door and walked in with Martin behind her. Laurel and Aiden were the first to greet them.

"Gosh I've missed you!" Laurel hugged Maggie.

"I've missed you too!" Maggie hugged her again, and when she pulled back there was a story dancing in her eyes, and Laurel knew what was coming.

Everyone suddenly started talking at once, and Maggie and Martin found themselves being embraced by their friends. Questions flew around the room until Aiden whistled and brought the commotion to an end.

"Let's all go out to the deck. Grab a drink and something to eat and then we'll all be ready to hear the news that Maggie and Martin want to share with us."

The commotion began again, but this time it was more like organized chaos as everyone followed Aiden's instructions. Laurel and Aiden brought more food and drinks out to the deck as everyone finally settled down.

Maggie glanced around to her oldest and dearest friends and then looked at Martin. He reached for her hand as she cleared her throat and began.

Time seemed to stand still as they all looked at her with pleading eyes.

"Well, as I'm sure you've guessed, Martin and I have some big news to share." She paused and took a deep breath as Martin squeezed her hand. "We're moving to Spain."

A collective "WHAT?!" exploded among the friends. Laurel jumped up and grabbed Maggie in a huge hug. Then Martin was enveloped in her hug.

"Oh, Maggie, Martin! That is amazing! I know how much

you love it there. Oh my gosh! I can't believe this!" Laurel hugged them again.

A frenzy of hugs, congratulations, and a barrage of questions assaulted Maggie and Martin. Aiden watched and then at the right moment, whistled again. They laughed as they all sat and turned their attention to Maggie and Martin.

Martin took over the announcement. "We know you have a million questions. Let me see if we can answer them for you. As you all know, we just returned from our annual trip. What was supposed to be our normal vacation," he paused and smiled at their friends. "You know, great food, hours every day spent on the beach, exploring—"

Lena interrupted. "Yes, we know how rough these vacations are for you both. Really, we do. We feel bad that you have to go through this torture every year, but just get on with it, Martin!"

Once the laughter quieted down, Martin continued, "While we were there, I had a couple of meetings with an investment group that is looking to build a new resort with two golf courses. I've been in contact with them for a while, and well, the project is going ahead, and they've hired me to design and build the courses."

"Congratulations, Martin! That is great news! You deserve it!" Brad said, holding his glass up in a toast.

"Thanks, Brad. It's a huge project and I'm excited to be a part of it." Maggie stood next to Martin holding his hand.

"As the project will take about four years, we've decided to move there for that period."

Maggie smiled, "A project this size will require Martin to be there much of the time. And..." she looked into Martin's eyes and squeezed his hand, "we don't want to spend that much time apart. So, moving there is the best solution for us. For now."

"Of course, that makes sense and to be able to live in your happy place. Wow!" Cassie smiled at Maggie. "We're going to miss you though."

"And we'll miss all of you." Maggie said as Martin wrapped his arm around her shoulder.

"We're very excited about the opportunity and as you said, Cassie, it is our happy place. We know it's a huge change but wait until you hear the rest." Martin said.

"First, I think we need to have a toast. This is exciting news and although we will all miss you, please know that we are happy for you both." Lena raised her glass. "To following your dreams! Congratulations!"

"Cheers."

"Salut."

"Congrats."

Everyone clinked their glasses together and hugs were shared before the story continued.

Maggie's smile made her eyes sparkle with the excitement she was feeling.

Martin continued. "We found an old Spanish country house to rent in a tiny village."

Maggie laughed. "Um, yes, a tiny village which just happens to be in a vineyard."

"WHAT?!" Laurel is the first to get the question out.

"It's an amazing story. A couple of years ago, our friend Xavi took us to this village. It was harvest time. We watched as the grapes were picked by hand and then brought to the crusher." Martin winked at Maggie as she took over telling the story.

"We wandered through the little village and then walked around the vineyard. We hugged a 1,400-year-old olive tree. Then we drove to another village for lunch. It was such an amazing day."

Martin cleared his throat. "So, we were wandering around Sitges looking at the real estate windows displaying houses for rent. We knew we didn't want to live in town, as there are festivals all the time and too many tourists in summer. Anyway, we saw an announcement in the window and the house looked incredible.

Old country home that had been renovated with a private garden."

Maggie chimed in. "Then we saw the name of the village. It was the same one Xavi had taken us to. We looked at each other and said, 'we know where that is.' We jumped in the car and drove up there to look at it."

Martin continued. "We were shown the house by a wonderful lady. As we walked around the house, we both kept saying, 'this is perfect.'"

"And it is! Wait till you see the photos." Maggie added.

"We then met with the owner of the village and vineyard. We all just clicked and well, we signed a lease for the house."

"Wow, you certainly didn't waste any time," Brad said. "Congrats!"

Laurel hugged them both again. "Not only are you moving to Spain, but you are going to live in a vineyard! I can't believe this. I'm so excited for you guys."

"I have a question. How quickly are you moving?" Holly asked.

"Six months."

"What are you going to do with all of your belongings and your house?" Cassie asked.

"We've decided to have a major purge. We'll ship some stuff—clothes, sentimental things, photos. But we aren't shipping any furniture. It just isn't cost effective." Martin said, and Maggie leaned her head on his shoulder.

"Honestly, we've accumulated so much stuff. Stuff we just don't need. The houses there don't really have any storage. We won't have a garage. Walk-in closets are unheard of there, so we'll need to purge clothes as well. I'm actually looking forward to clearing out."

"As for the house, we're talking about putting it on the market." Martin sipped his cava.

Laurel's shoulders dropped. "Wait. That sounds like you're not coming back."